A BEAUTIFUL DISTRACTION

For a long time Rafe sat there, watching Anne as she slept. He touched her forehead and smoothed the hair back from her brow.

She is a distraction, José had said. *She will slow you down.*

Rafe couldn't deny the truth in those words. He would be able to travel a hell of a lot faster without her, if she would just tell him where the gold was. He could make her tell him, he knew. Maybe she was brave and maybe she was stubborn, but she was still a woman. Except every time he thought of threatening her, he felt a knot in his stomach.

What was wrong with him? He hadn't let anything get in his way in a long time. All he knew for certain was that he couldn't possibly hurt her. And he couldn't stand by and let anyone else hurt her, either.

Desert
Dreams

⚞ DEBORAH COX ⚟

HarperPaperbacks
A Division of HarperCollinsPublishers

HarperPaperbacks *A Division of* HarperCollins*Publishers*
10 East 53rd Street, New York, N.Y. 10022

Cover illustration by Vittorio

First printing: January 1995

Printed in the United States of America

HarperPaperbacks, HarperMonogram, and colophon are trademarks of HarperCollins*Publishers*

❖ 10 9 8 7 6 5 4 3 2 1

In loving memory of my father,
Jimmy Cox,
and my brother,
Rusty.

And for
Julia Terry
for being a friend
through the darkest times.

On all the line a sudden vengeance waits,
And frequent hearses shall besiege your gates.
—Alexander Pope

1

He guided his horse through the crowded street with casual ease, one hand on the reins, the other resting on his thigh. His gaze never wavered from its direction straight ahead, but Anne Cameron would have been willing to bet he was aware of everyone and everything around him. There was the look of the predator about him, the menacing watchfulness of an animal on the scent of its next kill.

Anne felt his tension in the hollow thumping of her heart. She wiped the sweat from her brow with the sleeve of the shirtwaist that had been white that morning when she'd put it on. A warm whisper of a breeze caressed her hot skin, as a rivulet of moisture trickled between her breasts in the blazing September heat.

Drifter. She'd seen his type before. There had been plenty of them along the Mississippi River, rootless men who wandered from town to town, game to game, dangerous men who had nothing to lose.

Not until he'd passed down the street did Anne notice the body slung crosswise behind the saddle. The horse's movements caused the corpse to sway in a macabre dance, arms and legs dangling on either side of the animal.

She shuddered with revulsion. San Antonio, Texas, in 1863 was nothing at all like Natchez, Mississippi— on the surface, at least. You'd never see a man ride down the street with a body draped over his horse, even in Natchez-under-the-hill, the part of the city she was familiar with. But life in Natchez-under-the-hill was cheap, and it was evidently cheap in Texas too.

The man with the corpse stopped before the jail. He swung down from the saddle and walked around to the side of his horse. At the same time, a tall barrel-chested man emerged from the jail. He came to stand beside the body and raised the lifeless head by the hair to get a look at the dead man's face.

Anne strained to hear the words that passed between the two, but the din in the street was too thick. She took the opportunity to study the gunfighter more closely. Her gaze slid down from his dark head to his broad shoulders to his narrow hips, where a gun rode low against his thigh. At that instant, she looked up and met his gaze.

He smiled, touching a finger to his hat, sending a jolt of excitement tempered with fear through her body, and she averted her gaze quickly. A cold knot bottled in her chest, stealing her breath. It was a warning she dared not ignore. She'd disregarded her intuition before and paid a terrible price.

"There's gonna be trouble."

She turned at the sound of a deep male voice behind her to see a whiskered, white-haired man standing in the open doorway of the hotel. He nodded toward the horseman who had just dismounted in front of the jail. "*Pistolero*. Prob'ly a bounty hunter."

Anne moved past the whiskered man into the relative coolness of the hotel. She stepped up to the desk, placing her gloves on the polished surface, trying not to think about the gunman.

"See those men on the other side of the street?" the whiskered man persisted.

In spite of her resolve to remain detached, Anne peered through the open door at two dangerous-looking men lounging across the street in front of the saloon, their eyes fixed on the gunfighter.

"Vigilante scum." The whiskered man withdrew from the doorway with a scowl and walked around behind the shiny mahogany desk.

"Mark my words, somebody's gonna be dead before this day's over." He opened the large ledger book with a snort. "Minutemen, they call themselves. Their leader, Captain Asa Mitchell, vowed to punish criminals and traitors. Thing of it is, they're deserters and desperadoes themselves. They carry out their own brand of justice.

"Just last week, they hung a man for getting drunk and turning over a few chili stands in Alamo Plaza. Took him out of jail and strung him up from a chinaberry tree. Few months ago, they hung twenty men in one week."

Anne closed her eyes tightly. Her temples were beginning to throb. She didn't care about this town or chili stands or hangings. Her too-large boots had rubbed blisters on her ankles and heels, despite the thick woolen socks she'd stuffed into the toes to make them fit better. All she could think of was taking those boots off, along with the rest of her clothes, and soaking in a hot tub.

"I need a room," she said finally.

The innkeeper turned the guest register around without another word and waited for her to sign her name.

"Pedro!" he called as Anne finished writing. A Mexican youth appeared, smiling brightly from beneath a large straw hat.

"Take Miss"—he glanced at the register for her name—"Miss Cameron's baggage upstairs, pronto!"

The Mexican bobbed his head and lifted the carpetbag Anne had dropped at her feet. She followed him toward the staircase.

One more night in a hotel.

One more night and a stagecoach ride and she'd be in Ubiquitous, Texas, where she would start her new life. Finally she would have a home, a real home that didn't float up and down a river, with Aunt Marguerite. She could almost imagine her aunt's face. She would look like the miniature of Anne's mother, who had died when Anne was seven. Her house would smell like home-baked bread. It would be white with a large porch on the front. They would sit and laugh together at dusk like the families she'd glimpsed in Natchez, the part above the bluffs where the decent folks lived, and in Baton Rouge, and in Vicksburg. . . .

Anne only hoped Aunt Marguerite had received her letter. She'd posted it from Natchez on her way out of town. There hadn't been time to wait for a reply—it would have taken weeks to reach her, if it reached her at all—so she had taken a chance and struck out for Texas.

She moistened her parched lips. The taste of Texas trail dust was bitter on her tongue. Her gaze returned to the spot where the *pistolero* had been standing, but he had turned to follow the sheriff into the jail. She glanced across the street at the two vigilantes, who were still watching and whispering to each other.

If there was going to be trouble, as the innkeeper had predicted, she hoped it would wait until she was well on her way.

Sheriff Jim Conner opened the door to his office and stepped through. He didn't pause or speak as he crossed the dark room to sit in the leather chair behind his cluttered desk.

The gunfighter stood in the doorway, his right hip against the doorjamb, his left thumb hooked in his belt. He blinked his eyes until his vision adjusted to the lack of light, then pushed the hat back on his head. With sharp, wary eyes he studied the room, from the mountain of papers on the desk to the framed maps of Texas and the southwestern territories on the wall behind it.

He moved across the room slowly and lowered his tall frame into a straight-backed chair.

"You said you had papers?" Conner asked gruffly.

The bounty hunter sat forward and dug in his shirt pocket. Peering back at the sheriff with an unrelenting stare that never left Conner's face, he withdrew a sheet of paper, unfolded it slowly, and placed it on the desk.

Conner pulled a stack of WANTED posters from his desk and rifled through them, his hand shaking slightly despite his best efforts at control. He produced a newer version of the poster the gunfighter had provided.

"This must be your lucky day. Looks like the price has gone up. He's worth five hundred today. He's wanted in El Paso, so I'll have to send for the money. It should be here in three or four days."

"How about a little advance? I could use a bath and a drink or two."

"What the hell do you think this is?" Conner demanded. "Let's get something straight, friend. I don't like you and your kind. In fact, I wouldn't spit on you if you was on fire."

The gunfighter ran a hand over his beard. His eyes remained indifferent, but his annoyance showed in the tightening of a jaw muscle. Slowly, he rose to his feet, gripping the edge of the desk. As he leaned toward Conner, the sheriff couldn't help but lean back, away from the threat in the gunman's tightly coiled stance. Without volition, Conner's gaze shifted to the gun on the edge of his desk. He'd never reach it in time—and both men knew it.

"The feeling's mutual, sheriff. But the sooner I get my money, the sooner I'll be outa your town. I've been on the trail for weeks."

"Being a bounty hunter's a tough job," Conner said, swallowing his fear. This was his town. He was the law here. If he started letting men like this one push him around, he'd be out of a job—or dead.

"The way I figure it, I need . . . oh, three nights of rest here in San Antonio to recover. Now, I can start with tonight, or I can start in three days when the money comes."

Conner studied the man who hovered above him. He wrinkled his nose in disgust. The bounty hunter reeked of death. Those unnaturally pale eyes stared back. A chill crept down the sheriff's spine at what he saw—or, rather, what he didn't see—in those eyes. They were blank, as barren as the desert, as emotionless as the gun strapped to the bounty hunter's thigh. Conner didn't want trouble, and he had a feeling that the sooner this man was out of town the better for everyone.

He expelled an angry breath as he turned, opened the safe behind him, and dropped a small money pouch on the desk between them.

"There's a hundred dollars in gold in this bag," he said, as he wrote out a receipt and shoved it across the desk. "I'm sure you know the procedure. Make your mark at the bottom."

The sheriff watched the man move the ink quill across the paper.

"So you can write," he said with a snort. "Just what the world needs: an educated bounty hunter."

The gunman returned the quill to its well and slid the receipt forward. The name Conner saw there made his stomach tighten in disgust.

"Rafe Montalvo," he read aloud, then added, with more than a little sarcasm, "I didn't know I was talking to a legend."

Montalvo took the bag and turned it upside down. Gold coins clattered loudly against one another as he emptied the contents into his palm, counting the coins in a gesture Conner knew was meant to rankle him. Apparently satisfied, the gunman returned the coins to the pouch. "I knew you were a man of reason."

After dropping the money pouch into his shirt pocket, Montalvo picked up the wanted poster he'd brought with him and began refolding it. "Mind if I keep this for a souvenir?" he asked, then slipped the folded poster into his other shirt pocket.

Conner rose from his chair, glaring at Montalvo. "You just make sure you stay out of trouble, you hear me? All I need's half an excuse, and I'll have you in jail faster'n you can draw that pistol of yours."

Montalvo's lips curled in a taunting smile. "I hear you, sheriff. Thanks for the warning."

*   *   *

Rafe Montalvo stepped out of the sheriff's office into the noisy street, adjusting the brim of his hat so that it shielded his eyes from at least some of the sun's glare. He glanced down the street, looking for the girl he'd seen standing in front of the hotel moments earlier, her curly pale-red hair peeking out from underneath a battered hat. She was gone now, vanished, as if she'd never been there at all, as if she was nothing more than a mirage.

Something about her had struck a memory deep inside him. Tall and fragile, she'd seemed out of place on the rough, dirty street. Her carriage, her manner, everything about her spoke of breeding and pride, despite her slightly shabby, travel-worn appearance. She was probably a refugee from the war.

Pain stabbed his gut as if someone had plunged a knife between his ribs and was twisting it slowly. There once was a time when women like that were a part of his life, but that was long ago, before all the killing started. She was like a ghost from his past, a past he would just as soon leave buried. Still, he couldn't help wondering what she was doing in San Antonio, especially now, when what little law and order there had been before the war had completely broken down.

Rafe shrugged the question aside as he stepped off the wooden sidewalk and strode toward his horse. She was nothing to him. A woman like her would cross to the opposite side of the street to avoid passing too close to a man like him.

As he lifted the saddlebags from the chestnut gelding's back, he caught sight of a short bald-headed man hurrying across the busy street toward him.

Undertakers, he could smell them a mile off. Smiling vultures. They were all the same, from their white aprons to their serene faces and calculating eyes that counted death as profit—just as he did. They were in the same business, he and the undertaker, the business of death.

As he slung the saddlebags over his shoulder, the short, smiling man stopped before him. "After you're done with the body, have my horse taken to the livery stable," Rafe said, without looking at the man. "Make sure he's looked after, and I'll make it worth your while."

He didn't wait for a reply but sauntered toward the saloon. What he needed was a shot of whiskey—make that a bottle of whiskey.

As Rafe walked, his gaze settled on the two men who lounged on the sidewalk in front of the saloon. The taller one he recognized as Tom McCoy. A cold menace emanated from McCoy as their eyes locked.

Rafe knew McCoy would make his play before long. Two gunmen in one town was one too many. And although Rafe didn't look forward to the inevitable confrontation, he would not run from it either. If McCoy wanted a fight, he would get a fight, and he would end up dead.

McCoy had made quite a name for himself in Texas, and when war came he joined the Confederate army. Rafe supposed army service hadn't been to McCoy's liking. So now McCoy was one of Asa Mitchell's Minute Men. Life, as he well knew, was full of ironies.

He smiled as he approached the pair, noting that McCoy had begun to squirm a bit under his unflagging gaze. He recognized the sign. McCoy would choke in a gunfight. According to McCoy's reputation, he had killed some dozen men. Rumor had it most of them were shot in the back. He'd have to be careful, but then, he could hardly remember a time when he hadn't had to be careful.

Brushing past the two men without a word, Rafe stepped into the cavernous saloon. The stench of stale beer and tobacco smoke stung his nostrils as he paused just inside the door to make a mental note of the positions of those present.

In less than a minute, he had measured everyone in the room. Two men played stud at a table, one smoking a cigar and laughing with the scarlet-clad woman who bent over him, revealing more than a glimpse of lush, full breasts. Against the bar stood a huge, rough-looking character, but his bulk was probably more fat than muscle, and his gun was strapped on like that of an amateur. A lone figure, a Mexican, sat in a dark corner. Rafe hesitated briefly as his eyes slid over this man.

Conversations died in mid-sentence as one by one the other occupants glanced up. Rafe crossed the room to the bar, his spurs jingling loudly in the suddenly quiet saloon.

The bartender ran a towel around the inside of a shot glass, while a bored-looking blonde in black and red lace and black net stockings leaned against the bar.

It wasn't much of a crowd, but that suited him fine.

"Bottle of whiskey," Rafe ordered, reaching into his shirt pocket for a coin.

"Yessir!" The bartender hurriedly placed a full bottle and a clean glass on the bar.

Aware that the blonde saloon girl was watching him, Rafe turned to face her, and she smiled in invitation.

Maybe later. She wasn't unattractive. He knew what

to expect of her, and he knew what she expected of him. Nice and neat, no complications, no questions.

"You got a clean room?" he asked the bartender as his gaze inched downward over the blonde's voluptuous body. Her breasts threatened to spill out over her bodice, and the way her skirt was cut in front, her long straight legs were visible to just above the knee. A familiar heaviness in his groin reminded him how long it had been since he'd been with a woman.

The bartender nodded, reaching under the bar for a key. "Room Two-B at the top of the stairs."

Rafe looked away from the woman. He took the key in one hand, the bottle and glass in the other, and moved toward the staircase. There he halted, glancing back at the bartender.

"What're the chances of getting a bath around here?"

The bartender smiled. "I'll see to it."

Less than fifteen minutes later, Rafe was relaxing in a large tin bathtub. He'd positioned the tub so he faced the door, a precaution he always took. His gun belt hung from a coatrack above his head within easy reach. A wooden chair stood beside the tub, a whiskey bottle and glass on the seat.

He closed his eyes, laying his head against the hard metal rim of the tub. Warm water soothed his sun-parched skin, washing away the tension along with layers of grit and grime. He relaxed for the first time in weeks, letting his thoughts wander.

Castroville. When he'd ridden into Castroville a few days ago, he hadn't been looking for trouble, but then he'd seen that familiar face on the street. He hadn't known the man's name until he read it on one of the old WANTED posters he carried with him and studied faithfully, but he could never forget that cruel face.

Rafe recalled how the outlaw begged for his life.

"*Madre de Dios,* don't kill me," he'd pleaded. "I have a family, a wife and children." The bandit fished in his shirt pocket and held up a fistful of banknotes. "*Mira,* I have money. I will pay you!"

"You're worth three hundred dollars dead," Rafe had informed him evenly.

When the outlaw went for his gun, Rafe had all the reason he needed to shoot him down like the animal he was.

Looking back on it now, he couldn't help but feel a certain disappointment. He'd wanted the bandit to die slowly, to suffer awhile. But then, he supposed, dead was dead.

Rubbing a bar of soap between his palms, he worked up a lather and massaged the bubbles into his itchy beard. He tried focusing on more pleasant thoughts, but those were few. The future was barren, empty. He lived from day to day, driven by demons he didn't dare stop to contemplate for fear they would overtake him.

The past was dangerous territory and best avoided. He hadn't allowed himself to think of it in a very long time—until he'd seen the girl on the street. Something about her had jarred his memory and shaken him to his core. A heavy sadness settled on his heart as her image returned to him. He steeled himself against it. One image led to another until he found himself thinking of the old days when his world had been as soft and civilized as the one that young woman had undoubtedly left behind.

He lowered himself farther in the tub, submerging his head, as if by doing so he could wash away the memories that clung to him like trail dust. Resurfacing, he concentrated on scrubbing the dirt from his hair and body. He emptied his thoughts of past and future and surrendered himself to the present, to sensation: warm water, coarse sponge, waning sun through dirty, torn curtains.

The bathwater was cool by the time he stepped out and toweled his body dry. Digging in his saddlebags for a change of clothes, he remembered the wardrobes of clothing he had once owned. Now he could carry all his possessions in a pair of saddlebags.

Damn. Why did the past suddenly seem to be forcing itself into his consciousness? Maybe it was being in Texas again after so long. Or maybe it was seeing José downstairs in the saloon.

Of all the people Rafe could have run into in San Antonio, José Carvajal was the last one he would have expected or wanted to see. Seeing him again brought all Rafe's secrets crawling from their dark hiding places.

A knock sounded on the closed door as Rafe fastened his pants. He whirled around, drew his revolver from the coatrack, cocked it, and leveled it at the door in one smooth reflex action.

"Who is it?" he called.

"It is I, José!"

Rafe uncocked the gun with a muttered curse, struggling to steel himself against the onslaught of memories that always lurked close to the surface. If anyone could unleash them, it was José. At least José had allowed him to finish his bath in peace.

Without waiting for an invitation, José opened the door and stepped inside. His eyes widened as he watched Rafe holster his gun.

"It has been a long time, amigo," said the Mexican.

He turned around to stick his head out into the hall, then closed the door behind him. "I have worried about you."

"Why is that, amigo?" Rafe asked.

José had an annoying habit of calling everyone amigo, a habit Rafe mimicked in the vain hope that the Mexican would get as tired of hearing it as he did and drop it.

José laughed, wagging a finger at Rafe. "Because I know you too well. I know how reckless you can be." He lifted the whiskey bottle, studying it with a shake of his head. "Rotgut." José wrinkled his nose, then uncorked the bottle and took a swig. "So, what brings you to San Antonio?"

"I ran into some trouble outside Castroville," Rafe replied, retrieving his shirt from the floor beside the tub.

"Who was it this time, amigo?"

Rafe dug out the WANTED poster he had shown to the sheriff earlier and handed it to José. The truth was, Rafe couldn't recall the man's name even now, but he knew José would recognize him. José knew every *bandido* and comanchero between the Red River and the Yucatán.

After retrieving a small pair of scissors from his saddlebags, Rafe returned to the mirror, wishing José would go away and leave him in peace. Only José knew the truth about what had happened that day in the desert.

A sly smile curved José's lips as he unfolded the poster and studied the familiar face. Light from the open window glinted off his gold-capped tooth. "You always were the one to take advantage of opportunity. That is why I have always liked you."

Rafe studied José in the mirror as he tossed the WANTED poster on the bed and poured whiskey into the glass. The Mexican's eyes danced with mischief, like a cat that had just swallowed a fat mouse.

Short and round, José didn't look at all like a ruthless *bandido*. Many men had underestimated him, because of his almost comical appearance, and many had lived to regret it. It was only because of his reputation that he was allowed to roam freely in this, a white man's saloon.

José held the glass out to Rafe, but Rafe reached for the bottle instead. The Mexican laughed heartily, then tossed down the glass of whiskey with a shrug. Rafe upended the bottle, relishing the fiery liquid trail that burned down his throat.

"But I think it must have been providence that brought you here," José said. *"Sí, la Providencia."* His hand shook as he turned the empty glass in his palm, studying it with a frown before continuing. "I have an amusing story to tell you, amigo."

Rafe turned to place the bottle on the bedside table. The sound of bedsprings creaking told him José had made himself comfortable, and he realized his visitor meant to stay awhile. Resigned, Rafe turned back to the mirror to trim his beard.

"A ship arrived in Matamoros two months ago, a French ship carrying six million dollars in gold for the Confederate cause."

In the mirror, Rafe watched the Mexican rise from his seat on the bed and move to peer out the dingy window. José was nervous about something. Rafe couldn't remember when he had last seen him so jittery; it could only mean trouble.

José turned and looked at Rafe again, shrugging at the question in his eyes. "I might have been followed, amigo. You can never be too careful. A million dollars is a lot of money."

"A million? A minute ago it was six million."

"Be patient, amigo. You see, this gold was received by a Confederate agent who found himself without means of transportation. Who could he turn to but the governor of Tamaulipas province? Of course, the good governor was more than happy to help. Like France, Mexico is neutral in the American war."

José's sarcastic tone wasn't lost on Rafe. He could well imagine how eager the "good governor" would have been to take a fortune in gold off the unlucky agent's hands.

"When the gold was delivered to the agent in Eagle Pass," José continued, "it was a million dollars short."

"And where is this gold now?" Rafe asked, his interest piqued in spite of his best efforts to remain uninvolved.

"I do not know, amigo, but I know the only man who does, and he is here in San Antonio."

"You do? Who?" He glared at José through the mirror, damning him for his theatrics.

"Luis Demas."

Rafe surveyed his own reflection in the glass, his expression carefully indifferent. He ran a hand through ink-black hair that fell to his shoulders in wet, unruly strands.

"The name sounds familiar," was all he said. He had never met Demas, but he knew everything he needed to know about him from his reputation and the company he kept. "Why are you telling me this?" If this were another of José's wild schemes, Rafe wanted no part of it.

"I have a proposition for you, amigo. All you have to do is help me find the gold."

"Hell, why should I help you? You don't know where the gold is. Luis Demas does. What's to stop me from finding Demas and going after the gold myself?"

"You owe me, amigo. Besides, I can give you something you want very badly. You help me and I'll help you. Surely you know who Luis works for. The man the governor trusted to transport the gold, the man Luis stole the gold from, is none other than your old friend El Alacrán."

The name was never far from Rafe's mind, but hearing it spoken aloud hit him with the force of a blow. His heart began to pound as tension built in every nerve and sinew of his body. He closed his eyes in a vain attempt to hold back the memories. In his imagination, he was in the desert again, a land wavering in heat. A column of smoke curled skyward in the distance, beckoning him. . . .

He pulled his mind back to the present with an effort, but not soon enough, not in time to avoid the tormented stare of those damning eyes.

"I don't need or want your help," Rafe said, in a voice that sounded strange in his own ears. "But I suppose I do owe you something. I'll help you get your gold as long as nothing gets between me and El Alacrán."

"*Sí*, I understand," José said quickly. "But if you find the gold, you will find El Alacrán. El Alacrán wants Luis alive. He doesn't just want to find out where the gold is, he wants to make an example of the thief. You know better than I that if El Alacrán gets to Luis first, there won't be enough of him left for the buzzards. I wouldn't want to trade places with him right now, not even for a million dol—"

José fell silent at the sound of a knock on the door. He swung around, drawing his revolver from the holster at his hip, while Rafe stood ready to reach for his own weapon, should the situation warrant it.

"Come in!" Rafe called.

As the door opened slowly, the noise from the bar downstairs preceded the blonde saloon girl Rafe had seen earlier. José lowered his gun and turned to glance quizzically at Rafe.

Rafe ignored him, focusing on the woman who had stepped over the threshold, and halted just inside at the sight of José.

"I'll come back later," she said.

José laughed, looking from Rafe to the woman and back again to Rafe, as he returned his gun to its holster.

"No, no," José insisted. "I was just leaving. I'll keep an eye out for our friend."

Smiling lewdly, José circled the girl, his gaze gliding over her boldly displayed body. He glanced at Rafe once more, winked enviously, and went out, closing the door behind him.

2

"Will you buy me *a new pair of boots?*" Anne asked, lifting her hem to display the ugly boy's boots beneath her skirt. "These were all I could get in Baton Rouge, and they're too large."

She hovered over the small table in the kitchen of their apartment while Papa counted the money he'd won that night: piles of banknotes and stacks of shiny gold and silver coins that shimmered in the lamplight.

"Sweetheart, I'll buy you a whole wardrobe full of shoes and hats and dresses if I have another couple of nights like this one."

He laughed the feverish laugh Anne knew so well, the giddy sound of a gambler who's hit a stroke of good luck.

Just one pair of boots, she thought, gazing around the shabby apartment. Just one pair of boots before it's all gone.

"But I did manage to pick up a little something for you." He kept counting and stacking coins as if he hadn't spoken, but Anne could see the corner of his mouth turn upward in barely suppressed laughter.

"What? Where? Give it to me, Papa! Please don't tease!"

"All right, all right." He chuckled. "It's in my coat pocket."

She ran to the chair in the corner where her father had left his coat when he'd come in, digging in the pockets until she discovered a heart-shaped locket on a gold chain. She held it carefully in her palm and carried it across the room where the light of the lamp would afford a better view.

An intricate filigree pattern adorned the top, and around the edges were garlands of golden roses. Her finger ran over the rough surface, feeling the texture before working at the clasp.

Disappointment rushed through her as she gazed at the portrait within, a likeness of a strange woman. She was quite lovely, with pale hair and high cheekbones, but she was utterly unknown to Anne.

"You didn't buy this, you won it," she accused, trying to keep the disappointment out of her voice. He must have won it very recently, perhaps tonight, because he hadn't even removed the former owner's portrait.

"What difference does it make? It's lovely, isn't it?" Papa had come to stand close behind her and gaze over her shoulder at the stranger's face.

Snapping the locket shut, Anne said, "Yes, it's lovely."

"It's only the beginning, Anne-Marie," he assured her with a pat on the shoulder. "I'll shower you with trinkets and clothes and everything your little heart desires."

Anne watched in dismay as he placed his hat on his head. Tall and elegant, Paul Cameron was still handsome, even at fifty. The graying of the hair at his temples only served to heighten his appeal. Women were drawn to him until they realized what a wastrel he was.

"You're not going out again—"

"Don't fret. I won't be gambling anymore tonight. In fact, I'll leave the money with you if it'll make you feel better."

"Then why?"

"I'm calling on a lady, if you must know." He winked and nearly skipped to the door.

"A lady, indeed! What sort of lady entertains men at this hour of the night?"

Papa opened the door and turned. His hand on the knob, he made a courtly bow. "That's for me to know, and for you—not to know."

She laughed, unable to resist his exuberance, as he danced out the door and slammed it behind him.

A gunshot broke the silence.

Anne jerked awake and leaped out of bed, her heart racing. Rapid gunfire riddled the darkness as she thrust her head out the window. A shadowed figure fell to the ground just within eyesight.

Papa!

Grabbing her wrapper, she ran into the dimly lit corridor, around a corner, and down the stairs, her heart pounding with fear, her mind racing.

Papa, don't die!

She ran into the street, her bare feet racing over the dirt surface.

"Let me through!" she demanded as she forced her

way through the crowd that had gathered around the fallen man.

You can't help him, a little voice told her. *Papa's going to die and you can't help him.*

So much blood, she thought, kneeling beside the injured man: blood everywhere. Nausea rose in her throat and she swallowed the fear that threatened to strangle her. Her trembling hands reached out to touch him as her mind recoiled from the fact that he was dying or dead.

"Papa, don't die," she whispered, past the tears that ran down her cheeks.

A shaft of light fell across the wounded man's face. It was the face of a stranger.

Anne pulled away in shock. This wasn't Natchez, it was San Antonio. Papa was already dead, had been dead for weeks.

Grief crushed her with an iron grip. She sat back on her heels, angrily wiping her tears. If only he'd stayed with her that night, if only. . . .

Damn you, Papa! Damn you for leaving me!

It must have been the dream. She'd awakened and thought she was still in Natchez. Papa had gone back out that night and he'd been killed, shot down like this nameless stranger.

"*Ángel.*"

The word was so faint, Anne wasn't sure if she'd heard it or imagined it. It took her a moment to realize what he'd said. When she did, she smiled down into the pain-filled eyes of the wounded man and shook her head. "No, I'm not an angel."

Something in his desperation touched her heart.

"He—he needs a doctor!" she cried, forcing her gaze from the bleeding Mexican.

A dirty, bleary-eyed man smiled down at her in a manner she knew all too well. Even across the distance that separated them she could smell the rank odor of liquor on his breath. She clutched her wrapper around her. A menacing silence fell over the group. She scanned the circle of a dozen faces, all staring down at her with similar expressions.

How could she have been so foolish? She'd run out into the street clad only in a thin nightgown and robe. A man had been shot and would probably bleed to death while the men who had gathered to gawk stood by and did nothing. And she knew all too well what kind of men would be out on the streets at this time of night.

Anne had bluffed her way out of tougher situations: there had to be a way out of this one. She could just stand up and back away, but they might not let her go. If only she had her pistol—

"Hell, ain't no doctor gonna treat no Mex!" the bleary-eyed man said, eliciting a round of laughter from the others.

"You should be ashamed of yourselves!" Anne cried, playing for time. "This man is a human being!"

The man closest to her turned his head to the side and spit a brown stream of tobacco juice that landed in the dust close to her foot. "Maybe he is and maybe he ain't."

"*Por favor,* I must tell you—"

The wounded man broke off, his face contorting as pain gripped his body.

Her gaze fell on the gun strapped to the fallen man's waist. Did she have time to grab it before anyone realized what she intended and moved to stop her? Did she dare?

*   *   *

Rafe Montalvo came awake with a violent start as the door to his room flew open and banged against the wall. José stood in the doorway, his body haloed by the light from the corridor.

Swearing under his breath, Rafe groaned and fell back on the bed. He hadn't even thought to go for his gun. The reflexes that had kept him alive for the past five years had failed him. One mistake like that could cost a man his life, especially a man who chased trouble the way he did.

"It's Luis!" José cried before Rafe could gather his wits. "He's been shot!"

Rafe sat up slowly this time and threw the covers off with a scowl. He paused and ran a hand through his hair, struggling to clear his sleepy mind. Luis Demas held the secret to a fortune in gold, gold that could flush El Alacrán out into the open. After five years of futile searching, Rafe realized that within less than twenty-four hours he might have found and lost the best chance he'd had to get close to the elusive bandit.

"Is he dead?" Rafe asked quietly.

"I don't know, but you've got to come with me! He's down on the street in front of the hotel. If he *is* alive, you've got to try and make him talk. If he's dying, maybe he'll tell you about the gold. He won't talk to me—me and Luis go way back. Hurry, amigo!"

Rafe stood and donned his pants quickly, then sat on the edge of the bed to jerk his boots on. Shoving his arms into his shirtsleeves, he stalked past José, grabbing his gun belt from the coatrack on the way out the door.

A full moon cast freakish shadows on the street where men shifted in a taut, uneasy circle. The hairs on the back of Rafe's neck stood on end as he approached.

The air throbbed with tension like the silent excitement before a hanging or a dogfight.

Instinctively, Rafe's fingers tested the strap on his holster. Blood pounded in his veins and tingled in his fingertips as his body prepared for a confrontation.

He shouldered his way through the crowd to find himself face-to-face with the young woman he'd seen on the street that day. The men had completely forgotten the injured man and were ogling her. She looked as if she'd been in bed. Pale red hair had worked its way free of the braid that hung down her back to her waist, framing her face in disarray. Her thin nightgown and wrapper didn't conceal her body as well as she probably hoped.

He clenched his fists at his sides, trying to think, to curb the irrational anger and fear that roiled inside his chest.

Christ, what was she doing out here this time of night? And how the hell was he going to get her and Demas out of this?

These men were teamsters and drifters, probably deserters from one army or the other. The streets belonged to them at night, the streets and anyone unlucky enough or foolish enough to wander into their territory. They recognized no law, and nothing in San Antonio would stop them from doing whatever they wanted to do under cover of darkness, least of all a skinny half-naked woman with a gun in her hand.

"You can't shoot us all," one of them said.

She pointed the gun straight at the speaker. "Maybe not, but I'll make sure you're first."

"Hell, she prob'ly can't even fire a gun."

In answer, she pulled the hammer back and cocked the pistol. "I can shoot the head off a one-eyed jack at fifty paces, so I can sure as hell put a bullet through this bastard's head from here."

Rafe stifled a laugh at her audacity. He didn't know if she was bluffing or not, and he didn't want to find out. Acting quickly, he said the first thing that came to his mind.

"Darlin', I've been lookin' all over for you! What the hell are you doin' out here in the middle of the street this time of night?"

"Well—" She turned to look at him. Her eyes widened, and confusion became fear.

By now he should have become accustomed to seeing fear in people's eyes, but he hadn't. It still caused a sick pain in the pit of his stomach. He wanted to walk away, to turn his back so he wouldn't have to see the expression on her face.

"Were you sleepwalkin' again?" He turned to the men who were gaping at him. "She walks in her sleep. The doctors can't do a thing about it."

Sensing movement to his left, Rafe gripped the hilt of his gun, gazing around the circle from man to man.

"This ain't none of your business." A man with yellow teeth and foul breath, the one who had been threatened with the gun, stepped forward.

He was big and burly, probably a teamster. He'd be hell in a brawl, but he probably couldn't handle a gun worth a damn.

"The hell it ain't," Rafe replied, his voice nonchalant. "She's my wife."

He moved closer to the young woman. She didn't seem to notice him until his hand closed over hers and the gun and she tried to pull away.

"Give me the gun," he urged softly. Her hands trembled beneath his but he recognized cold intent in her eyes and knew she would have killed as many of these men as she could have if they had made a move toward her.

Her wide, frightened eyes darted from him to the men who watched her with a predatory zeal. He knew she was weighing her options, trying to decide whether to take her chances with them or trust him. He didn't envy her position, but he hoped for both their sakes that she made the right choice.

She looked at him again, and the murderous glint in her eyes softened as she relinquished the weapon. Her eyes met his and he recognized the fear in their depths, fear and a silent plea that wrapped around his heart and shook him to his core. She was asking him not to betray her trust.

Rafe stuffed the pistol in his belt while his gaze moved inexorably over her thinly veiled body. The outline of her firm, round breasts and long legs sent the blood pounding through his body. A fierce arousal gripped him before he managed to tear his eyes away from her. The scent of lilac soap wafted to him as he turned to face the crowd. It was a moment before he could speak.

"I'm takin' my wife and her friend to the hotel. Anybody got any objections?"

"Señorita," the wounded man murmured, just loud enough for Anne to hear.

She'd almost forgotten him. She tried to listen to the conversation around her, tried to understand why she had relinquished her only means of self-defense to a man she knew to be a killer.

She'd lost control of the situation, if she'd ever had control of it. This stranger, this bounty hunter, had both of their lives in his hands. She trembled at the thought, shivering despite the heat at the memory of his gaze stripping the clothes from her body and the cold, hard glint she'd seen in his eyes when he'd looked into her face again.

"Por favor, señorita, you must listen."

His voice was so weak she could scarely hear him. Anne focused on the face of the wounded man. He probably wanted comfort, but she had none to offer. All her energies were concentrated on escaping this dangerous situation, all her senses focused on the man who had casually called her his wife.

"Please don't get excited. The doctor will be here soon," she lied, kneeling beside the Mexican again. She could smell the blood, and she knew he was dying.

"I want to make you a very wealthy woman," he murmured. "I can tell you where there is a million dollars in gold." He looked skyward. "Maybe this will make up for some of my sins."

Anne divided her attention between the delirious man and the drama going on around her. What if this bounty hunter failed to convince these men to let them go their way? There were almost a dozen of them. What could one man do? What would she do if they overpowered him? Surely someone—the sheriff, the vigilantes who controlled the town—had heard the shots.

"Come closer." The wounded man grabbed hold of Anne's arm and pulled her down toward his face. Something in his eyes stilled her, and the noise and tension around them receded as he started talking.

"The gold," he whispered. "It is hidden in a small church in a place called Concepción near Chihuahua, Mexico. There are some loose boards behind the altar. A million dollars. No one could find it if they did not know already where it was. Go there. It is yours. Do what you will with it." He licked his lips as he winced with another pain. "And now, I must ask you to do one thing for me."

"What is it?"

She waited while he coughed convulsively. He fought for breath, fought to speak.

"Get a priest," he murmured.

Those words were his last. His body went limp and his life escaped on a ragged sigh. She peeled his fingers from around her arm and stared down at his silent, empty body. His words echoed in her mind and she began to tremble.

Slowly she became aware of her surroundings again. The huge, dirty man she had threatened with the pistol earlier moved toward the gunfighter, but the man closest to him placed a hand on his chest, halting him. "Leave it alone, Jake."

"Shut up, Tucker, I ain't scared of this hombre," the other man replied, without taking his gaze off the bounty hunter. "And I don't believe this pretty little thing is his wife."

"Better listen to him, Jake," the bounty hunter said. The menace in his voice shivered down Anne's spine, and she wondered again if she'd made the right choice in trusting him. "You might not believe she's my wife," he went on, "but believe this. Either you back down or I'll put a bullet between your eyes and roll a smoke before you can clear leather."

"That's Rafe Montalvo," Tucker informed Jake. "I seen him gun down three *pistoleros* in Mesilla a few months ago. Ain't never seen nothing like it before or since."

A tick started in Jake's left eye. Anne held her breath

as Jake considered Tucker's revelation and his own options. She could almost see his bravado faltering. What sort of man could inspire that kind of fear by the mere mention of his name?

"Why don't you fellows move along now?" Rafe Montalvo suggested. "The show's over."

Slowly the disgruntled crowd began to disperse and the gunfighter turned his attention back to the wounded man and to Anne, who struggled to her feet.

"He—he's dead," she murmured.

The gunfighter stepped toward her and she took an involuntary step back. She noticed the tensing of a muscle in his jaw and the anger that flashed briefly in his eyes before he hunkered down next to the Mexican and placed a finger against the dead man's jugular vein.

"One minute he was alive and talking, and the next—"

"Talking?" The gunfighter stood and narrowed his eyes, cold, emotionless eyes that seemed more animal than human. "What did he say?"

He took another step and she backed away again, but this time he was quicker. His hand wrapped around her upper arm and she gasped as he pulled her up close to his face. She tried to jerk free but he only clutched her more tightly, his fingers digging into her soft flesh.

"What did he say?" he demanded through clenched teeth.

"You're hurting me!" She recoiled from the menace in his voice and in his pale, pale eyes. "He . . . he wanted a priest, but there wasn't time," she said, hardly aware of speaking the words. Her mind and body had gone numb with shock.

She wanted desperately to run, to escape back to her hotel room, but she doubted her legs would carry her, and she wasn't at all sure he would let her go. Swaying dizzily from exhaustion and tension, Anne feared she might faint for the first time in her life.

He's a killer, she thought. Their eyes met and she tried to keep the fear from strangling her, even as she fought the urge to look away.

A man who won't look you in the eye is a liar, and you can bet he's bluffing. Anne remembered her father's words from long ago, and she knew if she looked away first, this man would never believe her.

"That's all he said." She tried to jerk free again, hoping to take him by surprise, but the attempt failed, leaving her no choice but to try to face him down.

He stared at her for a long moment before his expression suddenly softened and he released her. His eyes reflected curiosity and something like tenderness as he lifted a hand toward her face. She thought he would touch her, and she flinched, her heart catching in her throat. But when his fingers were so close they could almost caress her temple, he stopped, a shadow of pain flashing across his face before he dropped his hand away. He turned to gaze down at the lifeless body.

"Well, I doubt that all the priests in Texas and Mexico put together could pray Luis Demas into heaven."

"What a dreadful thing to say about a dead man." She blinked to clear her dizziness, surprised she could speak at all.

"He was a bandit," he told her as he turned to face her once again. "He murdered and raped and stole and cheated all his life. Just because he's dead doesn't make him a saint all of a sudden."

"I know." Perspiration broke out over Anne's body. She struggled to still the tremors that gripped her and the nausea that threatened to overwhelm her. She heard him curse as the darkness at the edges of her mind closed in around her and she staggered toward the ground. He caught her and swung her up into his arms.

He smelled of soap and stale whiskey and cheap perfume—the kind that had often clung to her father when he would come home from one of his late nights on the riverfront. Strong arms surrounded her, one supporting her back, the other beneath her knees, leaving Anne no choice but to twine an arm around his neck. Conflicting desires—to remain there and to run as fast and as far as she could—warred within her.

His hard chest crushed her breast. She tried to shift her weight, but her efforts only increased the intimate contact. So she remained as still as she could, reminding herself that sensation could be dangerous and that sometimes warmth and security were cruel lies.

"Please, I'm all right," she managed to murmur.

For a moment she thought he hadn't heard her. He said nothing, just stared at her with those ice-gray eyes that saw far too much and revealed far too little. But the pain she saw lurking there terrified her.

"Which room is yours?" he asked as he carried her toward the hotel.

"I can walk," she said, stiffening in horror. "Please put me down."

He carried her into the lobby and up the stairs to the landing above. His gaze held hers as he lowered her feet to the floor, and his expression softened for a moment, or perhaps it was just the effect of the dim light on his face.

"Are you sure?" His gentle voice went straight to her heart.

Anne nodded, unable to speak, frightened by her profound reaction to him. She didn't want to feel anything for this dark, violent man. His intense gaze made her uncomfortable until he turned with a slight nod and retreated down the stairs.

What an odd man.

Somehow she sensed there was much more to him than met the eye. At first glance, he seemed to be nothing more than a cold-blooded killer, a man without conscience. Yet he had stepped forward and rescued her from a precarious situation. She couldn't help wondering why.

Absently, Anne reached up to touch the locket that should have been between her breasts.

It was gone. The clasp must have broken again. Her hand patted her bodice as she gazed down at the floor around her feet. She remembered having it when she'd returned to her room after dinner. She couldn't abide having lost it. Her father had given it to her the night he'd died.

What if it had fallen off in the street? Or maybe just downstairs?

Either way, she had to go back for it. Retracing her path through the hall and down the staircase, she had almost reached the lobby when she heard the sound of approaching footsteps. Ducking quickly around a corner, she pressed her body flat against the wall as Rafe Montalvo stepped into her line of vision in the parlor, a smoking cheroot in his mouth. The last thing she wanted was another confrontation with him tonight.

He paused and turned around to face someone inside the room, taking the cheroot from his mouth and rolling it between thumb and index finger.

"Look, I don't give a goddamn about Luis Demas," the gunfighter said to the bald-headed man who was standing in the doorway. "And I sure as hell ain't paying for his burial. As far as I'm concerned, you can take his carcass and drop it at the end of town. Buzzards gotta eat, too."

Anne clapped her hand over her mouth to keep from retching.

"Of course. Well, I won't take any more of your time, Mr. . . . ." The bald-headed man let the word trail off, as if expecting the other man to supply his name. When Rafe Montalvo didn't, the little man shrugged and walked toward the door, where he paused and said softly, "Whoever you are, death seems to follow you, don't it?"

Anne withdrew farther out of sight as the bounty hunter followed the other man toward the front door. Then she rushed headlong up the stairs, fleeing from those wretched words.

3

The stagecoach to Ubiquitous pulled out of San Antonio precisely at eight the next morning as scheduled. Anne sat in a forward-facing seat, resting her head against the door. She had hardly slept at all last night, and there was little hope of doing so now. The stage was hot and dusty, and it felt as if the driver were deliberately hitting every bump and gopher hole they encountered.

She closed her eyes against the sun's glare and tried to ignore the idle chitchat of the man who sat across from her. The smell of his cologne nearly stifled her in such close quarters. He appeared young and reasonably clean. Some women—perhaps most women— would find him attractive, but he had a weak chin and the practiced smile of a cardsharp. He was probably a lady's man too, Anne decided, shifting in a vain effort to find a comfortable position.

Not to be discouraged, the young man turned his attention to the matronly woman who sat beside Anne.

"You ladies been travelin' long?" he asked.

He was definitely a dandy, Anne thought, just like Borden McKenna, who couldn't stop talking if you put a gag in his mouth.

"All the way from St. Louis," the woman said. "I'm a widow, you know, going to El Paso to stay with my brother and his wife."

The woman's shrill whining voice grated on Anne's already raw nerves.

"I'm truly sorry, ma'am."

If the man wasn't a snake oil salesman, Anne thought wryly, he should consider changing vocations.

"It hasn't been easy," the woman went on. "No family to speak of—"

"Well, at least you've got your daughter with you."

Anne stiffened. He was fishing for information.

The woman rose to the bait. "Oh, we're not together."

Thanks, lady, Anne thought. Didn't anyone ever tell you not to confide in strangers? Now this slack-jawed snake knows I'm traveling alone.

The weight of the pistol in her skirt pocket reassured her. He seemed harmless enough, but she didn't trust him any more than she liked him. And after last night, she'd vowed never to be caught unprepared again.

"Well, ma'am, I don't mean to frighten you, but Texas is an awful dangerous place for a woman to be traveling alone."

"Thank you for your concern, young man," the matron said, a bit crossly, Anne thought. "But I've made it this far and I'll make it the rest of the way. The Lord is looking after me."

"I'm sure He is, ma'am, but, well, you're getting into

Indian territory once you leave Ubiquitous. Now that the army's gone east to fight the war, there ain't nothing to stop them savages from doing whatever they want."

Anne tried to ignore her fellow passengers. She had enough to think about without becoming involved in someone else's life, even for the duration of a stage-coach ride. But whenever she let her mind wander unchecked, it took her back to San Antonio and the words Rafe Montalvo had spoken to the undertaker, and a cold chill crawled up her spine.

She'd known he was a killer from the moment she'd first seen him. She'd recognized the ruthlessness in his eyes. Hearing those words seemed to confirm the worst.

Why had Rafe Montalvo, a killer of some notoriety, a man who had ridden casually down the street in broad daylight only hours earlier with a body slung over his horse, come to her aid? Why had he been there at all? It didn't make sense, unless—unless the Mexi-can who had died in the street hadn't been the only one who knew about the gold.

She told herself not to think about it. She'd never see Rafe Montalvo again, which was just as well, con-sidering the way she had instinctively reacted to him. Even if he hadn't been the most dangerous man she had ever encountered, bitter experience had taught her to distrust her own desires where men were concerned.

Never again would she allow her heart to overrule her mind or cloud her judgment. She'd let that happen once and lived to regret it. What a fool she'd been!

Borden McKenna had been charming and handsome enough to melt the heart of any innocent girl. But she should have known better. She'd grown up on river-boats and in river towns and she'd seen countless charming, handsome young men by the time she was eighteen. And though he'd possessed a silver tongue, she had learned from her gambler father to judge a man by what he did rather than what he said.

"Look into a man's eyes," Paul Cameron had told her. "You can see into a man's soul through his eyes."

But she had forgotten everything she'd ever been taught about judging character and integrity the minute Borden McKenna had turned his green Irish eyes on her and wooed her with that soft Irish brogue. He'd said he loved her . . . and he'd shown it by murdering her father.

"Boy, you must be a hundred miles away."

Anne glanced up at the smiling young man in the seat opposite her. Her eyes narrowed and she gave him her best don't-bother-me look, then gazed out the window again.

"I was just asking—"

"Don't." She jerked her head around, glaring at him. "I am not in the habit of talking to strangers, and I don't plan to start now."

The irritating young man had every intention of pursuing the conversation despite her harsh words, but at that moment the stagecoach rolled to a halt. She peered out the window but could see no change in their surroundings.

"Why are we stopping?" the older woman asked.

"Looks like somebody wants a ride," the young man replied.

Anne's heart stopped. Out the opposite window she could see Rafe Montalvo striding toward the coach, saddlebags slung over his shoulder, leading his horse by the reins.

He'd shaved his beard, but it was him, there could be no mistake. Her gaze slid down his broad chest to his slim waist and the black leather chaps tied on with thin leather thongs just below the waist. The faded denim of his pants showed through in front where the chaps didn't meet.

She gasped and looked away before he could catch her. She'd been staring at his—at the front of his jeans—for how long she couldn't say. The blood rushed to her face as she closed her eyes. She hoped fervently that the man across from her was mistaken, that Rafe Montalvo did not intend to ride the rest of the way to Ubiquitous with them.

She tried to slow her frantic breathing, tried to fight the rising alarm inside her breast. Then his deep, quiet voice reached her, rumbling over her nerves and causing her heart to flutter uncontrollably.

"Horse went lame on me," he said. "You got room for one more?"

"Sure thing, mister," came the driver's reply. "Throw your saddlebags up top and tie your horse to the back of the coach."

"Mighty obliged. What do I owe you?"

"Two bits."

She closed her eyes and tried to steel herself against his inevitable appearance in the tiny, cramped coach. No matter where he sat, he would be close to her. She didn't know if she could bear to ride for the next several hours in such close quarters with this man who stirred her emotions more than any man she had ever encountered. He represented everything she wanted so desperately to put behind her: danger, uncertainty, instability. And yet . . . and yet . . .

The coach rocked, and she knew he had thrown his saddlebags on top as the driver had instructed. In the next instant, the door close to her flew open and a shock flashed through her as his eyes met hers.

One corner of his mouth curved upward at sight of her, but she couldn't tell if he were surprised to find her there or not. He tipped his hat, causing the heat on her face to increase. She turned away, mortified by the gesture and by her reaction, her breath heavy in her chest.

"Ma'am," he said, removing his hat. He climbed inside and lowered his large frame into the seat directly opposite her.

She quickly shifted her legs to avoid contact with his, but he was so tall, he seemed to fill the entire coach.

The vehicle lurched forward suddenly, causing her leg to brush against his knee. She recoiled from the contact, struggling to control the rapid rise and fall of her chest by concentrating on something else, anything else, but it was impossible with him so near.

He smiled crookedly at her, and she turned her gaze to the window. Again her leg brushed against his, and again she jerked away as if she'd been burned.

A deafening silence fell over the coach. Even the annoying young man seemed to have nothing to say. He sat stiff and straight beside Rafe Montalvo, pulling his collar away from his throat as if it were suddenly too tight.

The heat in the tiny space increased. Anne fanned her burning face with her hand. She'd met men like Rafe Montalvo before, men who seemed to have death in their eyes, but she'd always managed to stay away from them. Until now.

She crossed her arms over her chest and ran her hands up and down her arms. What if he knew about the gold? The menace she'd glimpsed in his pale eyes last night on the street when he'd demanded to know what the dead man had said caused her blood to run cold.

She also remembered the shadow of pain she'd seen pass across those eyes. He was too dangerous, too complicated, too—too unpredictable. She didn't want to admit that he intrigued her nearly as much as he frightened her.

Was he following her? Maybe he was just traveling the same way. Why would he follow her . . . ?

A million dollars. She wrote the number in her mind and counted the zeros: six. It would be heavy. She had a twenty-dollar gold piece in her reticule. It would take fifty thousand of them to make a million. She didn't care that a million dollars would allow her to live like a queen. Today she would be starting a new life with her aunt in Ubiquitous.

Then why did you lie? a tiny voice inside her asked. Why didn't you just tell him what the Mexican told you about the gold?

She couldn't answer her own question. Maybe when she was safe and sound in her aunt's house, if he was still around, if that was indeed why he was following her, maybe then she'd tell him.

Leaning back against the seat, she tried to relax, tried to forget the man who sat across from her, his long legs practically wrapped around hers, his knees nearly touching her seat. She tried to think about Aunt Marguerite and the life that awaited her in Ubiquitous.

The image she had created of her aunt's house floated before her closed eyes, an image she'd carried with her all the way from Natchez. It would be cozy and full of nice furnishings and bric-a-brac, things her aunt would have picked out lovingly and chosen just the right place to display. Once she reached Ubiquitous, she would be living in the kind of place she had only glimpsed from outside.

What would it be like to sleep in the same bed every night, a bed that didn't roll and pitch with the river's current? She would eat off the same dishes every day, sit in the same parlor every evening, and wake up in the mornings without that disoriented feeling of not knowing exactly where she was.

A million dollars. No one could find it if they did not know already where it was.

Carefully she peeked at the gunfighter through slitted eyes. He'd pulled his hat down over his forehead. She knew he was staring at her. The hairs on her arms stood on end and her mouth went dry. And she knew in her gut that he was following her.

Anne climbed down from the stagecoach practically before it stopped rolling. She didn't know why Rafe Montalvo hadn't spoken to her during the excruciatingly long stagecoach ride, but she wasn't about to give him a chance now.

A little man with round wire-rimmed spectacles and thick, straight, nondescript hair peered back at her from the cool, dark interior of the stagecoach ticket office.

"Can you tell me how to get to Marguerite Tremaine's house?"

"Well, yes, ma'am. Turn left two blocks up the street. It's a big white house on the right. But—"

She didn't wait to hear what else the man had to say. This was the last leg of her journey, and nothing was going to get between her and her goal. She grabbed her carpetbag, stepped onto the planked sidewalk, and headed up the street, limping slightly because of the blisters on her feet.

Now that she had arrived in Ubiquitous, the first

thing she planned to do, once she was safely settled in her aunt's house, was buy a good pair of boots. In Natchez, there hadn't been time to purchase anything. She'd fled in the dark of night, fearful that Borden McKenna might make good on his threat and come to the apartment where she and her father had lived to get the money he claimed her father had cheated him out of.

Once she'd arrived in Texas, she'd found that the wartime shortage of supplies had driven prices sky high. She'd been reluctant to spend the money as long as the boots she had didn't have holes in them.

As she walked, she glanced up and down the street to make sure she wasn't being followed. It was late afternoon, and there was hardly anyone on the street. If Rafe Montalvo did try and follow her, she shouldn't have any trouble spotting him.

A smile curved her lips as she rounded the corner and looked up at the large two-story white house on the right. She couldn't have missed it if she'd tried. It was the only white house on the street.

Finally she'd come home!

Joy swelled in Anne's heart and clogged her throat. She walked toward the wrought-iron fence that surrounded the house. Inside that fence was everything she had ever longed for. Once she walked through the gate, her life would never be the same again. This was where she belonged, where she'd always belonged.

The sight of boards nailed to the front door stopped her in her tracks. She glanced around to make sure she hadn't overlooked another white house, but this was the only one on the entire street.

The gate creaked open under her hand, and she walked slowly toward the front portal. As she drew closer, she could see that something had been tacked to the door. She stepped up onto the veranda, and the bold print leaped out at her.

PUBLIC NOTICE

ESTATE OF
MRS. MARGUERITE TREMAINE

PROPERTY FOR SALE BY
BANK OF UBIQUITOUS, TEXAS

Anne tried to focus on the words that floated before her blurred vision. She wiped her forehead with the back of her hand. It couldn't be. *Estate* of Mrs. Marguerite Tremaine? Aunt Marguerite was dead? She read it again, and stunned disbelief slowly gave way to rage. She'd come all this way, for nothing. Nothing! She beat her fist against the boards.

Slowly, she looked around at what her mind hadn't allowed her to see before: the chipped paint on the house's facade, the weeds that choked whatever flowers might once have bloomed in the small garden.

Across the street, a light burned in a curtained window. Would whoever lived inside that house know what had happened? When? And how? There were so many questions.

Wrapping her anger and sorrow in a blanket of determination, she stepped down from the veranda and strode toward the large brick building, halting uncertainly at the door. Behind her, her aunt's house sat in the midst of its ruined yard.

She knocked, tentatively at first, but when there was no answer she knocked again, more insistently this time. Torn between the need to stay and wait and the urge to turn and leave, she slowly backed away. She had nearly reached the edge of the stoop when the door swung open and a small fragile-looking woman stood peering at her.

"May I help you, young lady?" the woman asked.

"Mrs. Tremaine," was all Anne could say past the tears that filled her eyes. Her voice trembled and she took a deep, steadying breath, gazing away from the sympathy in the little woman's face.

"Are you related?"

"I—I'm her niece f-from Natchez."

"Oh, dear, won't you come inside?"

"No," Anne said, taking another step back. She didn't think she could bear to be inside that bright, cozy-looking home, to see the way other people lived and to know that it would forever be a dream for her. She couldn't bear this woman's pity. "I just need to know—"

"Who is it, Sarah?" A man came to stand behind the woman. His eyes were wide and kind-looking, his demeanor and appearance as comfortable as the house they lived in.

The woman placed a hand on the man's arm. "It's Maggie's niece, come all the way from Natchez." She directed her next words to Anne. "It's been two months since Maggie took sick—"

"Two months?" Two months ago, she'd been living in Natchez with her father, only vaguely aware that Ubiquitous, Texas, and Marguerite Tremaine even existed.

"Consumption. She died about ten days ago."

"She was dead before I sent the letter," Anne murmured.

"It must be a shock to you, dear," the woman said. "Won't you come inside and have some tea? Perhaps some dinner?"

"By all means," the man insisted. "Maggie was a dear friend."

She was already off the stoop and on the sidewalk. "Thank you anyway, but I have to—"

Her throat closed, and she couldn't finish. Turning away, she picked up her carpetbag and hurried back toward the stage depot.

Rounding a corner, she stopped, and leaned against a pole for support. A sob escaped her control, and she clutched a fist to her chest. She would not cry. Crying did no good. It changed nothing. She was alone, more alone than she had ever been in her life, and she didn't know what to do.

The sky was darkening. She certainly couldn't stay here. She'd have to find a hotel. That should be easy enough. Hotels were one thing she knew all too well. There had been one right across the street from the stage depot.

With a tired sigh, she straightened her spine and turned away from her dream, back to the hotel.

She didn't know what time it was when she finally gave up trying to sleep and got out of bed. Somewhere in the town, a rooster crowed, so she knew it must be nearly dawn. Lighting a lamp beside the bed, she rubbed her face in an attempt to clear her head. Her mind raced, one thought tumbling over another like the churning of a riverboat paddle wheel.

Her aunt was dead, had been dead for ten days. Ten days! All her plans, all her dreams had been nothing but fantasies, and she'd allowed herself to believe them. Now she would pay the price in pain and disappointment.

She'd never had a home, never had any stability. Marguerite Tremaine had been her last hope, and now she was gone. Not only that, but she had spent nearly all her money to get to Ubiquitous. She was alone and practically destitute.

In all the world, she had no one. Her mother's wealthy Creole family in New Orleans had turned its back on them when her mother had married someone not of their choosing. Her father had no family. She had no one, nothing. Hopelessness and stark aloneness crushed her.

I could die and no one would care.

Kneeling on the floor beside the bed, she shoved her hand underneath the mattress, thinking about her father and reliving the night of his death over and over in her mind.

Until her father had been shot on the street in Natchez, she hadn't realized that blood had an odor or that death had an odor. Smelling it again just last night had brought back a flood of memories.

She closed her eyes tightly. Her mind played the "what if" game. What if Papa hadn't gone back out that night? What if he hadn't cheated at cards in order to win? What if Borden McKenna hadn't caught him? What if Borden McKenna had truly loved her?

As her hand closed around the object she had been groping for beneath the mattress, she tried to empty her mind. She pulled out the worn leather pouch and sat on the bed once again, stroking the bag's soft surface.

She'd made the running bag in Baton Rouge. Even now, she could almost hear the cannon fire from the ships on the river that had sent her and the rest of the population fleeing through the streets in the middle of the night.

The running bag could be attached to hooks sewn inside the waistband of her skirt so that she could flee at a moment's notice without leaving behind her most prized possessions. At the same time, she could keep her hands free. It had worked well, and she had kept it, even after her father had sent Borden McKenna to Baton Rouge to find her and bring her to Natchez.

Opening the bag now, she spread its contents on the bed, trying not to think of the past. She had enough to worry about in the present.

She picked up a folded piece of paper, a letter from her father. He'd written it to her in Natchez while she'd been in Baton Rouge, but he had never gotten around to posting it. She'd only found it after the funeral. She couldn't bear to look at it. The pain of his death was too fresh still, so she stuffed it back inside the pouch and went on to the next item, a small bottle of perfume. Uncorking the bottle, she held it beneath her nose.

"Jasmine," Borden McKenna had said. "It suits you, Anne. Lovely, delicate, but strong."

A growl rumbled up from her throat. She might shed a tear now and then over her father's death, but she'd be damned if Borden McKenna would ever make her cry again. She placed the bottle on the bedside table and returned the rest of her possessions to the pouch, all except her money.

She'd been hoarding money and hiding it from her father all her life. If she had not, they surely would have starved to death. She had managed to save a small nest egg, which she had been forced to use in Baton Rouge to support herself and later in Natchez

to support both of them. But she still had most of the
silver and gold her father had won that last night.
She'd left the folding money behind. Confederate
money was hardly worth the paper it was printed on.
Silver and gold, now that was a different story. Harder
to carry, true, but silver and gold would always hold
their value.

She began to count. How much would the bank ask
for her aunt's house—a thousand dollars? Two thousand dollars? More? It was a large house, as large as
some of the fine homes in Baton Rouge and Natchez.
But she had no idea what a house like that might be
worth here.

"Five hundred dollars," she said aloud when she'd
finished counting, five hundred and whatever she had
in her reticule.

She might not know much about property values,
but she guessed that five hundred dollars wouldn't be
nearly enough to buy a house like that. And even if it
was, how would she live if she bought it with every
penny she had? There weren't many things she could
do to earn a living. She could sew, but she hated
sewing almost as much as she hated being poor.

The only other skill she possessed was gambling,
and she could not possibly stoop to making her living
gambling. She'd rather starve.

A million dollars in gold. The words of the Mexican
haunted her. She'd tried all day to forget them. She'd
told herself she didn't want the gold; she would be per-
fectly happy with a simple life with her mother's sister.

But that wasn't to be. Marguerite Tremaine was
dead. And Anne had nothing. As always she would
have to rely on herself. If she wanted that house, and
she wanted it desperately, she would have to have

money. In fact, if she wanted to *live,* she would have to have money.

It is hidden in a small church in the town of Concepción, near Chihuahua. Mexico. No one could find it if they did not know already where it was.

She blinked wearily. Her eyelids were heavy, and suddenly she wanted to sleep and not wake up for two days.

Her hand closed around the perfume bottle on the bedside table, and she carried it across the room to the open window. The sky had begun turning pink and soon the sun would be high overhead. If she allowed herself to fall asleep now, she wouldn't wake up until late afternoon, and she needed to be at the bank when it opened this morning.

Leaning out the window, she dropped the perfume bottle. It shattered on a below her window and she smiled with satisfaction. Why she had kept it for so long, she couldn't say, but it felt liberating to let it go. She made a silent vow then and there never to think of Borden McKenna again, never to look back, to keep her eyes fixed on the future.

She reached up to touch the locket that wasn't there, and the pain of loss twisted in her heart. It was the last thing her father had ever given her, that and the money spread on the bed before her now. She would go to the bank and try to turn that inheritance into a home. Perhaps her father could provide something for her in death that he never could have given her in life.

The dream was always the same: the smell of burning wood, the heat of the desert, the eyes consumed with a pain so horrible it was unimaginable. God, he could never forget those eyes, pleading with him, begging him—for what, he didn't know: for salvation, for an end to the unbearable agony . . .

Rafe heard the crack of a gunshot, as if from miles away, and bolted upright with a gasp. He was panting and covered with sweat. It took him a moment to get his bearings and remember where he was.

Texas; yes, Texas. Five years separated him from that hideous memory, five years and a thick wall of defenses.

"It was just a dream," he told himself over and over again, chanting the words as if they could protect him.

But nothing could protect him. Nothing could wipe out the past. The pain was every bit as strong today as it had been then.

He squeezed his eyes shut and ran a hand through his damp, tousled hair, then threw off the covers and got out of bed.

In the early morning darkness, he stumbled to the washstand across the room, poured water into the basin, and splashed it over his face and bare chest.

"Goddammit!" he said aloud, bracing himself with his hands on either side of the washstand, shivering in the aftermath of the dream. It was always like this afterward: the tremors, the nausea, the impotent fury.

The dream had haunted him for five years now, but lately it seemed to be visiting him more often than usual, as if his own mind were attacking him. It would give him no rest until he took the vengeance that had been his single reason to go on living and fighting, even in the darkest times when he would have almost welcomed death.

Grabbing a towel, he dried his face and chest. Useless regret and guilt twisted in his gut until he found it almost impossible to breathe.

Even time couldn't dull some memories.

He studied his reflection in the cracked, faded glass. Running a hand over his stubbled chin, he tried to remain detached, tried not to study too closely the man who looked back at him, afraid of what he might find there. He'd been chasing after animals for so long he had almost become one of them. His single-minded quest for vengeance had left a permanent scar on his soul. It showed in his eyes; he didn't have to look to know that.

He walked across the room to the corner where he had dropped his saddlebags, closing his mind against the vestiges of the nightmare, against any emotion. It was his only defense, and it was getting harder to maintain with every day that passed. A constant battle raged inside him, a battle for control. If he ever lost control, he didn't want to contemplate what might happen.

Goddammit! I won't let it get to me, I won't! he thought, shoving the dream back into the deepest recesses of his mind as he dug in the bag for a clean shirt.

Slowly the trembling stopped and his breathing returned to normal.

As he unfolded the shirt, something fell out and hit his bare foot. He bent down and retrieved the locket by its gold chain. Looking at the trinket made him think of its owner, and a bitter smile twisted his lips.

He held the locket close to his nostrils, even as his cracked thumbnail worked at the catch. It still smelled of her, a faint, hauntingly feminine scent that was hers alone.

"Empty," he said aloud as he pried the locket open like an oyster.

The locket was of the finest gold, crafted with care by a master jeweler. The piece might easily be an heirloom. And yet its owner could not find one image among all her possessions dear enough to wear close to her heart.

Nothing about her made sense. She was like a puzzle, and none of the pieces fit.

He shouldn't care, he reminded himself. The less he knew about her, the better. She was a complication, nothing more. She'd already cost him four hundred dollars in bounty money.

But the memory of her soft skin, her dark violet eyes, and the way she'd felt in his arms made him wish that things could be different, that *he* could be different.

Rafe snapped the locket closed and curled his fist around it. No, he reminded himself, she was more than a distraction. She just might be the only person alive who knew Luis Demas's secret. It didn't matter who she was or why she was here. He didn't care about her lies or her secrets or the emptiness this locket seemed to speak of.

He crammed the locket in his saddlebags and dressed quickly. As he tucked his shirt into his pants, he reminded himself that he was only here to find out what, if anything, Demas had revealed before he'd died. He had somehow to convince the girl to tell him what she knew about the gold, the gold that would lead him to El Alacrán. Finding El Alacrán, after all, was the only thing that really mattered.

4

The road to Castroville might be wide and well marked, as the blacksmith had assured her it would be, but the surface left much to be desired. By midmorning, Anne had been jostled and jolted until she was certain her body must be covered with bruises. Her hands felt as if they had been cut to shreds, despite the heavy leather gloves she wore.

She decided that this part of Texas must be the closest thing to hell on earth. In fact, had anyone asked her for a description of hell, this would have been it. The sun pressed down on her like a scorching flatiron. The barren terrain stretched as far as the eye could see in all directions. With the exception of an occasional cactus, not a tree dotted the desolate landscape. There was no water, no shade, nothing but the monotonous yellow-gold desert sand.

Once again, life had set her on a course not of her

own choosing. The words of the banker, Mr. Sampson, echoed in her mind. "I'm sorry, Miss Cameron, but without collateral . . . "

She knew he hadn't been sorry. He hadn't cared one bit about her or her problems. He'd wanted her gone. She'd known from the first caustic words he had spoken to her that the battle was lost.

"You have no guardian, no husband, no job, and only five hundred dollars to your name. To be frank, if I sold the house to you, I would be doing so with the knowledge that you are incapable of repaying the mortgage."

"I told you," she said through clenched teeth, "I will be receiving a large sum of money soon."

"Yes, you told me, but you were unable to tell me where it is coming from. It's not an inheritance. You have no prospect of employment. What do you plan to do, rob a bank?" He ended with a laugh.

"Something like that," she murmured under her breath.

"I'm sorry, Miss Cameron, I didn't hear you."

"Nothing like that," she said. "It's a gift."

"Try to see this from my point of view," he said slowly, pronouncing each word succinctly. "You are asking me to take a terrible gamble."

Mr. Thaddeus P. Sampson of the Bank of Ubiquitous had been unmovable. The house would be auctioned off at the end of the month.

Left with no other choice, she had taken the greatest gamble of her life. From the bank, she had gone directly to the livery stable, where she had paid a fortune for a team and wagon and directions to Castroville, the next town on the road to Eagle Pass.

The blacksmith in Ubiquitous who had sold her the worn-out wagon and pair of swaybacked horses had warned her that by sundown she'd regret deciding to make the trip. She was already wishing she hadn't started, and, if her estimate was right, there were still several hours of daylight left.

She couldn't remember the last time she'd gotten a good night's sleep. Right now she thought she could sleep for a week. The heat of the day, the monotony of the terrain, the rhythmic swaying of the wagon contrived to lull her. If not for the frequent deep ruts that jarred her to the marrow, she could easily have nodded off.

And then, without warning, a violent, erratic movement from one of the horses shattered her boredom. She pulled back on the reins as the horse on the right reared and bumped into its companion. The other horse took up the panic, and they both leaped forward, nearly jerking her from the seat.

Terror tingled down her arms and set her heart pounding. They were galloping across the desert, leaving the road behind as they cut across the wild, arid land to the right.

The wagon lurched and bucked over the uneven ground, throwing her out of the seat and sending her crashing back down on it, tossing her from side to side as she fought desperately to stop the frenzied horses.

She remembered the brake at her left. If only she could reach it. Carefully she inched across the seat, lifting her left foot, slamming it against the lever, screaming when it broke off

In the next instant, the back end of the wagon flew into the air. A back wheel broke off and rolled away across the desert. She braced herself to keep from being thrown out. The wagon tilted dangerously toward the missing wheel. She lost her seat and nearly flew from the careening vehicle. Wood began splintering as the wagon hit another bump. As the horses broke free, she had the presence of mind to let go of the reins to avoid being pulled from the wagon and dragged to her death.

Dust settled slowly around the wagon, but she was unaware of anything but the fact that she had somehow survived. Her heart thundered in her breast; the breath hissed between her teeth. She fought the trembling that possessed her, and the sobs that threatened.

Tears formed in her eyes and she steeled herself against them. It gave her something to concentrate on other than the fact that she had almost been killed. Never had she been so close to death. She kept seeing the scene over and over again in her mind. If she hadn't let go of the reins . . . if the wagon had turned over, as it easily could have . . .

She tried not to think about it, sitting still and quiet in the wagon until her heart rate slowly returned to normal. In the distance, the horses had stopped running and stood nuzzling the ground for something to eat, as if nothing unusual had happened.

"Damn!" she said, angry now.

The desert was quiet again, quiet and desolate. She surveyed her surroundings, and a sob broke through her control.

Dear God, where was she? How was she going to get out of this?

She had lost her hat somewhere in the tumult. It seemed foolish to fret over something as inconsequential as a lost hat, but without it she had no protection from the sun. Her cheeks were already growing hot. Without the shade of the hat's brim to shield her eyes from the sun's brightness, she could hardly see.

"Damn."

On weak and unsteady legs, she managed to move

toward the side of the wagon. It shifted beneath her weight. She gasped and stopped until she had a feel for how to proceed without upsetting her perch. Slowly she worked her way to the edge and climbed down.

Think, she told herself. There's got to be a way out of this. How far can I be from Castroville?

She gazed at the sky and knew it was well past noon. She'd been traveling for more than four hours. It would take much longer than that to return on foot. The blacksmith had told her it would take around eight hours to reach Castroville. She was better than halfway there.

The horses were useless to her. She didn't have the slightest idea of how to take their harnesses off. And even if she did, she'd never ridden a horse in her life, and she had no desire to start now.

Maybe she could walk the rest of the way. But she didn't know exactly how far it was. Maybe she should just stay put. The blacksmith had told her the road would be crowded with cotton wagons going south and supply wagons coming north.

But in their frenzy, the stupid horses had carried her out of sight of the road. No one would ever find her if she didn't get back to it.

A shrill cry drew her attention. High overhead, a buzzard soared in a leisurely pattern, watching and waiting.

Scanning the horizon once more, she spotted the wagon wheel. It was a good distance behind the wagon. She started walking toward it. If she could roll it to the wagon, maybe she could put it back on.

When she reached the wheel, her spirits plummeted to a new depth. The spokes were shattered. It was useless. She let out a growl of frustration, kicking the wheel with all her might.

The buzzard cawed loudly. Drawing her loaded pistol, she took aim and fired at the circling bird, though it was far too high to be in any danger.

"Go away!" she shouted. "I'll be damned if I'm going to die in this godforsaken hell!

"Damned bird. Damned stupid horses!" She kicked the wheel again but derived even less satisfaction than she had the first time.

Someone had to come along. They just had to. As much as she disliked being at anyone's mercy, she would gladly welcome help from the devil himself.

"Help!" she shouted across the flat barrenness.

When she got no response, she decided her only chance was to walk back to the road.

Lifting her skirt, she marched back to the wagon. She'd fetch her carpetbag and canteen and strike out to the south. That would take her back to the road, she was certain of it.

But when she reached the wagon, she had another unpleasant surprise. The canteen, a last-minute purchase, was gone. It had been thrown from the wagon. Worse than that, her carpetbag was missing as well.

She spotted something white blowing in the scant breeze behind her and knew with heartsick dread that it was one of her petticoats. The carpetbag had broken open and her worldly belongings were strewn over half of Texas.

"My money!"

Why had she transferred most of the money from her running bag to her carpetbag last night? It had been heavy around her waist. She'd thought it would be safe there for one day. Now she'd probably never find it in the dust and dirt.

Lifting her skirt, she ran across the uneven ground in the direction of the petticoat. The carpetbag lay on the ground nearby—empty. She picked it up and began running willy-nilly around the area she had just traversed in the runaway wagon, scooping up dresses and stockings and undergarments as she went. She threw them in the back of the wagon and set about searching in earnest for her money, digging in the dirt for scattered coins.

Sweat streamed down her face and into her eyes, blinding her. She wiped it away impatiently with the sleeve of her shirtwaist, ignoring the burning thirst that built within her and the punishing heat of the sun on the back of her head, but she recovered precious little of the money she'd had that morning.

Finally, she dropped to the ground in exhaustion, panting for breath, battling against the anger and fear that clogged her throat. Her dress, wet with perspiration, hung on her like a damp rag. Lifting the mass of unruly hair that had come loose, she allowed the scant breeze to touch the moist skin beneath. The sun was so hot she could feel her scalp burning.

A knot of fear lodged in her breast as she realized she'd die if she stayed here. Her situation was hopeless, utterly hopeless.

She tied a shirtwaist around her head to protect it from the sun. Her frenzied running had taken a toll on her energy, but she refused to acknowledge it. Without the rest of her money, she would never make it to Concepción. If she looked hard enough, she was bound to find it.

But before long she was utterly worn out by fatigue and a burning thirst. She'd searched every inch of the terrain she'd crossed in the runaway wagon. It was no use. She couldn't stay here.

Collapsing, she sat by the wagon, her back propped against a wheel.

No water, no shelter. The road was her only chance.

She had to make it to the road. She squinted and shook her head, but the dizziness persisted.

"Well, I'll just have to walk fast, that's all," she said aloud, gasping for breath. She ran her dry tongue over parched lips, grimacing at the acrid taste of desert dust.

"I'd rather die walking than sitting here waiting." And with that, she struggled to her feet and headed south toward the road.

Rafe Montalvo steered his horse off the road, following the path the wagon had taken. He could tell by the tracks that the horses had bolted and headed across country. A knot of dread formed in his gut and he tried not to speculate what might have happened to the driver as he came across pieces of debris: clothing, splintered wood, a canteen.

He dismounted at sight of her canteen. Picking it up, he shook it and the water inside sloshed around. Wherever she was, she was out of water. If she was alive, it wouldn't be for long.

Damn. It was beginning to look as if she might have survived the wreck of the wagon, but if she'd been out here without water for long, she was probably sick or dead.

Something in the distance caught his eye as he started to mount his horse: an abandoned wagon. He reeled from the images that sight stirred in his mind: blank eyes staring at him, a sky full of buzzards. . . . He shook his head to clear it, his chest rising and falling with the force of his ragged breathing.

This was Texas, not Mexico. The woman he sought now was a stranger, a stranger who was stupid enough to strike out on her own in the desert.

He wiped the sweat from his face with his shirt-sleeve and swung up in the saddle, sending his horse galloping toward the wreckage.

How she had managed to keep the wagon from rolling over and crushing her, he couldn't imagine. He pulled his horse to a stop, surveying the damage with a shudder, trying unsuccessfully to shake the image of what might have been. In his mind he saw her pinned underneath the wreckage, her dark eyes staring lifeless at the faded sky.

Where could she have gone?

Dismounting again, he walked slowly around the wagon, looking for signs that would tell him what he hoped for: that she had unhitched the horses, mounted one, and ridden back toward the road. What he found made his blood run cold.

The horses had taken off to the north; it was obvious from their tracks that they were still harnessed together. Wherever the girl was, she was on foot.

Unscrewing the cap from the canteen, he surveyed the horizon in all directions. He had to find her. He only hoped he wouldn't be too late.

Too late.

The thought sent his mind catapulting backward through the years, back to Mexico and another desert and another woman. He'd been too late then, too late and too careless. He'd allowed himself to fall into a carefully laid trap. Since that hideous day, he'd learned much about the desert, about survival, but he hadn't learned to cope with the kind of gut-wrenching fear he felt right now.

He forced his mind back to the present. It couldn't happen again. He wouldn't let it. He'd find her if it was the last thing he did.

A set of small booted footprints that led away from the wagon drew his attention. She'd been running, the idiotic woman. Damn. What was she doing out here alone? She didn't even know enough not to expend that kind of energy in the desert, where just standing still sapped a man of all his strength.

He had gone to the hotel looking for her around noon, intent on reasoning with her. She couldn't handle a job like this—taking a million dollars in gold from Lucifer himself. He'd hoped to convince her with logic. But when he'd described her to the hotel clerk, he'd been told she'd checked out that morning.

Even with all the delays he'd encountered, Rafe had been able to set out a little past noon. If she'd started out at daybreak, as he suspected, she would have reached this point around noon, five hours ago. And five hours was a long time to be in this heat without water.

The first time, he'd caused it all. Everything. The first time had been an act of vengeance, to teach him a lesson. He had drawn first blood. It didn't matter that it had been by accident. If he hadn't been so blinded by ambition and his quest for justice, it might have all been avoided.

Innocent blood for innocent blood.

The first time had put a headstrong, overzealous West Point army officer in his place. This time, he wasn't to blame. If the woman died, it would be because of her own foolishness. Still, he couldn't just let her die.

He mounted again and followed the footprints. At least she'd had the sense to head south toward the road. Maybe she'd been picked up by a cotton caravan on its way to Eagle Pass. Maybe she'd crossed paths with outlaws or comancheros.

Stop it! he told himself. He'd go mad if he didn't stop thinking about the past. It was the desert, he knew, the heat, the emptiness, the buzzard circling slowly overhead in the distance. . . .

His heart froze in sudden realization. Driven by fear, he spurred his horse into a gallop, heading straight toward the buzzard, dreading what he might find when he reached whatever the carrion bird had in its sights. He almost prayed, something he hadn't done since that other day in the desert so long ago.

God doesn't live in the desert.

She lay there beside the road, so still, so quiet. He leaped from his galloping horse and ran to her. She didn't react when he lifted her head. Her face was beet red from a vicious sunburn.

A soft moan escaped her parched lips. He laid her down gently, ran back to his horse, and returned with a canteen.

"Ma'am, ma'am!" he called, lifting her head again. "Do you hear me?"

She winced and groaned but didn't open her eyes. He held the canteen to her lips and tilted it slightly.

"Drink," he commanded, gently but firmly.

She swallowed the liquid and wanted more, but he knew her stomach couldn't take it. Her eyes opened. When she looked up at him, he recognized the signs of dehydration in her dull, cloudy pupils. She wouldn't have lasted much longer.

"Papa," she murmured. "Papa, why didn't you come?"

Picking her up, he carried her to his horse. He managed to mount with her in his arms and turned his horse to the west, hoping the water hole he had seen on his last trip through this way was still drinkable. At least there would be shade and a good place to set up camp.

"I thought you weren't coming, Papa," she murmured against his chest. He resisted the urge to comfort her, to smooth the damp hair from her face and soothe the crease of pain on her forehead.

"Please don't ever leave me like that again," she pleaded in a childish voice. "I'll be good, I promise."

Nudging his horse into a walk, he held her closer against him. He told himself it was to keep her from falling, but something in her helplessness and her determination touched a part of his heart he'd thought long dead.

Swallowing convulsively, he tried to remember that she was a complication and nothing more.

The sun had been down an hour before the girl stirred, sat up, and looked around in confusion. Rafe said nothing, just continued stirring the beans in the pot over the fire. Her eyes bored a hole in him. She didn't seem exactly happy to wake up and find she'd been rescued by him. He couldn't say he blamed her, but still it annoyed him. He could have left her there to die on the side of the road. He could have done a lot worse.

He ladled a plateful of beans and took them to her with long, impatient strides.

"It was me or the buzzard," he told her. "Sometimes you have to take what you can get."

She sat where he'd propped her against his saddle, her hair in disarray around her shoulders, her clothes covered with a thin coat of Texas dust. She gazed up at him and the plate he held out to her without comprehension.

"Maybe you would have preferred the buzzard," he said. At least she was alive. Now she was about to tell him everything he wanted to know about Luis Demas and a million dollars in gold, whether she knew it or not.

Finally she moved, dropping her gaze to the plate he pushed toward her, crossing her arms over her chest, and turning away.

For a long moment, he studied her delicate profile,

her soft skin marred by the ravages of the Texas sun. Her arms folded beneath her breasts caused her chemise to gape open, drawing his gaze to the hint of creamy white flesh beneath.

"Here, eat this." He held the plate of beans out to her, but she continued to ignore him.

Spoiled rotten, that's what she was.

He could just imagine what her life must have been like. He could imagine it because it had once been his life too. She was obviously used to getting her own way through temper tantrums and tears. But those tactics didn't work out here.

"This might not be up to your usual standards, but you have got to eat something. If you refuse, I'll have to feed you myself."

She jerked her head around, glaring at him. When her first attempt at speech yielded nothing but a hoarse croaking sound, she cleared her throat and tried again. "You wouldn't."

"Do you really want to find out?"

She still refused to take the plate. "What are you doing here?"

He held out the plate silently, determined not to speak until she took it. Finally, she accepted the food with an angry sigh.

"You're welcome." He walked across the small camp. Taking the beans from the fire, he sat across from her, using the wooden stirring spoon to eat directly from the pot.

"You've been following me since San Antonio," she said.

Rafe blew on a spoonful of beans to cool it and watched her as he ate. The warm glow of the fire reflected in her dark eyes and seemed to set her pale red-blond curls ablaze. Even in the dark, he could see the redness of her skin and knew she would suffer in the morning.

"It's a good thing for you I *was* following you," he finally replied. "You know, in some countries if someone saves your life, you become their slave forever."

"Why are you following me?"

His gaze slid down her neck to her breasts beneath the stark white fabric of her chemise. He'd unbuttoned her shirtwaist so she could get air. He'd even mopped her heated face and chest with his wet bandanna. The chemise was still damp and clung to her in a way that made his blood grow warm.

Even if there hadn't been a million dollars in gold and El Alacrán's scalp to consider, she would have been worth chasing into the desert. Whether he would have done so or not was another matter, but there were a lot of reasons why a man would pursue a woman like her.

"Eat," he ordered again, returning his attention to his own dinner, struggling to forget the glimpse of her inviting skin, the firmness of the flesh beneath her gaping bodice. "We'll fight later."

"I'd rather fight now."

He looked at her across the fire once again, and once again his eyes dropped to the damp material stretched across her breasts. She pulled the blanket he'd wrapped around her closer together in front. When his gaze lifted to hers, she met it squarely.

"I couldn't take advantage of your condition like that, ma'am," he said. "You're far too weak to put up a good fight. Now eat."

"It wasn't a coincidence that you stopped the stagecoach yesterday and got on. And your horse seems to have made a miraculous recovery. I want to know why. What are your intentions?"

Ignoring her, he took another bite of beans. She was regaining her strength. Maybe she'd be able to travel in the morning after all.

For a while there he hadn't been sure. She'd been pretty far gone when he'd found her that afternoon, but he'd managed to get enough water down her so that the suppleness had returned to her skin. Now she was strong enough to wage a verbal battle with him.

He wondered if she had any idea how lucky she was. She was still glaring at him, waiting for him to respond to her challenge, but he wasn't going to speak another word until she started eating. She knew it, too. Finally, she gave up and began digging the spoon into the beans and shoving them into her mouth.

"Are you always so stubborn?" he asked with an involuntary grin.

"Yes."

"Well, it almost got you killed this time." A cold tremor coursed through him again as he thought of her out here alone. He shouldn't care. The only thing he should care about was the gold. "What the hell were you thinking, setting out alone like that?"

She took another bite of beans and swallowed them before answering. "I've got to get to Eagle Pass."

"Why?"

"My mother is sick," she murmured, refusing to meet his gaze.

Not a very good liar, he mused as he grinned at her crookedly. "The first rule of lying is that the lie has to be at least halfway believable."

She threw her plate down with a loud, angry crash. "You don't have to tell me about lying. I've been lied to by the best of them."

"Have you now?" Her voice was becoming more

and more shrill. He hoped she wasn't going to get hysterical.

"Don't look at me like that."

"Like what?"

"Patronizing. Like you think I've never had a problem greater than a—a torn stocking."

"I know, you've been through a war. You're a seasoned veteran, aren't you?"

"I have been through hell, Mr. Montalvo!" Her voice rose in the silence. "Or at least I thought I had been through hell until today. Today I found out exactly what hell is."

He smiled cynically at that naive statement. Looking at her angry countenance and the slight trembling of her lower lip, he felt a little sorry for her. She hadn't known what she was getting into when she'd struck out on this adventure. His gut clenched at the thought of what might have happened.

"No, you didn't," he said quietly, suddenly unable to meet her angry gaze.

"How would you know?"

He tossed the dregs of his coffee into the fire, fighting to subdue the demons of memory. "Because I've *been* to hell, lady," he said, in soft, measured tones, "and this ain't it. So why don't you just tell me what Luis Demas told you in San Antonio."

"I don't know what you're talking about."

"You've got two choices. Play dumb and I'll leave you here to fend for yourself. Level with me and I might agree to help you."

"I never asked for your help. Never!"

"You need it now. You know it and I know it."

"Well, if you know so much already, why should I tell you anything?"

He smiled in spite of his anger. "You're a natural-born bluffer, aren't you?" He noticed the angry tilt of her chin but continued undaunted. "You're not about to admit to anything until you know what I know. But you'd better understand this. Your time is running out."

He dumped what was left of the beans in the fire, then tossed the bean pot aside as he stood and walked toward his horse.

"Wait!"

Her threadbare voice reached out to him, tugging at his soul, and he knew she had mistaken his actions. She'd believed he was leaving now. He turned to face her as he reached his horse, his heart aching at the defeat in her eyes, even though he knew he would use her misinterpretation to his benefit.

"Gold." She was nearly whispering.

"Where?"

"I won't tell you. I'll take you there, but I won't tell you where it is."

Damn her stubbornness. He should just show her how easily he could make her tell him what he wanted to know. So why didn't he? Maybe he was just as much a fool as she was. He picked up his bedroll where he'd dropped it earlier.

"Get some sleep," he said harshly.

"Then you'll help me?"

"Help you? Yeah, since you're hell bent on getting yourself killed—or worse—I'll help you." He threw his bedroll on the ground beside the fire and kicked it out until it lay flat.

5

     Felipe Delgado, known to allies and ene-
mies alike as El Alacrán, sat at a table in a cantina in
San Tomas, Texas, with a weeping mulatto girl of perhaps sixteen on his knee. His left arm encircled her
slim waist. With his right hand he lifted a glass from
the table beside him and tossed down a shot of tequila,
then poured himself another and downed it as well.

They had crossed the Rio Grande in broad daylight,
riding into the sleepy little town before sundown, forty
bandidos—Mexicans, Americans, Indians—loaded down
with weapons, sunlight glinting off silver studs and the
weapons they fired into the air.

The citizens, an equal mixture of Mexican and Anglo,
had run for safety, knowing there was none to be found.
It was not the first time *bandidos* from across the border had vented their savagery upon San Tomas.

The sounds of sporadic gunfire, women screaming,

and men laughing reached El Alacrán from the street outside, and his lips curved into a cruel smile. There had been nothing in this stinking town to warrant his interest, not enough gold to fill a single saddlebag, not enough jewelry and silver to fill even one wagon. It would have been a complete waste, if not for the women.

He laughed, squeezing the girl on his lap tighter, enjoying the smell of her fear and the feel of her squirming body against his groin.

She was probably a virgin, he thought, as he plunged a hand inside her loose peasant blouse and closed his fingers over a soft young breast, eliciting a cry from her. His mind reeled from the tequila and from the exhilaration of today's violence; his body pulsed with anticipation.

Still, he remained lucid enough to think of his options. If she were a virgin, he could demand a high price for her on the other side of the border. But his body quickened when he imagined how tight she would be, how she would scream and fight when he took her, and he knew he would not be delivering a virgin to Piedras Negras, not this one anyway.

He wrapped his right hand in the girl's dark hair, pulling her head down to him, capturing her lips in a brutal kiss. He ignored her flailing hands, which pummeled and clawed at his shoulders and arms, laughing deep in his throat at the excitement her ineffectual efforts aroused in him

The door to the cantina opened and closed behind him, but he didn't bother to turn and look. His men were positioned outside. No one who posed a danger to him could get past them.

But when he heard a chair scrape away from the table where he sat, he glanced past the struggling girl to see Diego Muñoz turn the chair around and straddle it.

El Alacrán released the girl's head. She tried to escape him but he held her easily, controlling her with one arm while he poured another drink and waited for his most trusted man to speak.

"Luis finally showed up in San Antonio," Muñoz told him.

El Alacrán's chiseled features shifted almost imperceptibly at the announcement, but he held his silence. Muñoz dropped his gaze, so El Alacrán knew there was more.

Muñoz took a deep breath and resumed, "Luis is dead, jefe."

"Dead?" El Alacrán bellowed, his deep baritone voice ricocheting off the stone walls of the cantina.

"He was shot by vigilantes."

"*¡Perdición!*" El Alacrán swore. "How did this happen?"

Muñoz shrugged. "I do not know. We watched him all night. He got away from us only for a moment."

"And did you get close to him? Did he talk?"

"*No* and *sí* jefe. I did not get close to him, but he did talk, only not to me. There was a woman."

"What woman?" El Alacrán banged his fist on the table, nearly upsetting the bottle of tequila.

"I do not know. I'd never seen her before—a *gringa* with flame-colored hair. She ran out in the middle of the street. I saw Luis talking to her just before he died. There was a man with her: Rafael Montalvo."

For a moment, El Alacrán sat stone-faced; then he began to laugh mirthlessly. "So, my old friend Rafael. It seems we are destined to meet again."

"That's not all, jefe." Muñoz swallowed convulsively, and El Alacrán knew he was prolonging the moment when he would have to impart whatever information he still possessed.

"Out with it," the comanchero growled.

"Valdez, he's dead too. Montalvo shot him near Castroville a few days ago."

El Alacrán's smile faded; his expression darkened. "¡*Perdicion!* He is killing off my men one by one, the bastard!"

Valdez's death had nothing to do with Luis Demas, he knew. Valdez's death was part of another matter between him and Montalvo, a matter he had considered long settled. He hadn't seen Rafael in five long years and had begun to believe that his adversary must have gone east to fight in the gringo war. But then he had reappeared on the border and started systematically going after all the men who had ridden with him five years ago.

It had to stop, and soon. But right now he had more urgent matters on his mind.

El Alacrán rose from the chair, still holding the terrified girl by the waist. She renewed her struggles with the same results as before. She was no match for him, and he had no intention of releasing her.

"What do you want me to do?" Muñoz asked.

"Rest!" El Alacrán said, his voice booming in the small barroom. "You've earned a little enjoyment, my friend. Then tomorrow you can take three men and return to San Antonio. Bring them to me—both of them—alive. I leave tomorrow for Chihuahua. And take Carlos with you. It's about time he grew up a little."

Muñoz watched as El Alacrán dragged the girl through a door to the left of the bar. The nervous bartender scurried over to the table with a fresh bottle of tequila and a clean glass. Muñoz gladly accepted both.

He had fared much better with El Alacrán than he

had dared to hope, but he knew that, for all his surface calm, the chief was close to exploding with rage at that moment.

He heard the girl scream from the adjoining room, followed by the bandit's merciless laugh. Lucky for him, El Alacrán had another object for his fury tonight.

Muñoz opened the tequila bottle and poured a glass-ful, which he drank in two gulps. Tomorrow he would make the long ride back to San Antonio. He'd have to take El Alacrán's little cousin. When would El Alacrán accept the fact that Carlos Delgado didn't have what it took to be a comanchero? The *niño* nearly fainted at the sight of blood.

Well, he would worry about that tomorrow. Tonight he was determined to enjoy himself. And with that decision made, he grabbed the tequila bottle by the neck and sauntered out of the cantina, intent on find-ing some suitable outlet for his own frustration.

The first thing Anne felt the next morning when she woke up was pain. It started at the top of her head and spread down her body to her feet. Her muscles and bones ached every time she tried to move, but she man-aged to get to her feet.

She stood on legs that threatened to give way beneath her and gazed around, sighing in despair.

Desert stretched as far as the eye could see, a world of brown and gold and faded green. A few small, pitiful trees lined the stream, but they provided no shade from the sun's glare.

Even though the morning was still young, the sun was hot enough to cause her face to burn painfully, and she held a hand to her brow to shield it. She'd lost her hat, along with nearly everything she owned. A little money and her most prized possessions were in the running bag she still wore inside her skirt, but other than that she was destitute. She certainly didn't have enough money to make it all the way to Concepción, Mexico— wherever that was.

At least she was alive, thanks to Rafe Montalvo. Why? If someone had to rescue her from her own foolishness, why did it have to be him?

After the near disaster in San Antonio, he must think her completely addlepated. And now this. She hated looking foolish more than anything—except maybe dying in the desert.

He was following her; if she'd thought so before, she was certain of it now. He'd admitted it last night, didn't he? Or had that been a dream?

Last night was not much more than a blur. She remembered waking to find herself propped up next to a fire. He must have found her where she'd passed out beside the road and given her water. He'd also loosened her clothes while she was unconscious; she couldn't help wondering what else he might have done.

How could she trust him? All she knew about him was that he killed people for a living, he was following her—and he had saved her life. If not for him, she'd be dead right now.

A chill ran up her spine at the thought that the only thing standing between her and death was a cold-blooded killer.

She groaned. There were other parts of last night she remembered as well. It hadn't been a dream. She'd admitted that she knew where the gold was, and he'd agreed to help her find it. Had she made an alliance with the devil himself?

He was nowhere to be found this morning, and she thought for one heart-stopping moment that he had left her. He seemed capable of anything, even of leaving her stranded to die in the wilderness. But if that had been his intention, why hadn't he done so yesterday instead of stopping to help her?

She squeezed her eyes shut and tried with all her might to remember more of last night. He'd given her something to eat, she remembered, and he'd questioned her about the man in San Antonio. Had she told him anything else? If she had told him the location of the gold, he was probably halfway to Concepción by now. She swallowed the fear in her throat.

Maybe he'd never been there at all. Maybe he'd been a figment of her imagination. But there was the coffeepot on the fire to be explained. She hadn't thought to bring a coffeepot or coffee, and she didn't have the slightest idea how to start a fire.

But then, she shouldn't have needed either coffee or a fire for an eight-hour trip. She should be in Castroville by now, comfortably ensconced in a clean hotel room, eating a decent breakfast in the hotel restaurant and planning the next leg of her journey.

For once, something ought to work out right for her. As if it wasn't bad enough that her father had died in her arms and she'd been forced to flee to Texas, she'd arrived only to find her aunt—her last hope for a normal life—dead too. Now she was stuck in the middle of nowhere with a gunfighter . . . unless, of course, he had run off and left her.

Which would be worse, she wondered, to be stranded in the desert with a man like Rafe Montalvo or to be stranded alone?

There was no time to formulate an answer. In the

next moment, she cursed the feeling of relief that washed over her as she caught sight of him in the distance, riding toward her.

She needed him. It was a bitter pill to swallow, but she would be a fool not to admit it. She needed him, perhaps more than she had ever needed anyone before in her life.

The aroma of brewing coffee drew her to the fire. With an effort, she pushed thoughts of Rafe Montalvo and her reaction to him to the back of her mind.

She found a clean tin cup where he'd undoubtedly left it on a boulder he'd converted into a makeshift table. There would be no cream, but it was better than no coffee at all.

When she lifted the pot by its handle, a searing heat scorched her hand and she screamed and dropped it. Coffee went everywhere—down the front of her shirtwaist, on her hands and arms.

Tears sprang to her eyes as she grasped her hand, blowing on her reddened fingers.

"Are you all right?"

Out of the corner of her eye, she saw Rafe Montalvo pull his horse to a halt and leap from the saddle. He rushed toward her, and the pain and frustration inside her burned her soul as the coffeepot had burned her fingers.

"No, I am not all right!" She took a step back, her heart pounding with anger and a mixture of emotions she tried to deny. She wanted to cry from the pain in her fingers and the confusion in her heart.

"Let me see." His soft voice reached out to her, making her shiver.

"No!" She whirled away. "Why can't you leave me alone? I don't want your help."

"If you don't do something about that burn, it'll blister."

Reason returned to Anne. Her hand hurt like hell. But she'd be damned if she'd go to him. She stood where she was, and he came to stand next to her.

"Are you always this grumpy in the morning?" he asked as he took her hand.

"What do you expect? I've lost everything—my clothes, my money, everything I own! And I feel like I've been run over by a freight wagon!"

She couldn't tell if he was listening to her. He seemed intent on her hand, and then he released it and returned to his horse. He took something from a pouch he had tied around the saddle pommel, and came back with it and a long, lethal-looking knife. It was some kind of plant and he was cutting a piece of it.

"What is that?" she asked suspiciously.

She didn't want to give him back her hand, but he didn't ask. He simply took it.

"What is it?" she repeated.

"Hold still."

He pulled her hand closer to examine it, and she stopped struggling. Her skin was warm, her hand trembling so badly she knew he could hardly see the burn.

Except when he'd caught her when she'd almost fainted back in San Antonio, she had never been this close to him before, close enough to feel the heat of his breath on her wrist, close enough to hear the rich tone of his voice. Her breath turned shallow.

"Hold still," he commanded again.

"I . . . I can't." She hated the way her voice shook and hated him for the way he smiled at her, as if he knew better than she did why she couldn't still the tremors that assaulted her.

The plant rendered a cool jelly that soothed her skin. She surrendered to the feel of his calloused hands on hers as he spread it on her sunburn.

"Your hands are cut pretty bad."

She wasn't listening. Her gaze was riveted on the white scars that encircled both his wrists like bands. They must have been there for quite some time, judging by their appearance, and she wondered, with a sick feeling in the pit of her stomach, how he had gotten them. What could have caused such wounds? She wanted to ask but couldn't find her voice.

"What the hell are you doing in Texas?" he asked.

His voice was hoarse in her ear, and soft, almost caressing. It was a quality she had never heard in a man's voice before, and she found herself explaining.

"My father died." She pulled her hand away because she couldn't stand the contact any longer. "I had an aunt in Ubiquitous. She died too, before she received my letter telling her I was coming."

Why had she told him that? She had all but admitted she was alone in the world, alone and defenseless— except for the gun hidden in the pocket of her skirt. But even that had done her precious little good since she'd arrived in Texas. A sob welled up from her throat, but she forced it down.

Rafe Montalvo didn't say anything, but his eyes seemed softer. In fact, his whole countenance seemed less formidable, or maybe she just saw what she wanted to see. Then he squeezed the piece of plant over his fingers and touched the salve to her cheek.

Startled, she jerked her head back, and the softness in his features vanished. The cold, hard stranger returned in an instant. He handed her the green shoot from the plant.

"Aloe. I got it for your sunburn. It's a kind of lily. It'll soothe some of the pain and might keep your skin from peeling too bad."

With that, he turned away and started breaking camp. She watched with a twinge of regret as he took the coffeepot to the nearby water hole and washed it out before rolling it and the tin dishware into his bedroll. He had surprised her, touching her like that, and she had pulled away instinctively. Had her actions somehow hurt or angered him? He was so closed up, it was impossible to read him.

When he finished retying his saddlebags, he turned to look at her. "You need to . . . take care of anything before we get started?"

Rafe stumbled over the words, and she found it unaccountably funny that a man who killed for a living and had done God only knew what else could be so flustered talking about bodily functions.

"Yes," she admitted.

He nodded toward a clump of bushes to her right. "Behind those bushes is a good place."

"I couldn't!" she said, mortified by the very thought.

"You'll have to," he said with a half smile. "There's no outhouse here, no chamber pot. Unless you want me to hold—"

"No!" She gave him her best scowl. He was trying to embarrass her, and she'd be damned if she'd let him see that he had succeeded.

She turned and stepped behind the bushes. When she returned to the camp, as quickly as possible, he was mounted on his horse.

"Give me your good hand." He reached toward her expectantly.

She crossed her arms over her chest and stared up at

him, her jaw set in that stubborn expression he was already beginning to dread.

"Isn't there another way?" Fear showed clearly in her eyes and trembled through her voice.

"Not unless you want to walk."

She glanced around as if searching for some means of escape. "The wagon?"

"What about it?" He tried to keep the anger from his voice. He could understand her reluctance to be close to him, but there simply was no choice.

"You could put the wheel back on. Then your horse could—"

"You've seen that wheel. The spokes are broken. Even if I could put it back on, my horse is no draft animal. And even if he were, the horses you started out with took off in the harnesses, remember? Now give me your hand. We're wasting time."

"I can't."

Anger and disgust mounted within him. Did she loathe him so much? Didn't she know he was trying to save her life? Or would she die rather than accept help from the likes of him?

"I'm not going to bite you." And I'll try not to contaminate you, he added to himself. "If you don't give me your hand, I'll climb down and pick you up and throw you over the back of this horse."

"Stomach down, like a corpse?" she challenged.

He smiled at her nerve. "Are you this disagreeable with everyone or do you save it all for me? I'm trying to help you."

"I didn't ask for your help."

"Well, I'm getting a little tired of reminding you where you'd be right now without it. We're wasting time."

He waited, his hand outstretched. She glared up at him, her shoulders squared, her lips drawn in a taut line. He found himself in a stare-down with a woman, a contest she was destined to lose.

As he predicted, she looked away first. What he didn't expect was the change in her expression when she looked up at him again. She bit her lower lip. He knew she was struggling to keep her chin from trembling.

Anger coursed through him, anger and regret. She must think he was some kind of animal. And what else was she supposed to think? The first time she'd seen him, he'd ridden into town with a dead body. But, dammit, he'd saved her from those men in San Antonio, and he'd saved her life yesterday. That should count for something.

"I . . . the truth is I've never ridden a horse," she admitted. "They frighten me."

The tension drained from his body as he realized that the terror in her eyes was directed at his horse and not at him.

He grinned slightly at her confession, gazing down at her with new understanding. "All you have to do is give me your hand and put your left foot in the stirrup. I'll pull you up behind and you can hold on to me. We'll take it slow."

She seemed to be lost in indecision as she studied the massive chestnut.

"You can't walk the rest of the way to Castroville," he told her. "We're only a little better than halfway there."

A sigh escaped her, her shoulders slumped, and she stepped forward timidly.

"Left foot in the stirrup," he directed, holding the prancing gelding as still as he could. She lifted her foot toward the stirrup. "Trust me."

"The last man who said that to me killed my father," she said, as she placed her small hand in his.

He nearly lost his hold at that unexpected confidence. He didn't want to wonder at its meaning. He didn't want to know anything about her, not even her name.

As her foot touched the stirrup, he tightened his grip on her hand, pulling her up quickly. In an instant, he noticed her boots. They were badly worn boy's boots. Again, he kept his questions to himself. The less he knew, the better.

He heard her gasp as her body hung suspended in the air for an instant before her right leg came down on the other side of the horse and she settled behind him. She wrapped her arms around his waist as if holding on for dear life. Her body trembled against his. Her soft breasts pressed against his back, eliciting an immediate response from his body.

He straightened uncomfortably in the saddle, clearing his throat. "You don't have to hold on so tightly. We're going to take it slow and easy."

The death grip on his torso eased, and he was able to breathe again, even though her nearness still disturbed him. But her grip tightened once again as the gelding started forward. And once again her feminine curves burned into his flesh through his shirt and the familiar tightening in his groin sent a shudder through his body.

"I thought all southern ladies learned to ride before they learned to walk."

"I never had a reason to learn," she replied, loosening her grip once again as the horse settled into a sedate walk.

"Maybe in the city you can get everywhere you need to go by buggy, but out here you just about have to know how to ride to get by," he said a bit harshly, angered by her helplessness and by his body's unbidden response to her.

"I'll manage. I always have."

He snorted. "Yeah, but now you don't have a daddy to take care of you."

She stiffened in reaction to his words. "You don't know anything about me or my family."

"You're right, I don't." And I don't want to, he added silently, spurring his horse into a slow trot, putting an end to their conversation and maintaining his distance for a little longer.

6

By the time they rode into Castroville a little before noon, Rafe held the sleeping woman in front of him, her head resting against his chest. At some point during the ride, he realized she was too tired to hold on, so he had stopped and rearranged them. She'd roused long enough to protest, then fallen back to sleep almost immediately.

He had stopped repeatedly along the way, forcing her to drink water in small amounts. He thought he had rehydrated her body. But she was weak and feverish, and he worried that she might not recover.

If she died, the secret of the gold would die with her, and so would his best chance of luring El Alacrán out in the open.

El Alacrán was a spinner of webs. He set traps and then waited to strike where the enemy was most vulnerable. Strike and retreat, that was El Alacrán's way.

Strike when the enemy least expected it, then retreat to a place where the enemy would not or could not follow.

The trouble with catching El Alacrán had always been not knowing when or where he would strike. This gold represented Rafe's first opportunity to predict El Alacrán's actions and seize the upper hand.

He told himself that was the only reason he cared one way or the other what happened to this fragile spit-fire of a woman whose name he didn't even know. Then he realized he'd been thinking of her as Christina, but this was not Christina. They resembled one another physically; they were the same height and, judging by the way this one felt in his arms, the same weight. They possessed the same ivory complexion that blistered too easily in the torturous Texas sun, and the pale hair, though Christina's had lacked this fireglow. They both came from the East; neither of them was equipped to cope with life in this brutal land.

Of course, Christina never would have jumped on a wagon and headed into the desert alone. But her reck-lessness made this woman's situation even more dangerous than Christina's had been—that and a million dollars in gold.

Dammit, he didn't want to think about this girl who slept against his chest. He didn't want to wonder about her or worry about her or compare her to Christina, whose only mistake had been that she had married the wrong man.

But she needed help, she needed something he couldn't give her. She needed medical care, a doctor, and as they rode down the main street of Castroville, he tried to remember if he had seen a doctor's shingle when he'd been here a few days ago.

He pulled back on the reins, stopping his horse just

in time to avoid running over a boy who had darted in front of him from between two overburdened freight wagons. The boy never even saw him as he wove his way across the crowded street and disappeared into the crowd on the opposite sidewalk.

Castroville had been a sleepy little town on the way to nowhere until the war, when the blockade had diverted the only foreign trade enjoyed by the present Confederacy. Now the narrow streets bulged to the point of bursting with traffic they were never designed to carry.

The Rio Grande represented the only Confederate border that couldn't be blockaded by the Union. With the sympathies of the government in the northern provinces of Mexico squarely behind the Confederacy, trade flourished. One consequence was the sudden growth of many small towns that, like Castroville, just happened to lie along what had become known as the cotton road. Another consequence was lawlessness.

He studied the signs outside the buildings. At the end of the street, he found one that read CLARENCE STONE, M.D.

His burden stirred as he dismounted, carefully holding her so that she didn't slip from the saddle until he could catch her.

Standing at the foot of a long flight of wooden stairs, he studied the arrow that pointed up. Painted on the arrow was the word DOC.

"Shit," he muttered. "Why can't anything be easy?"

He took a deep breath and started the long climb to the top. Why the hell would a doctor open an office at the top of a long, narrow flight of rickety stairs? Hauling an undernourished woman to the top was hard enough. It would take two or three grown men to get a wounded or sick man up there.

By the time he reached the top, he was out of breath. He used his foot to pound the door, since both of his hands were occupied.

A short man with white whiskers and round wire-rimmed glasses came to the door almost immediately, gazing at him with curious intelligence.

"What have we here?" he asked in a gruff voice.

"Let me in, doc, she's dehydrated and feverish."

"Well, come on in."

The doctor held the door open as Rafe entered.

"Through here," the doctor said, walking past him again and opening a door at the other end of the room. "Put her on that bed."

Rafe did as he was told, laying her gently on the narrow cot. Rolling up the sleeves of his starched white shirt, the doctor moved to a basin of water, and washed his hands thoroughly, then turned to look at Rafe as he dried them. "Who is she?"

"My wife." It came out without hesitation, just as it had in San Antonio.

He'd been practicing what he would say since he'd realized how bad off the girl was. If he told the doctor she was his wife, he'd be able to stick close to her. He had an appointment with destiny, and he wasn't going to let anything happen to the one person who held the key to his entire future—and his past.

"Well, loosen her clothes so she can breathe."

"Right." He worked at the fastenings of her shirt-waist. She moaned low in her throat but didn't open her eyes.

"Sunburned pretty bad." The doctor spoke from behind him. When he turned to look at the older man, he saw accusation and a bit of anger in the sharp blue eyes. "How'd you let that happen?"

He'd practiced that part of the lie too. "We're newly-weds. We ran away. Her daddy didn't like me, so we eloped. We were supposed to meet up on the road between Ubiquitous and Castroville, but she got lost. There was an accident. I was lucky I found her."

The doctor eyed him for a moment, running a hand over his whiskers as if digesting what Rafe had said. "So when did you get married, before the accident or after?"

Stunned and furious at his blunder, Rafe stood staring at the astute old man for several seconds, trying to decide how to lie his way out of this corner, when the woman on the bed moaned again. "Doc, she's real bad."

"Hmmm," was all the doctor said. He ran a hand over his chin, studying the patient. "What's her name?"

"Huh?" He pretended not to hear the question as his mind grappled for a name, any name.

"Her name. You're married to her, you must know her name."

"Christina. Christina Holden."

"Well, Miss Christina," the doctor said as he turned back to the bed, "let's see if we can fix you up."

"I'll wait in the other room."

Rafe left the examining room and waited impatiently, pacing back and forth in the small antechamber, while the doctor made his examination. He tried not to worry, tried not to care, but he did care, and not only because of the gold. Something about this girl made him want to protect her.

What was it? Maybe she reminded him of himself when he was younger—stubborn, willful, unwilling to accept his limitations. He hoped she would learn the lessons life had in store for her easier than he had.

He stopped pacing and stared out the window, gazing down at the activity on the street. The rest of the world was going on as usual, but for him everything beyond this window had all but ceased to exist.

Squeezing his eyes shut, he tried to block the image of the girl who lay unconscious in the adjoining room. His gaze followed the dusty street to the edge of town. He could leave now; he could get on his horse and ride away and never look back.

True, he didn't know where the gold was, but he was beginning to wonder if finding out was worth the risk of being close to her and allowing her to burrow even deeper into his heart. There had to be another way. There were a lot of reasons why he couldn't risk letting someone get too close.

At first, it was simply the resemblance to Christina that had drawn him to her against his will. But the more he was around her, the weaker the resemblance became.

Christina had been so fragile, so helpless, so delicate. This girl was fragile, yes, but certainly not as helpless as he had thought. He was beginning to recognize a kind of determination in her that he'd never seen in a woman before. It baffled him because he had assumed that she had come from much the same background as Christina—privileged and pampered.

The door to the examination room opened; the doctor stepped through with a grim, serious expression on his face.

"How is she?" Rafe asked.

"She's pretty dehydrated. Probably has sun poisoning, but she'll recover. She's young and strong."

"Can I see her?" It seemed like the right question to ask.

"I gave her some laudanum. She's sleeping now."

"Thanks, doc. I need to leave her here for a while. I've got to see to my horse and try to find a place to stay the night."

"Won't be easy. Bunch of rowdies burned the hotel down. There ain't nowhere else to stay in town. You planning on being here long, you and your—wife?"

"Just till she recovers. We're heading for Uvalde. I've got a job waiting for me there." Lying had always come easily to Rafe.

"Well, you can stay here until she's fit to travel."

"Thanks, I appreciate it. I'll be glad to pay whatever you think's fair."

"Oh, don't worry about that. I never was one to stand in the way of true love."

It was easy enough to find José late that afternoon. He was in the cantina, the kind of place they'd visited frequently during their long association. It was a small windowless adobe structure, filled with the too-sweet odor of cheap perfume and the even more offensive stenches it was meant to disguise.

"Amigo," the Mexican called with a broad smile. "Sit. Tequila?" He offered a bottle, but Rafe turned up his nose in disdain.

"Isn't it a little early for that?"

José laughed, setting the bottle back on the table. "It is never too early for tequila, amigo. But tell me, what have you been up to since I last saw you?"

Rafe turned a chair around so that it faced away from the table and sat on it backward, crossing his arms on the back. He'd agonized all day over how much to tell José. He knew how ruthless José could be when money was involved, and even though the Mexican might consider them partners, he had his own goal, and nothing was going to stand in his way, not José and his greed, and not the girl.

"Well, she knows, but she's not sharing. She won't tell me, but she says she'll show me where it is."

José studied him intently for a few moments before throwing up an arm in dismissal. "Not a problem, amigo. It should be easy to convince her to talk. Use some of that gringo charm of yours."

Rafe snorted. "I ran out of that a long time ago."

José leaned toward him with a conspiratorial wink. "Then do whatever you need to do. *Dios,* if I didn't know better I'd think you were going soft."

"I just don't seem to have much of a stomach for torturing women."

"Of course not, amigo," José agreed. "You would not have to torture her. It would take very little, a twist of the arm maybe, and she would tell you whatever you want to know. I only hope you are not becoming distracted."

José narrowed his eyes and leaned forward.

"Must I remind you of all that El Alacrán has done to you? Have you forgotten how close to death you were the day I found you in the desert where El Alacrán left you? Do you remember how the buzzards circled overhead? Do you remember the one that landed on your chest and—"

"Enough!" Rafe bellowed, suddenly aware that he had begun massaging his wrist. He stopped, glaring at the other man. "You've made your point." A blind fury seized him. It would have been easy at that moment to kill José. What was happening to him?

"And all your fine manners and your *aristo* blood

and your fine education were useless," José went on. "You were as helpless as a babe. If not for me—"

Rafe took a deep breath, struggling to control the rage that threatened to erupt into violence.

"You don't have to remind me, goddammit! You saved my life and taught me to survive. I owe you my life. Is that what you want to hear?"

He knew José was intentionally pushing him, and, damn him, José knew exactly how to do it and how far he could go before Rafe exploded. But even though he recognized the game, he could not control his own reaction.

"I think you are going soft," José repeated, "now that your belly is full and your wounds have healed. Maybe you don't have the stomach for vengeance any longer."

Rafe slammed his fist on the table, nearly toppling the tequila bottle. "The only thing that will heal my wounds is El Alacrán's blood."

"The woman is a distraction, amigo," José said calmly, "a beautiful distraction, but a distraction just the same. She will slow you down. She will get in the way."

"I know. I'll handle it."

"Good."

"We're heading for Eagle Pass. I suggest you stay out of the way for a while longer. By the time we reach Fort Inge, I'll know everything Luis Demas told her."

Rafe returned to the doctor's office around dusk, no better off for the tequila he'd consumed. Sometimes he wondered why he bothered to drink at all. He couldn't seem to get drunk. No matter how much he swallowed, all he usually got for his troubles was a roaring headache like the one that throbbed behind his temples now.

He pushed the door open to find the doctor sitting beside his patient.

"How is she?" Rafe asked, dropping his saddlebags and bedroll inside the door.

Pressing a finger to his lips, the doctor lifted a tray with a cup and bowl on it and stood up. Rafe moved silently to the door, holding it open as the doctor walked through into the waiting room.

"She took some broth and water," the doctor said, indicating the tray.

"I bought her a nightgown." Rafe held a package toward the doctor as if to prove his words. "She lost hers when the wagon overturned."

Dr. Stone wrinkled his nose. Rafe wondered if he could smell the liquor on his breath. "Whatever you say, mister." He turned toward a door to the right that Rafe hadn't seen before.

"Where are you going?"

"To bed. My apartment's downstairs. Wake her every couple of hours and see if she can take a little water. That's the best thing for her. And keep her face and hands doused with the salve beside the bed." With that, he left the room, closing the door behind him.

Rafe went back into the examination room and stood uncertainly just inside the door. He listened to the soft, rhythmic ticking of the clock on the far wall, the sound of shuffling footsteps descending an unseen flight of stairs, the shallow breathing of the woman who lay on the small bed. The kerosene lamp on the table beside the bed cast elongated shadows on the far wall.

His bootheels scraped on the hardwood floor as he walked toward the bed, his eyes fixed on the still, silent form under the white sheet. He didn't want to see her sun-reddened face resting on a white pillow, or the cascade of wild red curls that spread around her head like a storm cloud, or the bandaged hand that rested softly on top of the covers. He didn't want to feel his chest constrict at her innocence and vulnerability.

Everyone looked vulnerable and innocent in sleep. If she opened her eyes right now and saw him standing over her, she'd probably fly into a rage.

He smiled at the image his thoughts evoked.

"I didn't ask you to help me!" she would shout. "I didn't ask you to care about me!"

What was he thinking? She'd never accused him of caring, and he didn't, goddammit. He didn't care about her. He couldn't afford to. All he cared about was El Alacrán. The only reason he hadn't left her on the side of the road was that she knew where the gold was—the gold that would lure El Alacrán out of hiding.

He sat on the bed and laid the package containing the new nightgown on the nightstand. Then he touched her shirtwaist. His fingers trembled as he started to work at the buttons.

There was something profoundly intimate about undressing an unconscious woman. It troubled him more than it had last night; then it had been dark and he had stopped after he had loosened her blouse. He wanted desperately to maintain his distance, but he could feel the barrier around his heart cracking a little more with every button he unfastened.

When the garment was open it revealed a much-mended chemise that he'd glimpsed the night before. He hadn't realized he'd been holding his breath until he released it in a great sigh.

She moaned and murmured something incoherent. Her face was red from sunburn, her lips raw and cracked. Already her nose was beginning to peel, but at least it hadn't blistered.

He couldn't resist the opportunity to really study her closely for the first time. Her cheeks were hollows beneath high, delicate cheekbones; tiny, pale freckles dotted her nose. Her lips were full, but not pouty like Christina's, and slightly parted in sleep. His gaze slid down her throat to a fragile collarbone—farther down to the shadowed valley between firm, round breasts that disappeared beneath the frayed and faded chemise.

When he'd undressed her last night, she'd been so ill he hadn't been able to think of anything but keeping her alive. This time was pure torture. This time his hands ached to feel the softness of her skin; his heart ached to keep her out of danger, to send her back where she'd come from.

Guilt gnawed at him. It was as if he were violating her privacy. He knew how angry she would be if she knew what he was doing, but she'd been wearing the same clothes for at least two days. They had to come off, if for no other reason, than for the sake of cleanliness. Tomorrow he could find a laundress and have the garments washed. Her hair needed a good scrubbing too, but there was no help for that as long as she was ill.

"Sit up a little, *chica*," he whispered. He slipped his hand behind her neck and pulled her up gently.

She sat obediently, but her eyes remained closed. "Why don't we live in a house like other people, Papa?"

He tried to ignore the little-girl voice as he pushed a sleeve of her shirtwaist down her arm.

"When can we have a house? When, Papa?"

He slipped her other arm out of its sleeve, dropping the blouse to the floor. The chemise was tucked inside her skirt. He would have to remove the skirt first.

Easing her back down to the bed, he pulled the covers away, trying hard not to notice the taut nipples that pressed against the sheer fabric of her chemise. With one hand on her hip, he pulled her toward him, then held her on her side until he found the fastenings of her skirt. He worked them free, then hooked his hand in the waistband, pulling the back of the skirt down over her hips.

He released her and she rolled over onto her back. All he had to do was pull the skirt down her legs, and he stood and moved to the foot of the bed to accomplish that.

It was then he noticed that she was still wearing her boots. He'd glimpsed them before when he'd pulled her up on his horse. They looked even more disreputable on closer inspection. Ugly, clumsy boy's boots.

He untied the laces and pulled the first one free. A wadded-up sock fell out of the toe, obviously put there to make them fit her small foot better. A semicircle of red blisters ringed the back of her heel. How had she managed to walk, let alone run?

Quickly he removed the other boot, trying to remain detached.

When he pulled the skirt free, he heard a loud *thunk* on the floor and found the pistol she had bragged about being proficient with. He retrieved it from the floor with a smile. It was an old seven-shooter. If she could shoot—what had she said?—the head off a one-eyed jack at fifty paces with this gun, she was a better shot than he was.

He carried the gun and the skirt to a chair in the corner and was folding the skirt when he noticed something heavy around the waist. Turning the skirt inside out, he found a leather pouch hooked inside the waistband.

Pretty clever, he thought, as he studied the pouch, wondering what had prompted her to create such a thing. Maybe she had been in the path of the enemy army at one time and had used it to guard her jewels or whatever she prized. He thought of the locket he'd found, the locket with no picture in it, wondering, with a twinge of guilt, if it had been a prized possession.

And in spite of his vow to remain detached, he wondered what else she might have hidden away. Surely she wouldn't have been foolish enough to make a written record of what Luis Demas had told her. Surely not. But if she had, what better place to keep it than in a secret pouch inside her skirt? And even as he argued with himself, he was drawing the pouch open, looking inside.

First, he pulled out a worn deck of playing cards. Why the hell would anyone care enough about a deck of cards to hide them like that? He examined them closely to see if there was anything significant about them. They weren't marked or made of anything precious. It didn't make sense, and his curiosity was piqued almost beyond reason.

The cards went on the nightstand with the other things, and he returned his attention to the pouch.

Next he found a bent, rusted horseshoe. He almost laughed aloud at that. She was frightened of horses, but among her precious belongings he'd found a horseshoe.

She must be superstitious, he thought, as he placed the horseshoe on the nightstand with the deck of cards. Next he pulled out a yellowed handbill that read:

OPERA COMEDIE
NEW ORLEANS, LOUISIANA
MAY 9, 1860

When he opened it, an envelope fell out. He picked it up and read the name: *Anne-Marie Cameron.*

He glanced at the girl in the bed. She wasn't just a girl anymore. Now she was Anne-Marie, someone who kept a horseshoe and a deck of cards in a secret pouch on the inside of her skirt.

Anne-Marie.

He closed his eyes and tried to forget, but it was too late. The mere fact of learning her name changed everything.

He placed the letter and the handbill with the rest of her treasures on the nightstand, then turned the pouch over, emptying the rest of the contents on the bed. There were shells for her gun and about a hundred dollars in silver coins. So she hadn't lost all her money in the accident.

"Anne-Marie," he whispered, "you certainly are a mystery."

The letter wouldn't contain a reference to the gold, he knew. She'd probably brought it all the way from wherever she'd come from. Still, he took the envelope from the nightstand and held it up to the light. The flap was open, so it would be easy to peek inside. She'd never know, but he would. A letter addressed to her would have to contain intimacies and details of her life that he didn't have a right to know.

But what if it contained a map to the missing gold? Or a quickly scrawled set of directions? He would have missed the best opportunity he might ever have to find out the location of the gold and leave her behind where she'd be safe.

He wouldn't even read the letter, he told himself. He'd simply look for scraps of paper stuffed into the envelope.

Convinced that his motives were noble, he opened the envelope and removed the folded sheet of paper. He shook the letter and the envelope, but nothing fell out. With a deep breath, he unfolded the letter. Nothing tucked inside. But before he could fold the letter and put it back in the envelope where it belonged, the first line leaped off the page at him in large, sweeping script: *Please don't be angry at me. . . .* He could not help but read on.

July 20, 1863
Dear Anne-Marie:

Please don't be angry at me for leaving you behind. I couldn't stand being trapped in Baton Rouge with no chance of leaving the city once the Union army occupied it. I still think it was the best place for you, under the circumstances.

I have found a place to live in Natchez. It's not much, but it's clean and cool in the evenings. I am sending a friend, Borden McKenna, to bring you safely to me.

Please don't be angry, Anne-Marie. Please come. You know I need you here.

Love, Papa

Rafe's throat constricted. What kind of man would abandon his daughter and leave her unprotected in a town that was under attack by an enemy army? Perhaps there had been relatives to rely on, but even so, any father should want to keep his daughter safe.

Anne-Marie's father seemed weak and irresponsible—first leaving her behind, then begging her to come to him when he needed her.

Why did Rafe care?

He folded the paper and slipped it back inside the envelope. It was none of his concern. All he cared about was the gold, and he hadn't found the slightest clue to its whereabouts. He put the letter and her other belongings back inside the pouch and laid it on the bureau.

Now that he'd stripped off her dirty clothes, he decided to leave her in her chemise. Her body and the sheets she lay on were covered with grime. Might as well save the gown until tomorrow night. Maybe she'd be well enough for a bath then. Besides, it would save him the torment of having to undress her further, something he didn't know if he would survive.

Remembering what the doctor had said about the salve on the nightstand, he took the jar and sat on the edge of the bed, gazing down at Anne-Marie as he worked the top off the jar.

A fine film of desert dust, mixed with salt from her own body, covered her skin. Even so, her beauty shone through, a simple unadorned beauty that made him think of wildflowers growing along a mountain path. Unlike the hothouse beauty of women like Christina, whose only occupation was her apperance, Anne-Marie's beauty was a natural product of who she was, a scrappy, stubborn woman with more courage than many men he'd known.

He poured water into a cloth he found on the bureau to wash away at least some of the dirt from her face, arms, and hands That accomplished, he dipped his fingers into the jar of salve and massaged it gently over her painfully red face. She moaned and shifted in the bed but didn't open her eyes.

The sunburn would be painful in the morning when she was awake. For now, he was glad the doctor had given her laudanum to help her sleep.

Avoiding the white bandage wrapped around her injured right hand, he applied the salve to the rest of her hands as best he could, trying not to think how small and delicate they felt. Her skin was warm against his, and soft, despite the calluses and scrapes caused by her struggle with the runaway wagon. He still shuddered whenever he thought of what could have happened.

"How could you be so reckless, *chica?*" Gently he ran a finger over her cracked, blistered lips, his heart constricting. "You could have died out there in the desert alone."

With his fingers, he dabbed more salve on her lips, then rubbed it in with a feather-light touch. Her soft breath on his flesh sent a shudder through his body. Soon he found himself imagining what it would be like to touch those lips with his mouth instead of his fingers, and he pulled away.

For a long time Rafe sat there, watching Anne as she slept. He touched her forehead and smoothed the hair back from her brow.

She is a distraction, José had said. *She will slow you down.*

He couldn't deny the truth in those words. She *was* a distraction. She *was* slowing him down. He would be able to travel a hell of a lot faster without her, if she would just tell him where the gold was. He could make her tell him, he knew. Maybe she was brave and maybe she was stubborn, but she was still a woman. Except every time he thought of threatening her, he felt a knot in his stomach. He was getting soft. José had been right about that, too.

What was wrong with him? He hadn't let anything get in his way in a long time. All he knew for certain was that he couldn't possibly hurt her. And he couldn't stand by and let anyone else hurt her, either.

He rose from the bed with a disgusted sigh. At the bureau he poured water into the cup, then returned to the bed and slid a hand behind her shoulders to pull her up.

"Anne-Marie, wake up," he coaxed. "You've got to drink some water." When she didn't respond, he shook her gently. "Anne-Marie."

"Leave me alone." She opened her eyes slightly, but he knew she was having difficulty focusing on him. "Why are you following me?" she asked.

Ignoring her question, he held the cup to her parched lips. "Drink." He tilted the cup and she swallowed obediently. "Good girl. You'll be good as new in no time."

"I'm not going to tell you where the gold is."

He smiled. "I know."

"Are you going to kill me?"

What must she think of him? What could she think of him? The first time she'd seen him, he'd ridden into San Antonio with a body slung over his horse. She was right to fear him.

"No, I'm not going to kill you," he replied soothingly, fighting against the regret that clogged his throat.

Gently he eased her back down to the bed. She closed her eyes and smiled slightly, and he wondered if she was already asleep again. He bent over slowly, placing a kiss on her forehead, then jerked back in shock because he hadn't intended to do that, hadn't even known he was going to do it until it was done.

"Good night, Papa," she murmured.

He stared at the water that was left in the cup, trying to sort out his feelings. Nothing made sense anymore.

Everything had seemed so clear just four short days ago. He had been certain he knew where he was going and how he would get there. Now he was beginning to question everything he'd done and everything he'd lived for over the past five years. And he didn't like it one little bit.

"Good night, Anne-Marie," he murmured, pulling the covers up to her chin. He stood and moved a chair beside the bed to start his night-long vigil.

7

Anne slowly opened her eyes and tried to adjust to her strange surroundings. She was accustomed to waking up in unfamiliar hotel rooms, and this must undoubtedly be another one. But she couldn't for the life of her remember where she was. She blinked her eyes to clear them, trying to focus on the room, but what she saw only confused her further.

The room was small and dark. Not a single painting adorned the walls. The curtains at the single window were plain and drab. There was no bureau, no armoire. She'd stayed in some disreputable hotels before, but never in a room so poorly furnished.

The bed was narrow and hard, the nightstand small and unpainted. A clock on the far wall ticked the seconds as she searched her mind for some explanation. She glanced at the clock—one o'clock. She'd slept most of the day away.

And where was Papa? She didn't remember where she was or how she'd come to be here, but she remembered Papa.

She must have been sick because he'd sat beside her bed all night long, smoothing the hair from her face, kissing her on the forehead. He'd forced her to drink and bathed her with a cool, damp rag.

But even as the thought left her mind, she knew something wasn't quite right. Papa was dead, or had she only dreamed that he'd been shot down on the street in Natchez? She'd seen it with her own two eyes, or had she? He couldn't be dead. Last night, he'd called her Anne-Marie. No one called her Anne-Marie except Papa.

Memories flooded her mind, despite her best efforts to hold them at bay. She didn't want to face the truth, but reality would not wait.

Texas.

Yes, she was in Texas. She'd nearly been killed in a wagon accident, and Rafe Montalvo had saved her.

"So, you decided to wake up!"

She started at the voice, jerking around to see a strange man standing in the doorway. He carried a tray as he crossed the room, studying her with intelligent eyes behind thick spectacles.

"I was beginning to think you were going to sleep forever," he said.

"Where am I?" she asked as he set the tray on the nightstand. "Who are you?"

"Well, you're in Castroville, and I'm Doc Stone." He sat on the edge of the bed, and she scooted over to accommodate him.

The doctor touched her forehead. She closed her eyes, comparing his touch with the one she'd felt last night. His hand was warm and soft, his touch firm but gentle. No, it wasn't the same at all. The other hand had been warm but not soft. The touch had been as gentle as the doctor's, but there was a natural ease in the doctor's touch, while the other had seemed somehow tentative by comparison.

"How did I get here?" Memories flashed through her mind: the wagon flying across the desert, the brake failing, Rafe Montalvo raising her head and pressing a canteen to her parched lips.

"Your husband brought you in," he said, withdrawing his hand.

"What?" She pulled the covers higher over her body, noticing her state of dishabille for the first time.

"Don't worry, ma'am." He patted her hand in a fatherly gesture. "Your husband took care of the intimate matters."

She felt herself blush to the roots of her hair, but she doubted the doctor would notice beneath the sunburn that she knew covered her fair skin. She didn't have to see it; she could feel the pain.

"Oh, he did!" she said through clenched teeth.

She didn't know if she was more embarrassed or furious at the thought of Rafe Montalvo undressing her. The audacity of the man!

"In fact," he said, craning his head to look around the room, "he told me he'd bought you a nightgown. I see he decided not to put it on you. There it is on the nightstand, still wrapped up."

She sank down on the bed, trying not to think about the possibility of Rafe Montalvo undressing her while she was asleep and defenseless. Even he wouldn't stoop that low, would he?

"I . . . " she stammered, "I . . . there was a wagon accident."

"Yes, your husband told me about it when he brought you in. Said you two eloped."

"Eloped! No. Yes." She swallowed hard, concentrating all her efforts on restraining her emotions. Why did she suddenly feel like crying? Why didn't she just tell this man the truth, that Rafe Montalvo was not her husband?

"Where—where is he?" she asked. "My—husband, where did he go?"

"Don't know," Doc Stone replied. He ran a hand over his whiskered chin, contemplating her question. "He left as soon as I came in to check on you this morning."

She pulled the covers even higher, all the way up to her chin. Had Rafe Montalvo slept in this room? Had he been here with her while she was unconscious?

The doctor's thumb on her eyelid startled her. She flinched until she realized what he was doing. He pulled the lid open in order to study her eye.

"Your eyes look clear today. You'll be fine, thanks to that husband of yours."

He's not my husband! she wanted to scream. She should tell him, so why didn't she? Maybe later. Right now, she was too tired to face the inevitable questions. And what did it matter? Rafe Montalvo must have found out what he wanted to know. Maybe she'd spoken the word Concepción in her sleep.

He'd left her behind. Men always left. He'd gone after the gold without her—her gold!

"Here," the doctor was saying. "I brought you some broth."

She turned away when he tried to hand her the small tray. "I'm not hungry."

"You're bound to be. Your husband said you hadn't eaten since night before last."

"How long have I been here?" she asked, not certain if she could endure another unpleasant revelation.

"Oh, about twenty-four hours."

"I've been asleep all that time?"

"Like I said, you were pretty bad off. In fact, I suspect your husband saved your life."

"I know," she said, the taste of betrayal bitter in her mouth. "Did you know that in some countries if someone saves your life you're their slave forever?"

"Well, no, ma'am, I didn't know that."

He moved the tray toward her again, and she took it automatically.

"It's true," she assured him, settling the tray carefully on her lap.

"Well, I know you want to please that man of yours and all, being newlyweds, but take my advice and don't be too quick to let him have his way. You'll regret it later, mark my words."

A thin, almost hysterical laugh escaped her lips. "I'll remember that."

The doctor stood to go. "You rest now, Miss Christina."

Her mouth dropped open. "What did you call me?"

"Miss Christina," he repeated. "Would you prefer Mrs. Holden?"

"Holden? My name is Anne."

"Really? But—" He stopped in mid-sentence and shrugged. "I could've sworn he called you Christina. Well, then, Miss Anne, rest awhile and I'll be back to check on you shortly."

She watched as he crossed the room to the door and halted with one hand on the knob. He ran his other hand across his chin before he turned to face her once more. "Is there anything you want to tell me?"

Her heart caught in her throat, and suddenly she

was desperate that he not know the truth. What would he think of her, a woman traveling alone with a man like Rafe Montalvo?

"No," she said, she hoped convincingly .

The doctor stared at her with his piercing blue eyes. It was a long moment before he nodded his head almost imperceptibly and left the room, closing the door behind him.

She lay in bed, listening to the ticking of the clock, imagining all the ways she'd like to kill Rafe Montalvo. For the second time in their short, unpleasant acquaintance, he had claimed they were married.

Of course she knew why he had done so this time. He'd needed a way to stay in the same room with her in case she talked in her delirium—which, evidently, she had done. Now he was on his way to Concepción to claim *her* gold.

Maybe he's just gone out for a while, she reasoned. Maybe there was something he had to do. Like what? Like kill someone else?

Damn him!

She should be glad he was gone, and she told herself she would have been if not for the fact that he was going to cheat her out of her fortune. He'd gotten what he wanted from her; now he didn't need her. He didn't care if she was stranded in a strange town, penniless and alone. She didn't matter to him.

But maybe he'll come back.

Pain knifed through her heart, and she closed her eyes against it. How many times had she wondered if Papa would come back?

"I just have one thing to do," he'd told her.

She remembered standing alone on the crowded New Orleans dock, clutching her small satchel and a tattered doll. She couldn't have been older than ten. She remembered how frightened she'd been by the crowd and the noise and the activity.

She had tried not to cry as she searched the crowd of adults who rushed past her as if she were invisible. She jerked at the sound of a riverboat's steam whistle, the familiar noise foreign and frightening.

He'd promised he'd be here. He'd promised, but he was nowhere to be found. She bit her lip to still its trembling.

"I just have one thing to do, Anne-Marie, and then I'll be there," he'd told her that morning.

He was going to sell her mother's jewelry, she knew, the jewelry he'd once promised she would have when she grew up. It didn't matter to her, nothing mattered right now except that she was alone and frightened and her father had lied to her.

Maybe he had left without her. Maybe he expected her to be on the boat instead of on the dock and she was going to be left behind. Maybe—

"Are you lost, *ma petite?*"

The man who had bent over her that day was Gaston, she later learned, a man who preyed on children, taking them off the streets of New Orleans and selling them into prostitution.

Even now, the thought sent a shudder down her spine. But at that moment her father arrived. . . .

There had been other times before that one, minor disappointments, when her father made promises he hadn't kept, but never had she felt so abandoned, so helpless. She had learned a hard lesson that day, one she had never forgotten: to trust herself and no one else. No one was going to take care of her, no one, not even her own father—least of all her own father.

Rafe Montalvo was no different, but at least she'd known what he was from the start. Still, she should be thankful he'd brought her to a doctor instead of leaving her in the desert to die.

"Good thing I didn't talk in my sleep before he got me here," she murmured.

Closing her eyes, she mentally counted the money she'd kept in her running bag and the few coins she'd managed to salvage from the accident. She gasped aloud as a thought came to her. He'd undressed her last night. What if he'd found her money and taken it?

She threw the covers off and sat up quickly, too quickly. Her head reeled, and she had to sit for several moments while her equilibrium returned. When she was able to maintain her balance and think clearly again, she stood shakily.

Her legs were weak, practically useless, but she managed to walk around the bed by holding on to the bedposts.

"My clothes!"

She searched the room, but her clothes were gone. Gone! Why would he take her clothes?

Her heart began to pound in alarm. Not only was she destitute and alone, she didn't even have clothes to wear. What was she going to do? She couldn't stay in this room forever.

Without warning, the tears came, like warm rivers running down her face. Her vision blurred, but she managed to see a pistol resting on the bureau across the room.

When she reached the bureau, she recognized the weapon as her own seven-shooter. At least he'd left her that! And why not? He had his own gun.

Her heart froze as she looked at the bureau more

closely and spotted her running bag. He must have found it when he undressed her. A cold dread knotted her stomach. Had he looked inside, gone through her personal belongings? Had he taken her money?

She picked up the running bag and returned to the bed with it. When the contents lay spread out on the bed before her, she released a sigh of relief.

He hadn't left her destitute, just stranded. That she could cope with. She'd been stranded before.

She was not quite strong enough to travel yet, but as soon as she was, she'd ask the doctor how to get to Eagle Pass. Maybe she could still beat Rafe Montalvo there. She could buy another wagon and team and . . .

Her thoughts trailed off. She knew she didn't have enough money to hire another rig and buy enough provisions to make it to Mexico. Thanks to Rafe Montalvo, she'd have to buy new clothes, too. She needed money.

An idea began to take shape in her mind as she gazed at the worn-out deck of cards that lay among the spilt contents of her running bag.

A poker game.

As much as she hated gambling, it was her only chance. She needed to find a poker game. She knew how to convince a group of men to let a woman play. Some would want to take advantage of her inexperience; others would be curious to see if she could play at all. Either way, they'd let her in. All she had to do was find a game, which shouldn't be too difficult. Wherever there were men, there were gaming houses.

Although she dreaded having to carry out her plan, she couldn't help smiling at her cleverness. It was the only way. Poker was her only skill, and she needed money badly, thanks to Rafe Montalvo.

Deep inside, she knew it was irrational to blame

Rafe Montalvo for all her misfortune. He hadn't caused the accident that had put her in this situation. Still, she needed a target for her anger and frustration, and he was the only one at hand.

Damn you, Rafe Montalvo, she thought as she began stuffing her belongings back inside the running bag. I hope you burn in hell!

"What are you doing up, young lady?"

Anne whirled away from the window, turning to see the doctor step into the room. She walked to the bed and flounced down, jabbing a finger into the jar of salve on the bedside table and applying it to her lips.

"I can't stay here any longer," she said, her voice thin with desperation. "I feel much better. I can't stand being closed up in this room."

"Well, I'm sorry I left you alone so long. It's been an unusually busy day. Two bullet wounds and a broken leg. I just got back to the office. You been drinking plenty of water?"

"Enough to fill a river!"

The doctor laughed. "Good girl. You hungry?"

"Yes." She hadn't realized how hungry she was, but just the word caused her stomach to rumble.

"Well, it's Saturday, and my housekeeper has the afternoon off. There's a café down the street. I'll go down and get us something in a while, if your husband isn't back soon."

She frowned. Pain stabbed her heart and she couldn't understand why. "Doctor, I want to thank you for taking care of me."

The doctor laughed shortly. "It's my job."

"You didn't have to sit beside me all night and—"

"I didn't," he replied, moving to the bedside table to retrieve the dishes he'd left there earlier. "I turned you over to your husband and he took care of you."

Her hand went to her forehead. No, she must have dreamed that part of it. No one, least of all Rafe Montalvo, had kissed her on the forehead last night. It had been a dream; that was the only possible answer.

But there were other parts of last night that she was just as sure she hadn't dreamed, like the gentleness of his hands, as he'd held her and tipped a cup to her lips, and the way he'd bathed her face and neck with a damp cloth and smoothed the hair from her brow.

She distinctly remembered the pressure of lips against her forehead. No, it hadn't happened. She'd imagined it.

"I need clothing," she told the doctor. She needed something, anything to occupy her thoughts, to keep her from wondering about things that were better left alone. "How can I get something to wear?"

"Well, your husband said he was taking your clothes to be washed. When he gets back—"

"He's not coming back."

"Now don't talk nonsense, girl, he's coming back, all right. Why wouldn't he? You're his wife. And he cares about you, that's plain to see."

She laughed bitterly. "No, he doesn't. And I don't care about him. I'm glad he's gone. But I can't stay here."

He studied her with an expression of compassion and confusion. "Where's your home? Your folks?"

Tears welled in her eyes and she blinked them away. The emptiness that was always a nagging presence threatened to consume her. "I have no family, no home. As for the man who brought me here, he's—"

The door from the waiting room opened at that

instant. The doctor and Anne turned together to see Rafe Montalvo enter. He stopped short, his gaze passing from Anne to the doctor and back.

She gasped, grabbing the blanket from the bed, clasping it in front of her. Her heart raced; suddenly she was trembling all over.

He'd come back. It was impossible, but there he was. He'd come back.

"There. I told you he wouldn't leave without you," the doctor said.

Mesmerized, she watched Rafe step across the threshold and close the door behind him. Her breath caught at the perfect symmetry of his body, the way he moved with the grace of a predatory cat. When he glanced at her, her blood ran cold and hot at the same time.

A warning sounded in her mind. She was feeling tender toward him because of the doctor's revelation and her own murky memory. She mustn't allow herself to forget that everything he had done had been calculated to get her to tell him the location of the gold so he could leave her behind.

She couldn't allow this newly discovered physical attraction or anything else to dull her reason. He might be the most handsome man she had ever seen, he might have spoken to her soothingly and touched her gently last night, but she couldn't afford to forget what he was and what was at stake here. It was more than gold. When he looked at her with those silver-gray eyes that reflected the light like shards of glass, she feared for her very soul.

"You seem to be much better," he said, his voice soft and emotionless.

"I am." Her heart pounded so fiercely she wondered if he could hear it across the room.

"Well, I'll leave you two alone," the doctor said, and it was all she could do not to beg him to stay. "And I'll leave that laudanum beside the bed in case you have trouble sleeping tonight."

The doctor was talking to Anne, but she couldn't tear her eyes away from Rafe Montalvo. He held her with a magnetism that was nearly overpowering, even from across the room.

"See you in the morning," the doctor added as he went out, leaving her alone with her nemesis.

Rafe stood where he was, studying her intently. His gaze moved from her face down her body and back to her face in a way that made her legs feel even weaker than they had before. She tightened her grip on the blanket she held to her bosom.

He took a step toward her and she backed away instinctively, eyeing him warily like a trapped animal, a defenseless deer stalked by a mountain lion.

"I had your clothes washed," he said, holding a package toward her, "and I bought you another shirtwaist. The one you were wearing looked pretty bad. And boots. I couldn't help noticing yours weren't quite the right size."

Her heart caught in her throat. Why? she wanted to ask. Why did he have to do something thoughtful just when she was telling herself to hate him? Her anger was her only defense against the unaccountable wave of pleasure and relief she had experienced at the sight of him.

"Why did you tell the doctor we're married?" she asked.

He shrugged. "It made things easier. How else was I going to explain that we were traveling together?"

"Well, if you were going to lie, you could have said we were brother and sister or cousins or—"

He shook his head. "Somehow I just can't picture you as a sister or a cousin."

She didn't want to explore his meaning. His look was anything but a brother's right now, and the expression in his eyes made her nervous.

"I think you told him we were married so you could . . . could undress me while I was unconscious and—"

His sharp laugh cut her off. "Lady, you were unconscious for about three hours before we ever got to town. I could have undressed you . . . I could have done anything I wanted to you any time I wanted to."

A sob broke through her control. She felt more vulnerable at that moment than she had at any other time in her life.

"Bastard," she whispered, barely able to speak at all.

"What do you take me for?" He made a move toward her and she shrunk away. "Do you think I'm so depraved I'd molest a woman who was barely alive? No, don't answer that. I don't give a goddamn what you think. In the first place, if I wanted to molest you I wouldn't wait until you were unconscious. I like my women with a little more life to them."

Anne clutched the blanket tighter, looking away before he could see the fear in her eyes. What he said was true. He didn't have to wait until she was unconscious to attack her if he wanted to. When they were alone together, as they were right now, she was completely at his mercy. She couldn't help wondering if he possessed any mercy in that cold, black heart of his. There certainly was none showing in his eyes. Right now, the only thing she saw in those silver orbs was anger.

"And in the second place," he went on, "don't flatter yourself. Have you looked in a mirror lately?"

She sucked in her breath at the insult but could find no words to express her hurt and contempt.

He tossed the package on the bed, took off his hat, and ran a hand through his hair. She watched in fascination as he regained the iron restraint he exercised over his emotions. She could actually see the change take place, as if he were a snake that had shed its skin, only to crawl back inside it. His face lost its rage. In fact, his expression seemed completely bland as he turned to look at her, as if the violent outburst of a moment earlier had never happened.

"Why did you think I'd gone?" he asked.

She tilted her chin to face him squarely, despite the pain lodged in her chest at the insult he'd delivered and the tumult of her emotions after what she'd just witnessed. "I figured I must have told you what you wanted to know while I was delirious."

With a short, mirthless laugh, he shook his head. "We're quite a pair, aren't we. We don't trust each other, we don't particularly like each other, but we've been forced together by fate."

He gazed at her for an infinite moment before releasing a sigh, and she had the unmistakable impression that he was either weary or heartsick. Now why had she thought that?

"We've been forced together by you, Mr. Montalvo."

"Are you hungry?" he asked, ignoring her statement. She nodded.

"You feel up to going out?"

"I don't think I could stand it in this room for another hour." She hated the desperation in her voice and the way it nearly cracked with emotion. He'd come back.

"Well, change clothes and I'll take you to the café for dinner."

"I need a bath."

Once again that unfathomable gaze traveled down her body. She quivered, tried to swallow, but her throat had gone dry.

Deny it though he might, she knew he desired her. What she didn't know was if he had the scruples to control his lust. She'd have to be a fool to trust him, knowing what she knew about him.

He smiled, rather wolfishly, she thought. "I'm sure the doc can help you."

He walked across the room, his bootheels loud in the silence.

Anne took another step back, out of his path, watching him as he reached the far door and turned to gaze at her one last time. It occurred to her then, and not for the first time, that perhaps she should be worried about trusting herself.

8

How have I come to this? Anne asked herself silently. All I've ever wanted was a home, a little peace and quiet, and look at me now.

She'd been in some desperate situations before, but never like this. Always there had been a place to run to, a refuge, if it was nothing more than a cheap, shabbily furnished apartment. Now there was nothing but desert, nothing but a vast, unfamiliar wilderness.

She hadn't had enough money to spare for better boots, so Rafe had bought them for her. They fit remarkably well, she decided, pulling her skirt up to look at the shiny black leather, especially considering he had bought them without knowing her size.

"Maybe you won't slow me down quite as much with a decent pair of boots," he'd said gruffly.

She'd have to be a fool not to accept them with her money running out all too quickly. Having to rely on someone else, especially someone like Rafe Montalvo, didn't set well with Anne. She could defend herself with the gun tucked inside her skirt pocket, but eventually she would run out of ammunition and she couldn't afford to buy more. If Rafe Montalvo deserted her, she would starve to death when she was no longer able to buy food. She felt her spirits sag under the weight of her vulnerability and defenselessness.

Around her spread the town of Castroville, a collection of clapboard buildings and canvas tents. Animals and wagons and men on foot crowded the dusty streets. It was a town like many others she'd seen since coming to Texas, but somehow it seemed dirtier, more dangerous, less permanent.

She sat on a horse in front of Rafe Montalvo because he'd said she was too weak to hold on to him, and she really wasn't sure which would have been worse—to be seated behind him, with her arms wrapped around him and her breasts pressed against his back, or to ride in front of him as she did now.

His strong arms encircled her. Too tired and too weak to prevent it, she leaned back against his hard chest. His breath caressed her ear, sending currents of sensation down her neck to her breasts. His hard, muscled thighs cradling her hips served as a constant reminder of his maleness and of her own vulnerability. She hoped fervently that he couldn't feel the trembling of her body, and she hoped just as fervently that their ride would be a short one.

The sounds of shouting, thundering hooves, and gunshots invaded her mind, interrupting her disturbing thoughts. Fear flashed through her as Rafe crushed her back against his hard chest with one arm and controlled his pawing, prancing horse with the other, guiding it to the side of the street.

A team of horses pulling a wagon rounded a corner and galloped toward them. The man on the seat was cracking a whip over the backs of the animals, shouting and urging them on. Other men rode on horseback beside the wagon, firing their guns in the air. People on foot scurried to get out of the way as the wagon and its outriders bore down on them, swept past, and stopped up the street in front of a large canvas tent.

The man climbed down from the wagon seat, laughing and dusting his pants with his hat. The horsemen dismounted and tied their horses to the hitching post. As they stepped onto the sidewalk, a woman with impossibly red hair came out of the tent to watch them, her hands on her hips, her legs planted wide, her head shaking back and forth in mock disdain.

Anne had seen "soiled doves" before in riverfront towns, so she wasn't shocked by the woman's presence or demeanor or revealing attire. Rather, she was more than a little curious. After all, in her experience, where there were women like that, there was almost always gambling.

Her plan was still fresh in her mind. She had to get away from Rafe Montalvo. Her mind told her to run as far and as fast as she could from the strange, violent man who had saved her life. It was her treacherous heart that had rejoiced at sight of him today, and she couldn't trust her heart. Borden McKenna had taught her that.

Rafe already knew she intended to travel as far as Eagle Pass, so she planned to take advantage of his protection and his money for a while, although she couldn't help wondering how safe she was. She didn't really have a choice.

Something disturbing and frightening had happened between them this afternoon in the doctor's office. Her body had responded to him, despite everything she knew about him, despite the fact that she didn't trust him. She didn't want to like him; she certainly didn't want to be . . . to desire him.

It was hard to admit, even to herself, that she felt anything but disgust for him. She had to get away before he found out where the gold was and abandoned her, yes, but now that wasn't her greatest fear. Her greatest fear was herself.

Rafe dismounted first. He reached up and took her by the waist before she realized what he meant to do. She placed her hands on his broad shoulders as he pulled her from the horse and planted her on her feet in front of him. His hands remained on her waist, his face close to hers.

Instinctively, she leaned away from him, putting as much distance as possible between them. She brushed against the horse behind her and it gave a snort. When she jerked forward, her body pressed against Rafe's hard form. Again she leaned away, mindful this time of the animal behind her. Trapped between a horse and an animal of a different kind, she had no choice but to stand her ground and hope that Rafe Montalvo couldn't hear the furious thundering of her heart.

Unable to hold his gaze, she glanced away. When she managed to look at him again, his face loomed even closer to hers. She would only have to tilt her head slightly and their lips would meet.

A strange languor spread through her body at the thought. The pull of his body on hers terrified her even as it thrilled her. She fought the instinctive yearning to lean toward him, to have his arms encircle her and pull her against him.

Grabbing one of his arms and prying it off her waist, she twisted away. When she reached the sidewalk, she turned to wait for him as he looped the reins over the hitching post and strode toward her.

He was everything she despised in a man. He had no moral fiber. He was a killer, just like Borden McKenna. But Borden was light, physically and emotionally. He was a dandy, a man who took nothing seriously, not even the business of killing. Rafe Montalvo, on the other hand, was all darkness, all shadows, all mystery. To look into his eyes was to look into an abyss.

She had learned early to read a person's eyes. Her father had taught her some of what she knew; the rest had come instinctively. For the most part, she wasn't even aware of the process. She did know that she could learn a great deal about people that way—most people. But some people had eyes that were hard to read. They were all closed up inside. Rafe Montalvo was such a man. You could never know what he had in his head, what he was capable of.

He stepped up onto the sidewalk, removing his hat in a gesture that was all grace and courtesy. He offered her his bent arm, as if they were entering a ballroom, not a barely decent café. She placed a hand on the crook of his arm and he guided her inside.

Immediately after they crossed the threshold, she had a sense of staring eyes, of conversations abandoned, of nervous anticipation. Customers packed the small restaurant to overflowing. Most of them were men with guns who looked nearly as hard and uncompromising as Rafe Montalvo.

Her grip tightened on her escort's arm. For once, she was grateful that he was so big and imposing, although she knew at the same time that he was the reason they had drawn so much attention. These men perceived him as a threat. Why shouldn't they?

She recalled the night on the street in San Antonio. At the time she had been so terrified, so determined just to survive, that she hadn't really absorbed all that had been said. Now she recalled that the men had known Rafe's name, and the fear evoked by that name had pulsated through the crowd. They had spoken of his prowess as a gunfighter.

Did these men know him by reputation too? How many people had he killed? Was that the source of his notoriety—bounty hunter, hired killer?

He steered her through the room toward a small table in the back that had been recently vacated. He held her chair out for her until she sat down, then took the seat across from her.

Conversations around them picked up, and the tension in the room seemed to lift.

"Do people always react that way when you enter a room?" she asked.

He smiled. "I was going to ask you the same question."

She bristled, remembering his earlier insult. "Don't try to be charming, it doesn't suit you. We already know what you think of my appearance. I am not the one they were looking at. I am not the reason they all stopped talking and turned to stare. They were afraid of *you*. The same thing happened in San Antonio, as soon as they learned who you were. Why is that, Mr. Montalvo?"

"Let it be," he said, his calm tone veiling a warning.

Rafe turned in his chair, giving her only his profile. He seemed to be searching the room for a waiter, but she sensed that his posture was intended to put an end to any further discussion.

"What are you afraid of?" she asked before her courage could falter.

He turned to face her, an ironic smile curving his expressive lips. "Afraid?"

"What is it you want to avoid talking about?" Her heart fluttered inside her chest. She could hardly believe her own boldness.

She wasn't at all sure she wanted him to answer the question. Did she really want to delve into his past? Were men like Rafe Montalvo born or made?

He glanced away again, and for a moment she thought he wouldn't respond. When he did, his voice was so soft she had to strain to hear him in the crowded room. "Before you start asking questions, you'd better make sure you want to know the answers."

To Anne's relief, the waiter arrived at that moment. They ordered steaks, and Rafe ordered a beer. She looked away in disgust as the waiter returned with the mug of frothy beverage.

"I see you disapprove of drinking," he said as he took a sip of beer.

"It leads to slothfulness and irresponsibility, like gambling. Either one can get a hold on a man and destroy him."

"You sound like the voice of experience," he said, and she knew he was patronizing her.

In truth, she hoped he would drink it quickly and order another and another. She needed him out of the way tonight. The alcohol would help her cause, but she had no intention of depending on that alone. She had left nothing to chance. The doctor's tiny vial of laudanum secreted away in her skirt pocket would guarantee that Rafe Montalvo didn't interfere with her plans.

"Do what you like, Mr. Montalvo. Drink to your heart's content."

"I intend to."

As she watched Rafe Montalvo drink his beer, she trembled at the thought of what she was going to do tonight. She'd have to wait until he and the doctor were both asleep, then sneak out of the office undetected. It would be late, and she didn't like being out alone after a certain hour, but it was a risk she'd have to take, and no worse than any of the other risks she'd taken since Papa died. Desperation had made her bold—and reckless.

He was staring at her, and her face grew warm under his scrutiny. Had he read anything in her expression?

"Your face is a window into your soul," Borden McKenna had told her.

She'd learned from her father to put on a blank poker face when she needed to, but when her guard was down, her emotions showed on her face as clearly as a reflection in a mirror.

Clearing her throat, she shifted nervously in her seat. "How much longer do you think we'll have to stay in Castroville?"

"That depends on how fast you recover."

"I feel fine."

"You don't look fine."

"I know. You've already told me." She remembered his earlier insult, then silently chastised herself for caring what he thought of her. "But we should at least move out of the doctor's office to a hotel, don't you think?"

"Can't," he replied casually. "Bunch of teamsters burned the hotel down and there's no place else to stay."

The waiter arrived with their food, and Anne dove into her steak with all the vigor of a starving field hand. It proved to be a little tough, but she was too hungry to care. She glanced up once to see Rafe Montalvo staring at her.

"The doctor has offered to let us stay with him until you're fit to travel," he said.

She swallowed the bite of steak, then replied, "I'm just a little tired. Maybe tomorrow. . . . "

"Why don't you just admit you're not cut out for this kind of adventure?" He leaned toward her, his arms folded on the table in front of his plate. "Tell me where the gold is and wait for me here."

He wasn't going to give up. Did he think her completely brainless? Did he really think there was a chance she'd tell him where that gold was?

"And you'll go and get it and bring it back to me, right?"

He smiled and picked up his fork and knife. "Right."

"I may be a bit reckless from time to time, but I'm no fool."

"A *bit* reckless?" He took time to chew and swallow a bite of steak before adding, "You nearly got yourself killed."

"That was an accident." She hated to feel the need to defend her actions to this man who had forced himself into her life. "It could have happened to anyone."

"Out here you have to be prepared for accidents. You have to know what you're doing."

"And you know what you're doing, don't you?" she asked.

But he wasn't listening to her. All his attention was focused on the front of the café. She took advantage of his momentary preoccupation, grabbing a small slice of onion from her plate and dropping it into her reticule.

"Stay here," he said, as he rose from his seat and went to investigate.

As soon as he was gone she dug in her pocket, taking out the vial she'd hidden there while she dressed in the doctor's office. She grabbed the cap and twisted, but nothing happened. Her gaze darted to where Rafe stood peering out the window. Her hands began to sweat, and she wiped them on the napkin in her lap. He'd be back any moment. If he caught her, she didn't even want to think about what he'd do.

She twisted the cap with all her might. Nothing. It wouldn't budge. Orange light reflected on Rafe's face as he talked with the man next to him.

"Damn!" she whispered.

Her heart pounded with the urgency of the situation. This might be her only chance to make sure that Rafe was safely out of her way tonight, and she didn't even want to contemplate what he would do if he returned and found her attempting to drug him. She held the cap in her mouth, clamping her teeth on it, then twisted with her hand.

The cap gave.

She finished untwisting it and dumped the entire contents into his beer mug. His even footfalls echoed behind her as she secured the cap, and he sat down just as she slipped the empty vial back into her pocket.

"What was it?" she asked, hoping her voice didn't tremble.

He picked up his fork and knife before replying. "They've started a bonfire in the middle of the street."

"Isn't there any law here?" She watched Rafe cut his steak and put a piece in his mouth.

He chewed and swallowed, shaking his head until he could speak again. "Just one man. Better eat if you plan to keep up with me."

She picked up her fork, but she'd lost her appetite. Staring at the mug, she wondered belatedly if she'd given him too large a dose. What if it killed him?

"You know, I can move faster and safer alone," he said.

Unbelievable! He seemed actually to think she would trust him enough to let him go on without her. She told herself she didn't care if it did kill him, though she wasn't quite convinced.

"And you can be all the way to South America before I know what's happened. I *need* that money."

"I told you . . . look, I'm only trying to save your hide."

"My hide is not your responsibility, Mr. Montalvo. I will take it wherever I want. If you try to leave me behind, I'll just strike out again alone."

He dropped his fork on his plate, the loud clatter causing her to jump. She could see anger in his eyes, in the clenching of his jaw, before he regained his air of indifference. "I know, I know. Why is this gold so important to you? Important enough to risk your life for?"

"Haven't you ever cared enough about anything that you were willing to die for it?"

She watched in amazement as the carefully constructed wall around him cracked, and for a fleeting instant she sensed she was seeing past the facade into the heart of the man. It was like that night in San Antonio when he'd caught her up in his arms and she'd glimpsed the unmasked pain in his eyes.

Then it was gone as if it hadn't been there at all. The crack closed and the hardness returned to his eyes.

"No," he said. "You about through wolfing down that steak?"

"But you haven't finished your beer."

He picked up the half-full mug and downed the contents, then slammed the empty mug down on the table. He dug in a pocket and took out several silver coins, which he dropped beside his plate. When he rose, she knew he intended to walk around to her side of the table and help her up. She stood before he had a chance. He smiled knowingly as he took her arm, guiding her out of the café and into the dark street.

The bonfire the revelers had built in the street had died to embers. The men who had been responsible for unwittingly providing her with the diversion she'd needed to drug Rafe Montalvo's drink must have drifted off to find other amusement.

Dozens of men wandered aimlessly in the darkness, their elongated shadows reaching from one side of the street to the other. Gunshots rang out sporadically, and voices shouted unintelligible words.

Instinctively, she moved closer to Rafe, who responded to her nervousness by tightening his hold on her elbow. It was a small gesture, but strength and confidence flowed from his body into hers. For a moment, she almost regretted what she'd done.

How long would it take for him to start feeling the effects of the drug? Would he make it back to the doctor's office? She certainly hoped so, since she'd never be able to carry him—or even drag him. What would she do if he collapsed now?

She didn't want to think about it. Instead, she turned her attention to the men milling about on the street.

"Why aren't those men fighting for the South?" she asked, more to take her mind off what she'd done than out of any real curiosity.

Rafe snorted in the darkness. "No future in it, no money to be made, too many rules."

The sound of raucous laughter across the street grated on her already frayed nerves. They were the same kind of men as the ones she'd encountered that night on the street in San Antonio, the same kind of men who roamed the streets of riverfront towns.

"But don't they care about the Confederacy?" she heard herself ask.

"Some claim to be loyal to the Confederacy, and some are Unionist to the bone. Of course, none of them are as loyal to any cause as they are to themselves. Whichever way the wind blows—"

"And what about you, Mr. Montalvo?" she asked. It was a question that had nagged at her almost since the first time she'd seen him. There was a war going on, yet this man seemed completely unaffected by it. "Why aren't you in the army?"

"The Confederate army?" he asked with a mocking smile, his white teeth flashing in the darkness. "Well, for one thing, I'm from New Mexico, not Texas, and New Mexico is Union."

"Then you're a Unionist," she accused.

She hated this war, hated both armies for disrupting the routine and fiber of her life, for adding to the hardships that had already been a part of her existence, but her heart remained loyal to the Confederacy. The South was her home.

"Didn't say that."

She couldn't see his face clearly, but she could feel his gaze on her, holding her with its magnetic power so she found it impossible to look away from his shadowed visage.

"Then what are you saying?" she asked a bit breathlessly.

He was silent for so long she thought he wasn't going to answer. Finally, he said, "I'm saying it's not my fight."

"You mean you have no opinion whatsoever?" Everyone had an opinion about the war.

"Didn't say that either."

"You certainly are being vague this evening." A loud

burst of laughter drew her attention to the door of the saloon, where two men staggered out, their arms locked together for support. "Maybe you're like those men. Maybe there's no money in it, and that's why you don't want to get involved."

"So you think you've got me all figured out."

She heard the sarcasm in his voice. Though she couldn't make out his features, she could well imagine his expression. His eyes would be narrowed, his lips curved up at one end in a mocking smile. The image of those lips touching her forehead flashed across her mind and she took an involuntary step back.

It couldn't have been him. It couldn't!

"I . . . I don't know anything about you, Mr. Montalvo, except that the first time I saw you, you rode into town with a body slung over your horse. Not a very good first impression, you must admit. And after that, you began to follow me."

"Was that when I saved your life?"

"You and I both know why you saved my life, don't we? I'm valuable to you. You need me alive because I know where the gold is and you don't. That's the only reason I trust you at all, you know. You need me."

Rafe untied the horse from the hitching post and swung up in the saddle. Someone fired a lamp near the window in the café. A shaft of light fell across his sardonic features as he reached his hand toward her and smiled.

"We may soon find out which of us needs the other more."

9

Anne's hand closed around the pistol in the pocket of her newly laundered skirt as soon as she reached the bottom of the staircase.

The night was dark, the street near the doctor's office quiet and deserted, but the hairs on the back of her neck prickled at the sounds of drunken revelry that reached her from the far end of town. She could see the lights from the big tent where she'd seen the prostitute earlier, and it was toward that structure that she made her way, her heart hammering inside her chest.

It was a terrible chance she was taking. Everything depended on the men in the saloon being too drunk to present a threat. She needed their judgment impaired in order to win the kind of money she needed. It was a big gamble, but she had no choice. She had to get away from Rafe Montalvo as soon as they reached Mexico.

She'd left him asleep on the floor. He hadn't moved,

even when she'd nudged him with the toe of her new boot. He should sleep the night away, after all the laudanum she'd given him. In the morning, he'd never even suspect she hadn't been in bed all night or that she had enough money to leave him behind.

Stopping at the door, she dug in her reticule for the piece of onion she'd taken at dinner. She rubbed it over her fingers and tossed it on the ground. One of her father's women, an actress, had taught her the trick. You rub onion on your fingertips, and then when you need tears, you just touch your fingers to the corners of your eyes.

Closing the reticule, she made her way through the door, hoping the trick would work. She'd never had occasion to use it before.

The hour was late, but the saloon wasn't nearly as deserted as she'd hoped. There were two poker games in progress and about twenty spectators spread out between them.

She studied the faces of the men at the first table. They seemed bland and harmless enough, except for one man with black slicked-back hair and sharp shrewd eyes, like those of an eagle or a hawk. He chewed on the stub of a cigar beneath his thin mustache, his lips curling in an unpleasant smile as he placed his cards on the table.

From the reactions of the other men at the table, she knew he'd won and she guessed that he was cheating. He looked the type.

She studied each player at the other table. There were four. The dealer looked like a farm boy, with a round face, dull eyes, and chubby fingers that fumbled over the cards. To his left was a small clean-shaven man dressed like a dandy. He seemed more interested in the saloon girl who stood behind his chair massaging his shoulders than he was in the cards.

Next to him was a huge brute of a man who kept drinking from the bottle at his side. His eyes were red, his hands unsteady. The last player was a man who resembled the ticket agent in Ubiquitous: small-boned, thin, with wire-rimmed glasses so thick they made his eyes appear twice their size.

She stifled a smile and made her way toward the second table.

"Do you have room for one more?" she asked.

The man with the glasses started as if he'd been prodded with a hot poker. He leaped to his feet, dropping his cards face up on the table—a pair of sixes, jack of diamonds, three of clubs, four of spades.

"Ma'am?" he said, grabbing his cards and overturning a beer in the process.

"Jesus Christ!" the drunken brute said, coming to his feet quicker than she would have thought him capable of doing.

A man in a white apron hurried over and mopped up the spill while the spectacled gambler apologized profusely and the brute cursed.

"Ain't no women allowed in here," the drunkard growled.

She looked pointedly at the saloon girl.

The man in the apron said "You wanna dress like her and serve drinks, fine. Otherwise . . . "

With a practiced sob, she touched her fingers to the corners of her eyes and the tears started.

"I . . . I don't know what to do."

"There, there, miss," the spectacled man said. He came to stand beside her and guided her gently to his own chair.

She was as good as in.

"My . . . my pa . . . he went to join the army. Got killed at Vicksburg. I need money to get to my uncle's in California."

"You ever played poker before?" the dandy asked.

She sniffed theatrically. "Well, no, but I—I'm sure I could learn. I'm a real fast learner." She withdrew the money pouch from her reticule. "I have fifty dollars." She dumped the money on the table before her to prove her words.

"I wouldn't feel right, taking your money," the dandy said. "Deal the cards, farm boy."

"But . . . but fifty dollars won't do me any good. I'd just as soon be broke. If I don't win enough tonight to get to my uncle, why, I . . . "—she gazed at the painted woman behind the dandy—"I suppose I'll have to find employment and stay here."

"Let her play," the spectacled man said. "Can't you see she's desperate?"

The dandy's gaze crept from her face down her throat to her breasts in a slow, assessing manner. She clutched her hands to her bosom and gave the man a look she hoped was a mixture of affronted modesty and shock.

The drunkard who had remained silent so far blurted, "Hell, I know how you can make twenty dollars real quick!"

"You shouldn't talk that way," the farm boy interjected. "Can't you see she's a lady? I say we let her play."

"Me too!" It was the man with the glasses. He dragged a chair from an empty table and sat beside her. She beamed at him appreciatively.

"Deal," the dandy growled. He turned to Anne. "You know how to play five-card stud?"

She gaped at him mutely.

"I'll explain," the spectacled man offered, and she was treated to a long, boring explanation of a game she'd been playing since age eleven.

She was careful to lose the first couple of hands, staying in the game long after she should have folded. Several spectators had drifted to their table, undoubtedly drawn by the sight of a woman gambler. Some stood behind her, looking over her shoulder at her cards, and she didn't want to appear too knowledgeable.

"Now, tell me again," she said, studying her cards intently. "Does a full house beat three of a kind?"

"Yes, ma'am, it does."

"And what is a straight?"

The dandy slammed his cards down on the table in disgust. "Haven't you lost enough money yet?"

"Leave her alone, dude," the farm boy warned.

She fingered her cards as if in indecision. She was holding two tens and three throwaways. She'd never be able to win outright with a hand like that, but if they fell for the bluff, she wouldn't have to show her cards.

"I'll hold on to these," she said with a smile.

"I fold," the spectacled man said in disgust.

"Me too," said the farm boy.

The dandy glared at her uncertainly, then gazed back at his hand. "Shit! I'm out too."

All eyes turned to the last man, the brute who sat slumped forward in his chair. His eyes had rolled back, and his head lolled from side to side.

"Mister, you in or out?" the farm boy asked.

When there was no response, the dandy poked him on the arm. "What's it gonna be?"

The drunk man belched loudly, then slammed his beefy fist down on the table. "I'm out . . . for good."

"You quitting?" the dandy asked as the drunkard began raking in his money. "Yep. Much as I'd like to stay for the fun, I've had it."

He stood unsteadily and stumbled away from the table. Anne placed her cards face down and reached for the small pot in the center of the table.

"What did you have?" the farm boy asked.

"Oh!" She turned to her mentor in feigned confusion. "But you said that if no one called, I didn't have to show my cards."

"Well, yes," the man with the glasses agreed, "but if you don't show us your cards, how will you ever learn?"

"The lady's right."

She gazed up to see that her champion was the black-haired man from the other table. He smiled down at her, and her stomach turned over.

"Mind if I sit in?" The man lowered his tall, lean frame into the recently vacated chair without waiting for an answer.

Her throat constricted. She tried to think of some excuse to turn him away, but the others were already welcoming him into the game and the cards were already being dealt.

The luck seemed to move around the table to Rollins, the lean-faced, black-haired man. Something in his eyes made her skin crawl. They were cold, bottomless eyes, as clear and sharp as a hawk's.

She played carefully, remembering to keep up the pretense of helpless ignorance, although she didn't think the new player believed it. He'd called her bluff more than once, and she'd had to change her tactics.

It wasn't long before the pile of money before her started to grow and the piles in front of the others, including the newcomer, began to dwindle. She decided to quit while she was ahead, something her father had never been able to do.

"Gentlemen," she said as she raked her winnings toward her, "it has been a pleasure, but I'm afraid I'm getting tired."

Rollins grabbed her wrist, his long fingers wrapping around it like a steel band. What she saw in his eyes when she looked at him made her blood run cold.

"Not so fast, girl. I think you cheated. I know you cheated, and I want my money back."

"Just a minute, mister," the farm boy broke in.

"Shut up and stay out of this, kid," Rollins growled, without taking his eyes off Anne, "unless you're ready to fight. This little lady's gonna give me back my money, and nobody's gonna get hurt, ain't that right?"

She moistened her lips and jerked her arm away, and he released her. There had to be a way out of this. She wasn't about to give this man anything. She'd won every penny of the money in front of her fair and square.

"I . . . I don't know what you're talking about," she said, stuffing money into her reticule and down the front of her bodice. "Why, I wouldn't know how to cheat."

Rollins snorted. "Don't try that innocent greenhorn act with me. You know the game, all right. If you were a man, I'd shoot you on the spot."

There was still a good bit of money on the table— *her* money—but she set her sights on leaving. Her heart pounding in her chest, she stood quickly and lunged for the door. But Rollins was too fast for her. Grabbing her by the arm, he pulled her against him, laughing at her futile struggles.

He held her around the waist with one arm while his other hand plunged down the front of her shirtwaist, pulling out banknotes and letting them fall to the floor.

She struck out, slapping him hard across the jaw. As soon as the sting of his skin against her palm brought her back to her senses, she regretted her rashness.

Rollins howled like a wild animal. He crushed the breath from her, and this time when his hand groped inside her blouse, it closed around a breast. His mouth covered hers before she could twist her head away. She tasted the foulness of his tongue as it sought to invade her mouth through her clenched teeth.

"You got some spunk, girl!" He growled. "God-dammit, I like a woman that puts up a good fight! I'm gonna enjoy taming you!"

With one hand, she pushed against his chest with all her might; with the other, she groped in her pocket, her hand closing over the pistol. She was about to shove it into his side when the change in his expression halted her. He glanced past her over her head. Tension tightened the muscles in the arm that banded her waist.

Before she could react, he produced a knife from somewhere and pressed it against her throat. She couldn't help the tiny gasp of horror that escaped her dry lips at the feel of cold steel against her flesh. Her fingers went numb. She dropped the pistol, well aware that he could slit her throat before she could squeeze off a shot.

"Don't try it, mister," Rollins warned, "unless you want her throat slit ear to ear."

In the corner of her eye, she caught sight of Rafe Montalvo. How had he known where she was? Why wasn't he sleeping after all the laudanum he'd swallowed tonight? It didn't matter. All that mattered was that he was here.

"Just want me a drink," Rafe said, easing his hand away from his revolver. He turned to face the bar as if he hadn't a care in the world. "It's no concern of mine."

This can't be happening, she thought, with the only part of her mind that was still functioning. It had to be a dream, a horrible nightmare. Rafe had to help her. He had to keep her alive. She knew where the gold was. Without her, he would never find it.

"C'mon, honey." She could smell the liquor on her tormentor's breath as he whispered against her ear. "Let's you and me go out back. You can show me what you been doing for our friend over there."

She gasped. He'd known all along that she wasn't alone and that she'd been lying.

"If you're good enough, I might even pay you."

She wanted to resist as he began dragging her toward the back door, but a slight pressure reminded her of the blade pressed against her skin. The tent full of patrons watched with only passing interest, among them Rafe Montalvo.

Then Rafe moved—slightly—but the movement caught her eye. It caught Rollins's eye as well and he swung back to Rafe.

"You got any objections?"

Rafe shrugged. "Yeah, I've got objections. You always do your fighting from behind a woman?"

Rollins laughed shortly. "Hell, a man needs a little security."

"I heard that about you, heard you were a coward."

"Do I know you, mister?"

Rafe smiled, but there was no humor in the gesture. "You know me, all right. We have a mutual friend, El Alacrán."

Rollins laughed again. It was a sound more like a snort. "Ain't seen him in four or five years. And I sure as hell don't remember you."

"We met five years ago in the Chihuahuan desert,

remember? You and a bunch of El Alacrán's men kidnapped a woman. . . . "

The knife shook against Anne's throat as a tremor ran through the man who held her. "I didn't have nothin' to do with that."

His grip relaxed for a fraction of a second, long enough for Anne to mount an escape. She struck backward with her elbow, landing a blow to the man's rib cage that caused him to drop the knife. She pulled away and tried to run but tripped over a chair, landing on the sawdust-covered floor at his feet. Dust and wood slivers stuck to her palms.

The barroom exploded in violence as both men drew their revolvers. Then both men fired as if at once, but Rollins was a split second slower. Rafe's bullet tore through Rollin's chest, and the impact of the shot sent him crashing into a table, which splintered under his weight. He fell to the ground with a thud.

Anne struggled to her feet, clutching the edge of the rough-hewn bar with one hand while she brushed the debris from her skirt with the other. Rafe Montalvo walked over to the fallen man and pulled out a piece of paper from his own vest pocket: a WANTED poster. He held up the likeness to the face of the dead man, then holstered his revolver and stood up.

"What the hell's going on here?" a voice asked.

Anne looked up from where she was gathering her money to see a man wearing a sheriff's badge walk in.

"It was a fair fight," someone said. "He saved this lady from that outlaw."

"Is that right, miss?"

She jerked around to face the sheriff when she realized he was talking to her. "Yes."

Rafe walked to the sheriff and handed him the

WANTED poster. The lawman took it and compared it to the face of the dead man. "It's Sam Rollins, all right."

A man came running in, tying a white apron behind his back. His neck was long, and he resembled a bird, with his long nose and skinny legs. He went immediately to the dead man, and took measurements with a tape measure he produced from his pocket.

Bile rose in Anne's throat at the callousness of the entire affair.

"Okay, mister, you can come by in the morning and collect your reward. Bill, can you get this mess cleaned up?"

The bartender nodded vigorously. "Go back to bed, sheriff, I'll handle this."

The sheriff snorted, and eyed the undertaker. "Looks like everything's under control. He'll be in the ground by morning. Of course, I'll hold out the cost of the burial."

"Is that necessary?" Rafe asked.

"Well, hell, he's gotta be buried, and you killed him. I always hold out the cost of the burial."

Through a fog of nausea and dizziness, Anne glanced down at the man who leaned over the body, measuring it for a coffin. A cold knot settled in the pit of her stomach. She was finding it difficult to focus.

"Are you all right?"

Startled by the voice so nearby, she turned to see that Rafe had come to stand close to her. When he reached out to take her by the elbow, she jerked away. A shiver of gooseflesh ran up her arm.

Nonplussed, Rafe took her by the elbow once again. This time he didn't release her when she tried to pull free.

"Come along peacefully," he said, his voice as soft and smooth as velvet yet as lethal as a snake, "or I won't be responsible for my actions. What did you put in my food anyway?"

She couldn't answer, couldn't speak. It took all her concentrated effort to keep up with him as he dragged her into the street.

The first rays of dawn tinged the sky with pink. The early morning air was cool and refreshing. She took several breaths; the dizziness that had possessed her lessened somewhat.

When they reached the bottom of the staircase that led up to the doctor's office, her fragile control broke. She reached out with her free hand and grabbed the banister, taking Rafe by surprise and halting him on the bottom step. His grip only tightened on her elbow.

"Let me go." She'd intended it as a demand, but her words came out sounding more like a plea.

She tried to pull away, but he didn't seem to notice as he forced her up the step so that she stood toe-to-toe with him.

Once again she tried to escape, but he grabbed her free wrist, pulling her roughly against him so that their bodies were almost touching. She could feel his strength and knew that to resist was futile. His angry eyes held hers captive. There was nowhere to run, no possibility of escape.

"Understand me," he said, his face a mask of stone except for the tightening of a jaw muscle. "You are going up the stairs. We can do it the hard way or the easy way. It's up to you, but if I have to carry you, I promise you, you'll regret it."

He let go of one arm, turned, and began walking up the stairs. She had no choice but to follow, though she dreaded what would happen once they reached the top. She didn't know him, not really. She didn't know what he was capable of, except that killing seemed to come naturally to him and he probably didn't possess a conscience at all.

When they reached the door at the top he opened it and dragged her through into the waiting room. Without hesitation, he hauled her into the room where they'd been sleeping, pulling her to the bed and turning her so that she faced him, her back to the bed.

"Sit," he commanded.

She did as he told her, sitting on the edge of the bed, watching as he went to the corner where he'd dropped his gear. He returned with a long coil of rope.

"What are you going to do?" Her voice cracked, despite her efforts to master her fear. A warning glance from those pale eyes held her pinioned.

"Hold out your arms," he told her when he was standing close before her.

She had to tilt her head back to look up into his rage-contorted face. "I will not."

Before she could think or react, he dropped the rope and grabbed both of her hands in his. She struggled with every ounce of strength she had left after her illness and the night's events, but he easily drew her wrists together, holding them with one large hand. Then he bent, retrieving the rope from the floor, and began wrapping it around her wrists.

The will to fight drained from her body. What was the use anyway? She sat helplessly as he secured her wrists and then pulled the free end of the rope through the wrought-iron bars of the headboard. When he seemed satisfied that he'd tied it tight enough so she couldn't work it loose in the middle of the night but still had enough slack to lie down, he walked across the room, where he dropped down on his pallet.

"I need some sleep, and this is the only way I can be sure you'll stay out of trouble."

She waited until the room was silent except for the incessant ticking of the clock. Then she lay down on her side, curled as best she could into a ball of misery.

"How did you know where I was?" she asked softly.

Silence met her question. Just when she began to think he was already asleep, an answer came from the darkness.

"I didn't. I just followed the noise."

"I don't understand. I put the whole vial of laudanum in your beer."

"That was one dose for you. Lucky for you, I weigh a hell of a lot more than you do."

Silence engulfed them again. A question nagged at her mind, and though she wasn't sure she wanted to know the answer, she knew she had to ask.

"If that man hadn't had a bounty on his head, would you have killed him to save me?"

"Sure." The answer came without hesitation. "You still haven't told me where the gold is."

She turned her head into her pillow and gave in to the tears that had been close to the surface ever since Rafe had appeared in the saloon, silent tears that streamed down her face and into her pillow.

After a while, her body yielded to exhaustion and she slept.

10

Anne couldn't repress or deny the thrill that coursed through her as she stood at the window, watching Rafe walk toward her in long fluid strides. He carried a saddle slung over one shoulder and led two horses with his other hand.

She should be furious with him after what he'd done to her last night, but she could feel herself being drawn to him against her will. She knew he would eventually betray her. He was a man, after all, and that was what men did.

Rafe had known the cardsharp who'd attacked her. She tried to remember what he'd said. Something about the Chihuahuan desert and a woman. . . .

With an involuntary shudder at the memory of Rollins, she turned her mind away. There were so many questions, and she wasn't at all sure she wanted to know the answers. She opened the door, and went down the stairs as Rafe drew near. He stopped before her and dropped the saddle over the hitching post.

Was he still angry? Would he tell her or just refuse to speak to her, as her father used to do? Punish with silence: that had been Paul Cameron's way of dealing with anger, and she half expected the same treatment from Rafe.

"What is that?" She nodded toward the extra horse, choosing to ignore what had happened last night for as long as he would allow her to.

"What does it look like? It's a horse."

At least he'd spoken to her, even if his sharp words cut her to the bone. They stirred the anger and regret she had warred with all morning.

What she had done last night had been foolish, she was willing to admit that. But it had nearly worked. It would have worked, if not for Rollins.

Inching closer, she glared at Rafe. "I know it's a horse, but why is it here?"

"It's for you," he replied, as he tied the end of the rope that was fastened to his horse's halter to the hitching post.

She tried to avoid his eyes, tried to pretend he wasn't still angry, by concentrating instead on the horse.

It was quite pretty, with a gleaming dappled-gray coat and large almond-shaped eyes. It seemed placid enough at the moment, but she kept her distance just the same. The animal's sheer size and, to her mind, unpredictable nature terrified her. It reminded her of the man who stood before her now, impatiently awaiting her response.

"You know I can't ride." She was careful not to look at him, afraid of what she would see in his eyes.

"Well, you're going to have to learn. My horse can't carry us both all the way to Mexico."

"Couldn't we get a wagon?"

"No!"

She recoiled from the violence in his voice and the anger in his expression.

She turned her attention to the horse, anything to avoid his fury, as Rafe continued. "I tried to convince you that you'd slow me down, but you wouldn't listen. I'm not going to let a wagon slow me down even more."

She reached out to touch the horse's muzzle. "I have a whole month to get the gold and get back to Ubiquitous with it, so I'm not in any hurry," she said.

"Well, I am. You don't think—"

Whatever he might have been about to say was lost when the horse snorted softly and moved its head toward her.

"It tried to bite me!" she cried, jerking her hand away.

"No, he didn't," Rafe assured her, in a voice almost devoid of patience. "He wants you to rub him like this."

He reached out, stroking the horse's muzzle from between the eyes all the way down to the tip of his nose, then withdrew his hand. She knew he was waiting for her to touch the horse as he had.

Tentatively, she followed suit, smiling when the animal stood still and allowed her to stroke his smooth muzzle.

"Its nose is so soft," she murmured, enjoying the closest contact she'd ever had with a horse. At the same time, she was all too conscious of the large mouth full of teeth so close to her hand and of the man beside her.

He was watching her. The pressure of his gaze upon her caused a stirring in her heart that she couldn't explain. His behavior last night was unforgivable, and yet she felt as if she were the one who should ask for forgiveness. She closed her eyes tightly. No, she would not apologize. She'd done what she'd felt she had to do.

If you have a passion for great historical romance, here's an offer you'll love...

4 FREE NOVELS

Reader Service.

Yes! I want to join the Timeless Romance Reader Service. Please send me my 4 FREE HarperMonogram historical romances. Then each month send me 4 new historical romances to preview without obligation for 10 days. I'll pay the low subscription price of $4.00 for every book I choose to keep--a total savings of at least $2.00 each month--and home delivery is free! I understand that I may return any title within 10 days and receive a full credit. I may cancel this subscription at any time without obligation by simply writing "Canceled" on any invoice and mailing it to Timeless Romance. There is no minimum number of books to purchase.

NAME

ADDRESS

CITY   STATE   ZIP

TELEPHONE

SIGNATURE

(If under 18, parent or guardian must sign. Program, price, terms, and conditions subject to cancellation and change. Orders subject to acceptance by HarperMonogram.)

"I used to love to go to the track and watch the horses run," she said, remembering the days when she used to go to the races in Natchez with her father. "But I've always been afraid of them. They seem so wild and fierce."

"Horses are animals," he said, "and you shouldn't expect them to act otherwise. But they are not unreasonable or vicious, except for the occasional rogue. You just have to know how to handle them."

Like you? she wondered as she continued to stroke the horse's silken nose. From what she knew about him, he could have been talking about himself.

"Is it male or female?" she asked instead.

"Neither," he said with a crooked grin.

"Neither? How can it be neither?"

"It's a boy, a gelding."

"Aren't male horses called stallions?" She knew that much. Young male horses were called colts and older male horses were called stallions. Her father had never mentioned geldings.

"Not always," he replied, amused for some reason she couldn't fathom. "Someday I'll explain the difference. Right now it's time for your first riding lesson."

He swung a collection of leather straps down from his shoulder. It was the first time she noticed the bridle.

"You put the bridle on," he instructed, holding it out to her.

She took a step back. "I can't."

"What do you mean, you can't?" he asked. "How the hell did you think you were going to make it to Mexico if you can't even put a bridle on a horse. How were you going to harness and unharness a team?"

His tone caused her to wince, but Anne stood her ground. "The man at the livery stable in Ubiquitous harnessed them for me. It was only supposed to take eight hours to get here, and I planned to take them to the livery stable here and—"

"Of all the stupid, irresponsible—"

"I had no choice!" Hurt and anger warred within her. She knew he was right; she had been foolish to think she could make it all the way to Mexico without knowing how to care for a team of horses. Still, he had no right to berate her so. She'd nearly been killed. Hadn't she suffered enough?

"Well, you're going to learn if you're going to travel with me. You hold the bridle like this," he said, holding one end in his left hand, while his right hand held the edge of the bit. With his left hand, he held the bridle toward the horse's ears. With his right, he pressed the bit against the horse's mouth. "You nudge his mouth with the bit until he opens it."

The sound of metal against teeth grated on her nerve endings. "Doesn't that hurt?"

Rafe slipped the bit all the way into the horse's mouth and the animal immediately began chomping on it. "No, it doesn't hurt."

"How do you know?"

"It doesn't hurt," he repeated. "Look, if it hurt, he wouldn't get used to it. If a horse gets a rock in his shoe, he limps. If a horse gets a burr under his saddle, he bucks. A horse isn't going to let you do anything to him that hurts without putting up a fight. Okay, now you fasten the chin strap and it's done."

Unsure how to proceed, she stepped closer to the horse. Two leather straps dangled on either side of the animal's head. Taking one in each hand, she drew them together just as the horse tossed its head.

She gasped and jumped back. "He won't hold still."

Rafe gave a short laugh. Leaning back against the hitching post, his arms folded across his chest, he watched her closely. "He's an animal, not a fence post. He knows what you're getting him ready for, and he wants you to hurry up."

"Well, I can't!" she snapped.

"That's all right. You don't have to do what he wants. He has to do what you want."

"Does he know that?"

"Yes, and he knows you're afraid, too. He can sense it."

"I'm not afraid."

"No, you're just shaking all over because it's so cold."

She moved toward the horse once again, gazing into the placid brown eyes, wondering if this animal could really sense her fear. She stole a glance at Rafe Montalvo. She didn't have to wonder about him; he knew when she was afraid. She wondered if he could read her other emotions as easily.

"Don't worry about me," she said as she grasped the two ends of the straps again. "I'll do it, all right?"

"There's nothing to be afraid of." He had come to stand close behind her, so close she could feel the heat of his body against her back. "I'm not going to put you on a horse and turn you loose."

Her fingers trembled as she managed to fasten the chin strap while Rafe Montalvo looked on.

"I told you," she said as soon as she finished. "I'm not afraid."

"Not too tight." Rafe reached over her, leaning into her back. A rush of heat spread like a brush fire through her body as the scent of lye soap and male flesh assaulted her senses. He slipped his hand between the chin strap and the horse's muzzle. "Make sure your hand fits under it. You want to be able to control him, but you don't want to choke him to death."

She moved away. She liked him like this—all cleaned up. Maybe she liked him too much. He seemed almost respectable. He hadn't shaved, but she was beginning to think she liked him better with a beard than without.

"What next?" she asked from a safe distance.

"The blanket and saddle. Blanket first. It protects his back from the leather saddle. Make sure it's straight and high enough on his neck so it won't slide down when you start moving."

Anne did as she was told, swinging the heavy, coarse blanket up onto the animal's back and adjusting it onto its neck.

"Now it's time for the saddle. I'll put it on this time and you watch."

He took a step toward the saddle, but she darted in front of him and reached it first.

"I want to do it. It's the only way I'll learn."

"It's kind of heavy," he warned.

"Just tell me what to do." She'd show him she wasn't as helpless as he thought.

Rafe murmured something under his breath about stubborn women, then said, "Okay, pick up the right stirrup and the girth. You do know what the girth is?"

She ignored the sarcastic question, picking up the right stirrup and a strap of leather she assumed must be the girth. "What next?"

"Lay the stirrup and the girth over the saddle out of the way. Then pick the saddle up by the horn and the back lip and carry it over to him."

Clearing the hitching post with the saddle was easy, but when she tried to carry it to the horse, it became too heavy and she dropped it in the dusty street.

Rafe came forward immediately, but she had already grabbed the saddle again.

"No!" she snapped. "I can do it. I just didn't expect it to be so heavy."

His booted foot in the middle of the saddle prevented her from lifting it again. "There's nothing wrong with admitting you need help sometimes, Anne-Marie."

She let go of the saddle and jerked back. "Don't call me that. No one calls me that but my father, and he's dead. How do you know my name anyway? You've never been curious enough to ask."

Her eyes widened as she suddenly realized there was only one way he could have found out. "You went through my things! You read my letter!"

Rafe lifted the saddle. "I was looking for information about the gold."

"So you could leave me behind. Bastard!" Consumed with anger, she forgot for a moment that she had planned to leave him behind, too.

He walked over to the horse and threw the saddle on its back. "You don't know what you're getting into here, Anne-Marie."

"I told you not to call me that!" Her skin had gone cold, despite the heat of the day. She couldn't bear the idea that Rafe Montalvo had gone through her private things, had read a personal letter.

"Then what should I call you?"

He pushed the stirrup and girth over the other side of the horse, then turned to gaze at her, leaning against the saddle on the horse's back.

"How about Christina?" she asked, her voice trembling with rage and dread. Did she really want to open up this subject?

He seemed to pale slightly at the mention of that name. Or was it just her imagination? He moved away so quickly she couldn't be sure, but she sensed a change in his demeanor as he leaned beneath the horse's belly to catch the girth.

"Why would I call you that?"

"The doctor said you told him my name was Christina." She'd wanted to elicit some response from him, but something in his silence and his manner disturbed her. She pressed on. "Who is she?"

"It's just a name I made up." He threaded the girth strap through the buckle as he spoke.

"I don't believe you." The words came out before she even formed them in her mind.

"I don't give a damn what you believe." His face had turned to stone, and he gave her the most implacable stare she had ever seen. It should have been enough to warn her, but she couldn't let it drop. He had reacted, and she wanted to know why.

"Let it be," she mimicked. "Every time I ask you a question about your past life you tell me to let it be."

"Are you watching what I'm doing?" he asked.

"I need to do it myself if I'm ever going to be able to do it on my own."

"So you can run away again?" Securing the saddle, he turned to face her with accusing eyes.

"I didn't run away," she replied. "I would have come back."

"What the hell did you think you were doing anyway?" He was angry now, and his anger sparked a like response in Anne.

"Quit trying to change the subject. You went through my personal belongings. That is inexcusable."

"Then I guess it won't do any good to apologize, and

there's no reason to discuss it. You won't excuse me and I won't ask you to."

She followed as he led the horse behind the doctor's office. He had succeeded in turning her away from the subject she'd wanted to pursue, the subject of a woman named Christina.

"You always mount from the left side of the horse," he said, as he came to a stop. "Put your left foot in the stirrup and swing your right leg over the horse's back."

He waited impatiently while she swallowed her fear and walked toward him. She obviously didn't know what to do.

"Take the reins in your left hand and hold on to the saddle horn with the same hand. I'll hold the stirrup straight. Just slip your foot in it and swing yourself up."

Other than when the outlaw in the saloon had pressed a knife to her throat, she couldn't remember ever being more afraid than she was right now. She stood close to the horse, reaching up to grasp the saddle and the reins. When she felt somewhat satisfied that she had a good enough grip, she looked down at the stirrup. How was she ever going to maneuver this?

She lifted her leg, and Rafe guided the stirrup until her foot felt secure.

"Pull yourself up and swing your right leg over," he told her.

She pulled with her arms and pushed with her left leg, but she couldn't make it. The horse's back was too high and she was too weak. Just when she was about to give up, a hand on her backside pushed her up and she stood in the stirrup, suspended in air, too terrified even to take exception to the intimate contact.

"Wait!" she cried in panic as the horse moved slightly.

Her right leg swung over the horse's back and she dropped none too gently in the saddle. With her right foot, she searched frantically for the other stirrup, but whenever she managed to get that foot situated, the other one would come out. The stirrups were too long.

"Take it easy," Rafe said gently.

Anne turned to look down at him, where he stood at her left, and drew some reassurance from the calmness in his eyes.

"Move your foot," he said, in that same soft, calming voice.

She did as she was told. Shifting in the saddle, she tried in vain to find a comfortable position. "It feels awkward."

"You'll be sore for the first couple of days.

His long fingers worked skillfully at adjusting the length of the stirrup. Watching, she couldn't help thinking how gentle and firm they seemed, those hands that could kill so easily. She remembered their strength when he'd held both her wrists in one hand last night, and she also remembered their gentleness when he'd applied the aloe to her burnt hand in the desert. He was a man of mystery and contradiction, a man who stirred her senses as much as he stirred her curiosity.

His task finished, he looked up at her, squinting against the glaring sun. "You didn't answer my question."

"What?" She'd been so absorbed in watching him, so completely mesmerized, that she had lost the thread of their conversation.

"What were you doing last night?"

He walked around the front of the horse, and then he was standing on her right. Without warning, his hand closed around her slender ankle.

She jerked away from the contact, adjusting her skirt when her motion caused it to ride up above her boot. He smiled up at her crookedly; her face grew hot as her heart began to pound hard inside her chest. She held her leg out of his way, trying not to think about how close he was to her or how his touch made her melt inside.

"If you wanted to get yourself killed, there are easier ways," he said.

"You went through my things. You know how little money I have. I needed more."

"So you could run away?"

"So I could survive, Mr. Montalvo. I learned a long time ago that people aren't always around when you need them, and if you can't take care of yourself, no one else will."

Rafe gazed up into her eyes for a moment before saying rather sadly, "How'd you get to be so old so fast?"

Tears rose in her throat; she wasn't quite sure why. For someone who never cried, she'd been close to tears more in the past few days than she had been throughout the rest of her life.

"My father used to say I was born old." She swallowed with an effort, forcing the tears down.

"Couldn't you have thought of a safer way to earn money?"

She laughed without humor. "Got any suggestions? The only things I can do are play poker and sew, and I hate sewing more than I hate gambling."

He walked around to the front of the horse, grasped the bridle, and started leading the animal forward.

She gasped. "What are you doing?"

"I'm going to lead him around in a circle and let you get used to moving. Put your weight in the stirrups and hold on to the pommel if you need to. As long as you stick with me, you don't have to worry about money. I have enough for both of us."

The tears in her throat were replaced by bile as she thought of how he earned that money, how he'd bought her a horse. She closed her eyes but the memory still came: Rafe Montalvo reaching into his shirt pocket, withdrawing a WANTED poster, holding it up to the dead man's face to see if the picture matched, arguing with the sheriff over paying for the dead man's burial.

"I'll pay you back every cent you spend on me," she told him. "I don't want anything to do with your blood money."

"Well," he said, without turning around, "that blood money's going to get you where you're going."

Silence stretched between them as he led the horse in a circle. She accustomed herself to the unusual feel of the saddle. There was something rather exciting about putting her legs around a living, breathing beast. She'd never put her legs around anything in her life before. It didn't seem quite decent.

She sat atop an animal that was capable of carrying her at speeds she could only imagine, an animal whose strength and stamina she could not fathom, an animal that could easily injure or even kill her should it decide to do so, but that had been gentled through centuries of breeding and training to the point that it would allow itself to be used for her purposes. It was thrilling and frightening at the same time.

She studied the back of the man who walked in front of her. He knew the secret of this animal. He knew many secrets, some of which she had no desire to plumb. He knew the secret of killing and then going on living as if it had never happened.

The scars that encircled his wrists intrigued her. She glanced at her own wrists. Although the rope had been gone when she'd awakened in the empty room this morning, the discoloration of her skin served as a reminder of her own humiliating experience.

Could a rope have caused the scars she had seen around Rafe Montalvo's wrists?

She didn't believe that the marks on her arms would scar, so if a rope had caused Rafe's scars, it must have been tied much tighter than the one that had bound her to the bed last night.

Or maybe it had been in place longer. She wondered if length of time had anything to do with the production of scars. Or maybe they had been made by iron manacles. Had he been in prison?

She wasn't sure she wanted to know any more about Rafe Montalvo than she knew right now. It seemed every time she peeled back a layer around him, she discovered something dark and vile. All she wanted was safe conduct to Eagle Pass. No matter what else she knew about him, she was beginning to believe he would not harm her.

"How many WANTED posters do you carry around with you?" she asked.

He didn't look at her or change his pace. "I've lost count."

They reached the point where they'd started. Rafe moved to the left side of the horse, reached up without a word, and placed his hands on her waist. She had no choice but to grab onto his shoulders as he pulled her down from the saddle and stood her on her feet before him.

He didn't release her as she'd expected. Instead, he stood with his hands nearly spanning her waist, his face close above hers. She glanced away when she could bear the intensity of those pale eyes no longer.

"You knew that man last night," she murmured softly. Her voice sounded strange in her own ears.

Rafe gazed at her in silence for a long moment. She couldn't look at him. The heat of his gaze on her was enough to cause her to squirm in his grip. His nearness violated her composure and stripped away her defenses. She wished fervently that he would back away or release her so she could put some distance between them.

"I had a poster on him," he said.

Closing her eyes tightly, she tried to resist the magnetism that sizzled between them, wondering if he could feel it too. "You . . . you said you'd met him in the desert. What happened? How did you know him?"

He dropped his hands away and she released a ragged breath, regaining her composure with an effort. Turning to the horse, he dropped the reins over the animal's head. "Let it—"

"Let it be?"

"I knew him, all right? I had tracked him before, when I was in the army."

Her heart lurched. This was more than he had revealed about himself since they'd met, and she had a feeling he hadn't meant to reveal even that. "You were in the army?"

"Let it—damn, I said I was in the army. He rode with a band of .. They used to raid along the Texas border when I was stationed at Fort Bliss."

"Why were you still tracking him?"

"*He* was tracking *us,* Annie. Don't you see? Do you think you and I are the only people who know about the gold?"

"I didn't know—"

"There's a lot you don't know."

"But if you weren't tracking him, why did you still have the WANTED poster? Why—"

She hardly saw him move before his arms closed around her. He pulled her against his hard chest almost angrily, knocking the breath from her for a moment. He held her tightly with one arm, lifted her chin with his other hand, and forced her to look into the silver depths of his eyes. And then his lips moved against hers, at first gently, then more demandingly.

Moaning against his mouth, she placed a hand on his chest and felt the erratic beating of his heart. Her mind told her to fight the strange languor that crept up her legs to possess her. Instead, she clung to him, parting her lips instinctively, feeling his tongue dart into her mouth. She tried to pull away from the intimate, shocking contact, but he held her tighter.

His hands slid down her back to her buttocks. With a gasp of shock, she tried to twist away as they clasped her flesh, pressing her against him. The hardness she felt through both sets of clothing stunned her.

She began to struggle in earnest. His breathing had quickened, his fervor growing until he was handling her roughly, all traces of gentleness gone. His fierceness terrified her because she was utterly helpless against his strength and because she almost wanted . . . wanted it to go on and on. She was on fire, as if all her life's blood had rushed to the surface of her skin. Her legs trembled so that she had to lean against him to keep from falling, even as she struggled to be free.

His mouth finally released hers, but he still held her in his arms. His eyes bored into hers, his face only inches above her.

"Why do you ask so damn many questions?" he asked breathlessly.

"Please let me go," she murmured, her gaze fixed on his mouth.

She could hear his shallow, rapid breathing, feel it in the rise and fall of his chest against hers. She tried with all her might to keep her own body from picking up the rhythm. Her heart fluttered uncontrollably as a war raged within her, a war of sense against sensation.

Relief washed over her as he dropped his arms and took a step back, but it was tempered with a strange regret. At least now she could think clearly. Silence stretched between them, an unbearable silence that she felt obliged to break.

"I . . . thank you for helping me last night," she murmured.

"I did what I had to do."

"You . . . you saved my life again."

"He probably wouldn't have killed you. He'd have convinced you to tell him where the gold was, but he probably wouldn't have killed you."

"I wouldn't have told him," she said in a voice that quivered slightly.

"Yes, you would have."

The implication that hung between them sent an army of gooseflesh marching over her arms and down her spine. "No, I—"

"Damn you, Annie, damn you."

She tried to pull free, but he refused to release her. Panic rose raw and bitter in her throat. "Please let me go."

She twisted away, and he let her go. She stood staring into the depths of his eyes for an endless moment. *Why haven't you forced me to tell you what you want to know?* she wanted to ask. *How long will you wait?*

Swallowing her fear, she backed away from him, then fled up the stairs as if the devil himself were behind her. Perhaps he was.

11

"Oh, God, the blood!" *he cried. His eyes blurred so he could hardly see to sight down the rifle. His hands trembled violently, but he managed to hold the rifle steady long enough to do what he had to do. The eyes: he would never forget those eyes, anguished, pleading. . . . He squeezed the trigger; a shot exploded, echoing through the empty desert. . . .*

"Mr. Montalvo, wake up!"

The voice barely penetrated his consciousness. Someone was shaking him. He opened his eyes with a start to see a face hovering close above his. She gasped and jerked away as he sat up, shaking his head to clear the fog.

"Are . . . are you all right?" She stood several feet from him, clasping her hands to her breast as if terrified.

He realized who she was—Annie—and he remembered where he was. They were still in Texas, not in the Chihuahuan desert. He'd been dreaming again.

"Damn!" He ran a hand through his hair, and a ragged sob escaped his throat before he managed in part to regain his composure.

"You cried out," Anne told him weakly. "A nightmare."

Her face reflected her fear. He closed his eyes, struggling for control as the tremors and nausea crept over him. There was no room in his mind right now for Annie or anything else but his own agony. The world seemed to be collapsing around him.

He didn't see her move, but he flinched away violently as a tentative hand touched his shoulder. "Don't!" He didn't want comfort, not from her, not from anyone. He didn't deserve it, and it would do no good anyway. Nothing would ease his pain but El Alacrán's blood, and he would not allow Annie to be sucked into his private hell.

He didn't want to look at her, didn't want to see the fear and confusion in her eyes. It would turn to loathing if she knew the truth.

"What can I do?"

"Leave me alone." He stood shakily, his body swaying as he stepped into his pants.

"But—"

"Go back to bed," he managed to grind out, opening the door and closing it behind him.

Anne couldn't move, could hardly breathe, even after she heard the outer door close and knew that Rafe had gone outside.

Oh God, the blood! His words ran down her spine like a cold hand. Never had she heard such raw anguish in a voice. She managed to move back to the bed and sit on the edge, hugging her arms around her body in an effort to stop the trembling that had seized her.

She remembered his face, a mask of pain in the light of her candle. She hadn't known whether to turn away and leave him with his nightmare or reach out to him. She'd decided on the latter, and she had watched in astonishment as he withdrew inside himself.

Even now, she longed to touch him, to comfort him. More than anything, she wanted to follow him into the night. Yet at the same time she was afraid, both of the stark nakedness of his scream and of the way he had said those words, as if they had been torn from his very soul.

Her heart ached when she thought of him out there somewhere, suffering with the demons that woke him in the dead of night.

The immense barrenness of the terrain stretched as far as the eye could see. Anne felt overwhelmed, as if she could be swallowed up by the vast sea of nothingness, never to be found again. How had she ever believed she could traverse this wilderness alone?

The desert spread out in every direction like a great brown blanket. Small, scruffy trees, which Rafe identified as mesquite, and towering saguaro cacti were the tallest structures on the horizon, though some of the wicked-looking brush grew taller than the horses.

The only animals they had encountered since they'd left Castroville that morning were rattlesnakes and large, ugly lizards. Certainly no other human beings had passed this way in a very long time—or maybe ever, Anne thought, with a mixture of fear and awe.

There was no trail she could discern. Yet Rafe seemed to know instinctively which way to go in this unchanging, monotonous landscape. They would be harder to track if they went through the desert, he'd said, should anyone wish to do so, and the route they were taking would get them to the Nueces River at least half a day earlier.

"Every moment counts," he had told her. She didn't doubt it.

The sun glared down on them like an angry god; the air dried her skin and caused her already chapped lips to hurt and dry out again. At least her new hat shielded her face from further burning.

A relentless thirst began to build inside her, growing more intense with every mile they traveled. Her teeth felt gritty, her tongue so thick and dry she could hardly swallow. She had to have water.

Rafe rode a few feet ahead of her, his back straight and implacable. She knew he was avoiding her, avoiding questions about what had happened last night. He'd been inching ahead all morning, ever since he'd refused her request to stop and rest. She spurred her horse forward until she was riding alongside him. Whether he liked it or not, she was still there, and he couldn't ignore her.

He glanced over at her, his expression stern and unreadable, then turned back to the terrain ahead.

"Please, I need a drink. Can't we stop—"

"No. I told you, we'll stop at noon and not before."

She stared at him, trying to formulate a rebuttal. He had no reason to be so angry with her and no right to push her so hard. Every part of her ached. Her thighs felt as if they had been rubbed raw. Her back hurt so much she could hardly stay in the saddle. But he didn't care.

Rafe nudged his horse into a faster walk, and Anne pulled back on the reins, allowing him to move ahead once again. She stared daggers into his back as she followed.

Damn him! Who did he think he was? He'd pushed all morning, knowing she was unaccustomed to riding at all, let alone for such long periods of time without a rest.

There was plenty of water in her canteen, but he wouldn't let her drink. He kept saying, Wait a little longer, a little longer. Well, she was tired of waiting. Did he want her to dehydrate again? Was that it? Would he leave her behind this time if she did?

Damn him!

The reasonable side of her knew it was irrational to blame him for her discomfort, but it was much easier and much more enjoyable than blaming herself.

He grew smaller as he rode ahead into the monotonous desert. When he was far enough away that she felt safe, she pulled her horse to a halt and grabbed hold of the canteen that hung from a leather strap tied around the saddle pommel.

The water was warm, but she couldn't get enough of it. Her body seemed to soak it up like a sponge. It was almost as if she could feel the liquid spread throughout every parched inch of her body. Never had anything tasted so wonderful.

A cry of alarm escaped her lips in the next instant as a hand jerked the canteen out of her grip. She looked up and gazed into the angry eyes of Rafe Montalvo.

Furiously he screwed the cap back on the canteen.

"What are you doing?" she asked as he lifted the canteen's leather strap from the horn of her saddle and tied it around his own.

He said nothing, just stared at her in unbreachable silence.

"But what if we get separated?" she asked.

He was taking her water supply, her independence. Now she truly needed him for everything. Her dark eyes asked for mercy, but not a flicker of emotion glimmered in his gray ones.

"You'd better hope we don't," he said, his voice soft.

Without another word, he wheeled his horse around and started off at a sedate trot.

She took a firm grip on the reins and the saddle horn and gently kicked her mount into a trot also. Fear still pricked the edges of her mind, but since they'd left town, she'd grown increasingly more bold in the saddle. She'd fallen enough times during three days of lessons back in Castroville to know she could be unseated without serious injury.

The longer she rode, the more her confidence grew. He couldn't just ride off and leave her as readily now as he had been able to do earlier that morning. And if he thought he was going to escape her that easily, he was badly mistaken.

"Do you always have to have your own way?" she asked as she drew up alongside him.

"Yes." He continued looking at the road ahead, all but ignoring her.

"I have something at stake here too, you know."

He seemed to relax in his saddle, but he still didn't look at her. "The only thing you have at stake right now is your life. All I'm trying to do is—"

"You're trying to punish me for playing cards in Castroville, aren't you?" She hadn't thought of it before, but maybe that was it. Maybe he was still angry over her attempt to escape. Even though she'd assured him more than once that she hadn't planned to run away, she knew he remained unconvinced.

He turned to face her for the first time, his gaze sweeping over her body in a way that sent a tremor racing through her.

"Miss Cameron, I don't think you understand the situation. As I've tried to explain before, there's a two-year drought in this part of Texas. We'd have been all right if that extra water bag hadn't sprung a leak. We may or may not find water in the next couple of days. If you drink all your water today, you could die tomorrow. I am trying to keep you alive. One mistake, and you'll end up feeding the buzzards."

Everything he said made sense. He sounded completely reasonable. But Anne was not in the mood for sense and reason. She was hot and thirsty and saddlesore, and spoiling for a fight.

"You have a lot in common with buzzards, don't you, Mr. Montalvo?" Her voice shook from the jarring motion of the horse beneath her. "Isn't that what you do? Wait for someone to make a mistake and then move in for the kill?"

Rafe slowed his horse to a more sedate walk, and Anne's mount followed suit.

"Buzzards don't kill," he said, smiling without humor. "They live off what other animals kill and leave behind."

"Precious little difference. You both live off the dead. Why do you do it?"

"Save your strength," he said quietly. "You'll need it out here."

She released a deep sigh of exasperation. He was right, of course; it was too hot to fight.

"It's so hot," she said, giving voice to her thoughts. "It's just as hot in New Orleans, but at least on the river there's water and shade. There's nothing out here but mile after mile of brush and cactus. At least at home when it's hot you sweat, and there's almost always a breeze off the river. Out here it's like putting your face near a glowing stove."

"It's not too late to turn back."

She glared at his stony profile. "I'm not turning back. I'm going to see this thing through if it's the last thing I do."

"It may well be." he said with a malevolent smile that sent a shiver up her spine.

"Stop trying to frighten me. It won't work."

But it was working. Nothing in this brown and green world held the smallest bit of familiarity for her. There was nothing she could cling to, no touchstone. She was completely adrift, depending on a bounty hunter for her very life.

"I guess that shows how ignorant you are."

"Ignorant! Why you—"

"I told you to save your strength, Annie. That's how you got in trouble the first time."

"What first time? What do you mean?"

"When the wagon turned over. You went running around in the hot sun instead of conserving your energy."

"How could you possibly know that?" Had he been hiding somewhere, watching her?

"I could tell by your footprints."

She gazed at him suspiciously. She'd read in dime novels about men who could track like that. Surely those stories were greatly exaggerated. But what other explanation was there? How else could he have known that she'd been running? Unless he'd gotten there first. Had he somehow gotten in front of her and waited? Had he intentionally frightened the horses?

"You must be very good at tracking," she said, try-ing to still the irrational doubts roiling inside her. "Did you learn that in the army?"

"Partly. Anything I didn't learn in the army, I learned in the desert."

She watched his face for any hint of untruth, but if he was lying he was a master at it.

The desert. Everything seemed to go back to the desert. What mysteries lay hidden in the barren expanse that spread around them on all sides? What had happened when Rafe and her attacker in Castroville had met the first time? She wondered about the woman Rafe had mentioned in the saloon, and her mind made a connection.

"Tell me about Christina. Is she the one you rescued in the desert from that man in Castroville?"

A taut silence stretched between them. She studied his profile, wishing she could read his mind. What went on in the mind of a killer? What was he remembering? The muscle in his jaw flexed, and she sensed a war inside him, a war for control of his mind and emotions.

"What makes you think I rescued anybody?" he asked quietly.

The venom in his voice turned Anne's blood cold. Was she on the verge of uncovering something really dreadful?

"Well, I just assumed . . . I mean, I thought you had."

Rafe pulled his horse to a stop and Anne did likewise. He turned in the saddle to look at her with an expression of utter impatience.

"It was a long time ago. It doesn't matter. Nothing matters right now but getting to the Nueces. If we don't make it in two days, we'll run out of water, and without fresh water . . . "

He let his words trail off, but his meaning was unmistakable. Without fresh water, they would die. Anne held her horse back as Rafe spurred his into a trot. She gazed skyward and prayed they would reach the river in time.

* * *

Rafe glanced over at Annie, barely able to make out her silhouette in the growing darkness. He didn't have to see her; he had committed her every feature to memory. Her dark eyes would be closed, her soft pink mouth slack. She must be exhausted, but she hadn't complained once since he'd taken her canteen from her.

They'd been riding hard all day. He'd pushed her beyond endurance, and she'd risen to the challenge. She'd lasted far longer than he would have thought she could, and her courage and determination tugged at his heart. She had no way of knowing what she was getting into.

She had no business out here; he knew it, and if she didn't know it yet, she soon would. Even though she'd kept up pretty well today, she'd be even more tired tomorrow. The water they had in their canteens would last another day, but that was all. He couldn't bear to think about what would happen then.

"Miss Cameron," he said, more harshly than he'd intended. He needed some diversion to push his memories back into the dark where they belonged.

She nearly jumped, and he realized she'd fallen asleep in the saddle.

"We'll be stopping soon," he told her. "Can you hold on for a few more minutes?"

"I'm fine," she mumbled.

"Good. We'll be coming up on a stream soon. We'll make camp there."

She nodded silently.

He had to admire her tenacity. She'd had a rough week, beginning with the wagon accident and ending today with hours of hard riding.

Christina couldn't have ridden so hard for ten minutes. But Christina would never have done anything as dangerous and reckless as starting out on a journey through nearly a hundred and fifty miles of desert with a man like him.

And Christina never would have gone to a saloon and charmed her way into a poker game.

He shuddered with fear and fury at the memory of that night. He hadn't lied when he'd told Annie he would have killed Sam Rollins even if there hadn't been a bounty on his head, even if he hadn't been one of El Alacrán's men. The knife pressed against Annie's throat had sealed the outlaw's fate.

How could he protect her if she insisted on getting herself into situations like that? Even now he was afraid to let her out of his sight for fear her own recklessness would lead her into more danger.

Stubborn woman. If only she'd listen to him.

He had felt a stab of guilt and regret the morning after the incident in the saloon, when he'd seen the marks left on her wrists by the rope. But dammit, he'd tied her to the bed as much for her own protection as for his peace of mind. There was an irrational rage that took control of him from time to time; he had actually been afraid that he'd turn it on her if she had tried another trick like that one.

Rafe wondered what Christina would think of him now. The man she had married was long dead, dead and buried with her in the Mexican desert. She wouldn't even recognize him today, and she certainly wouldn't like what he'd become.

He couldn't help comparing them, Annie and Christina. Annie would have completely overshadowed Christina's quiet gentility. Annie walked fast and made her own decisions, whereas Christina had deferred to him in all things. Annie spoke her mind and plunged into situations without considering the consequences. Christina had usually adopted his opinions, and she had possessed the temperament of a diplomat: slow to act, willing to go to any lengths to keep the peace.

His gaze traveled from Annie's shadowed face and squared shoulders down her body. The two women were about the same size. Perhaps Christina had been a trifle more delicate of bone, but he'd been able to buy clothes for Annie that fit because he remembered Christina's size. The shirtwaist Anne wore now, one that he had purchased, gaped open slightly across her breasts. Christina's breasts had been small and pert with dark brown nipples and—

Goddammit!

He closed his eyes tightly, glad for the darkness that concealed the emotion that must be etched clearly on his face. Why now? He'd managed all these years to keep the memories at bay, to forget everything that brought pain like a knife twisting in his heart. It was so much easier that way—easier to live with the loss and the crushing guilt.

The sky was darkening slowly, but he could still make out the shadows and contours of Annie's face. She gazed at him with those dark, mysterious eyes that had begun to haunt his sleep as regularly as the other eyes, the eyes full of pain and suffering. Would Annie's eyes ever look at him with that kind of anguish? The thought made him sick to his stomach. They would certainly look at him with disgust and loathing one day, and that was hard enough to accept.

"You said we'd be coming to a stream bed soon," she murmured.

"I know what I said," he retorted, unable to understand the cause of his rage.

A shaft of moonlight fell across Annie's face, and he was able to see the weariness etched on her face. Her head lolled from side to side as she struggled to stay awake a little longer. She ran her tongue along her lower lip in an almost childlike gesture. She was so fragile, yet so brave.

Damn her. She had a way of making him feel guilty and sorry and a lot of other things he didn't want to feel. All he wanted was to cut out El Alacrán's heart. He didn't care what happened after that, whether he lived or died. Annie could take all the gold and buy whatever she was so anxious to have, if she lived through the hazards that awaited them.

He'd carried the image of the dream with him throughout the day. They were getting closer to Mexico with every step. Mexico had been drawing him back ever since he'd left it behind less than a year ago.

He'd traveled this route so many times he could almost do it in his sleep. He knew what lay ahead: the Nueces River, a wide stretch of parched land leading to the Rio Grande, and, beyond that, El Alacrán.

What was he going to do about Annie? She was already beginning to toughen a little. A good thing. She'd need every ounce of strength and courage she possessed before this journey was over. He hoped it would be enough.

12

Anne didn't remember much about last night, but she did have a vague recollection of slipping from the saddle into Rafe's strong arms. She couldn't remember ever being more exhausted.

Rafe had taken care of her—again. She seemed to remember eating something, which he had undoubtedly provided. And this morning, when she'd awakened, she'd been wrapped in her bedroll.

As the miles slipped by, she found herself becoming more and more dependent on Rafe Montalvo, and she wasn't at all sure she liked it. She'd learned a long time ago never to depend on anyone but herself. Now it seemed she didn't have a choice. It was that or perish.

Her legs were stiff and sore this morning. The pain in her inner thighs made her wonder how she could ever ride when just walking caused such agony. Every muscle in her body seemed to ache and cramp as she made her way to Rafe, who was leaning against a scruffy-looking cottonwood tree.

A dry streambed wound its way through the desolate landscape, barely noticeable, except for the fact that it lay a little lower than the rest of the land. Brush and prickly pears dotted the streambed just as they did the rest of the terrain. She couldn't help wondering how long it had been since this stream had contained any water.

"We may not see water until we get to the Nueces," he said, without looking up, as if he'd sensed her presence.

"How far is that?" Fear tugged at her heart. If they ran out of water, they'd die; he'd said so himself.

"We ought to be there before nightfall, if we don't run into any trouble."

"Do you expect trouble?" She searched his eyes. He might not tell her the truth, but maybe she could read it in his expression.

"No, but you never know out here."

"How do you know the Nueces won't be dry too?"

He smiled, and she felt a bit foolish, as if she'd asked the question about the Mississippi. "Well, there's no way to be sure, but I've never known the Nueces to dry up. It's a big river, by desert standards anyway, so it would take one hell of a drought."

She swallowed hard. They would make it. They had to. Rafe knew this country as well as anyone else; he must know what he was talking about. "Do we have enough water?"

"Yes, if we watch it." He pushed away from the tree and made his way back toward camp. "We'd better get started. It'll be getting hotter as the sun gets higher. We don't want to be caught out in the middle of the open desert at the hottest part of the day."

He walked toward the horses, and Anne followed. She moved slowly, each step an exercise in agony that sent flashes of pain burning through her legs.

Reaching the horses, Rafe lifted her canteen from around his saddle horn and turned to give it to her, only to find that she hadn't yet reached him.

Her slow, awkward progress ignited a spark of both anger and admiration within him. He knew she'd sooner die than admit she was in pain and risk another lecture on her unfitness for the desert. Her eyes met his, and her nose lifted slightly at the expression on his face.

"You all right this morning, Miss Cameron?" he asked.

She glared at him. "I'll be fine."

He handed her the canteen, and she took it with a look of surprise.

"We might get separated."

"What if we do?"

The fear in her voice twisted his heart. "Don't worry. But you should have your own water supply, just in case. If we do get separated, just stop wherever you are and stay put. I'll find you."

Her expression doubtful, Annie gazed at him for a moment. She still didn't trust him, and he couldn't blame her. It showed intelligence on her part.

She took the canteen and walked around to her horse, winding the leather strap around the saddle horn. Reaching up to mount, she groaned and a grimace of pain wrinkled her forehead.

"You sure you're all right?"

She refused to look at him as she murmured, "Will you help me?"

"What? Annie Cameron admitting she needs help?"

"If you're going to make fun of me . . . "

Rafe had come to stand behind her. A tremor rippled through her body, and he wondered at its cause. Fear or desire or both? He couldn't forget the day he'd kissed her. She had responded to him in a way that had nearly driven him beyond reason. He had lost control for a moment and frightened her.

Did she remember the pleasure or the fear? He could hear the shallowness of her breathing. What would she do if he pressed his lips against the throbbing pulse behind her ear? He'd seen her watching him when she thought he wouldn't notice. He knew she desired him, even though she was a little afraid of him, and he also knew she was innocent. Was he enough of an animal to take advantage of her vulnerability?

At that instant, she twisted around to face him and jerked away as her body brushed his. The contact flashed through him like a bolt of summer lightning.

"Don't we need to get started?" she asked, her voice thin and unsteady.

He wasn't listening. His gaze traveled down from her eyes to her lips. The bottom one quivered slightly; he longed to touch it with his own lips, to feel that shiver spread over her body. He looked down to her throat and the white shirtwaist and the way her breasts rose and fell gently with her breath.

With every part of his being, he wanted her. The hard shell that had protected him from feeling for so long was beginning to crack; he was losing control. He didn't want to feel, didn't want to want. He tried to remind himself of his goal, of his reason for being here, but El Alacrán seemed very far away at this moment, and Annie Cameron was very near, too near.

The only reason she allowed him even as close as he was now was because she had no choice. If not for their common purpose—to find the stolen gold—she wouldn't come within ten feet of him.

He moved closer to the horse and she took a step back. "You don't have to jump every time I make a move, Miss Cameron. If I meant to harm you, I'd have done it by now."

He bent over, cupping his hands and holding them out to her. When she didn't react, he glanced up to see her studying him in wide-eyed astonishment. He straightened, pushing his hat back from his forehead.

"Don't you think I know what you think of me?" he asked impatiently.

"How could you?" Her voice trembled slightly. "I don't even know—"

"I am a bounty hunter," he said, angered by the light that flickered in her dark eyes, a light that seemed to offer redemption. Did she think she could save him from himself? "I kill for money. I live from day to day, never knowing when I'm going to meet a faster gun and end up dead. I have no principles. In any other circumstance, you'd put as much distance between us as you could, and you'd be smart to do it."

"Well, if all that's true, why should I trust you?"

"Because I don't have any reason to want to harm you."

"And you have a reason to harm the men you kill for the bounty on their heads?"

"To my way of thinking I do." He wished she'd stop looking at him as if he was some lost soul and she was a missionary sent to save him. His next words were calculated to put an end to any girlish fantasies she might have about softening his black heart. "Man's got to make a living. It's what I'm good at."

"Killing?" She stiffened, disgust apparent in her eyes. He knew a moment of regret, even though he had managed to elicit exactly the reaction he'd wanted—or thought he wanted.

"That's right," he said. What difference did it make? He and Annie Cameron might as well be a world apart. It was just a cruel joke of fate that they had met at all. He bent over beside the horse again. "Now, please, Annie, put your foot in my hands."

"Why?" The eyes that studied him reflected doubt and suspicion.

"Just do as I say. I'm going to give you a leg up so we can get going."

She stepped toward him, placing her left hand on his shoulders for balance as she lifted her booted foot. He dropped his hands and stood up with a sigh before she could plant her foot.

"Hold on to the saddle like I taught you. I'm trying to put you on the damned horse, remember?"

"Well, you don't have to curse at me! I've never done this before."

Her voice vibrated with pain and anger. He could almost hear the tears she fought to quell and damned himself for hurting her.

He said nothing, just leaned over to assist her. She grabbed the saddle by the back lip and the pommel but found she couldn't lift her foot high enough to place it in his hands without experiencing excruciating pain throughout her hips and buttocks. How was she ever going to ride all day?

His hand closed around her foot, and she began hopping on her other one, trying with all her might to steady herself, to pull herself up. But she lost her balance.

Before she hit the ground, he grabbed her, swinging her up into his arms as he had that night in San Antonio.

She struggled in his embrace, but in her efforts to

put some distance between them she only succeeded in increasing the contact, sending tremors of excitement through his body.

"Put me down!" she demanded breathlessly.

"Just wait. . . . "

"Put me down. Please!"

Rafe ignored her panic, her maddening nearness, as best he could. He carried her back to the horse and turned her, shifting her in his arms so he could lift her high enough to put her in the saddle.

She seemed confused to have both her legs dangling on the same side of the horse.

"Throw your right leg over his neck," he instructed, more gruffly than he had intended.

She did as he said, wincing in pain as she settled into the saddle. He stood close by, and she used him to lean on while she found her stirrups. When it was done and she was securely seated, he turned away and walked toward his own horse.

He too was in for a thoroughly uncomfortable ride this morning, but for a totally different reason.

They were later leaving camp than Rafe had wanted. The sun was high overhead by the time they crossed the dry creek bed to the other side. Neither of them spoke all morning as they traveled across terrain that was becoming more hostile with every yard they put behind them.

Even the most tenacious brush that could survive in these desolate conditions had been burned out by the horrendous sun and lack of moisture. Only the towering hundred-year-old saguaros dotted the parched landscape with any regularity.

At noon, they stopped at a place where two saguaros

stood close enough together so that Rafe could string a blanket between them for shade. He spread another on the ground to sit on.

Lunch was dried beef. It was barely palatable, but Anne managed to eat a small amount, knowing it was the last scrap of food she would get until they stopped for the night, and who knew when that would be?

She glanced over at Rafe where he lay on his side, his torso propped up on an elbow, to find him studying her intently. An instant, uncontrollable tremor rippled through her. It was maddening the way he could set her pulse racing with nothing more than a glance, while he seemed to remain completely unaffected.

"So," he said in a slow, lazy tone, "why is this gold so important to you?"

"Why do you want to know?" she asked suspiciously.

"Just trying to make conversation," he replied, as he rolled onto his back.

She decided it could do no harm to tell him. "There's a house in Ubiquitous. It belonged to my aunt. I want to buy it."

He laughed. "That's it? With a million dollars, you could buy the whole town. You could do whatever you want to do, go wherever you want to go."

"What I want is a home of my own and a simple life," she replied, trying not to be hurt by his attitude toward her dream.

"What about your family?"

"I don't have any family."

"Where are you from?"

"I was born in St. Louis. I've lived in Natchez, New Orleans, Vicksburg, Baton Rouge—"

"You mean your daddy didn't keep you locked away on the plantation?"

"My daddy was a riverboat gambler. I've never even seen a plantation except from the river."

Why was she telling Rafe Montalvo her life story? She hadn't intended to, but once she'd started she couldn't seem to stop.

"My mother came from that kind of world. She was a New Orleans Creole. Her family owns one of the biggest sugar plantations in Louisiana, or they did before the war."

"Well, you should have gone and stayed with them instead of coming here after your father died. It would have been safer."

She laughed mirthlessly. "They wouldn't have anything to do with me *or* my father. My father wasn't one of them. He was a Yankee from Pennsylvania. He came down to New Orleans on a riverboat and sneaked into a Mardi Gras ball, and that's where he met and fell in love with my mother. Her family disowned her when she married him. My father didn't die in the war. He was gunned down on the street in Natchez for cheating at cards."

"Like father, like daughter."

Her body vibrated with anger. "I don't cheat, Mr. Montalvo. I don't have to cheat. And if I did, no one would be able to tell." He'd goaded her into revealing too much about herself, when she knew nearly nothing about him. "What about you?" she challenged. "Do you have family?"

"I have a brother."

"In New Mexico? Do you ever go back there?"

He hesitated for a moment before replying. "We don't get along."

"But he's your brother. Surely—"

"He hates me, Miss Cameron," he said sharply. "And I can't say I blame him."

"You drive people away."

He quirked an eyebrow at her, then gave a frown of annoyance.

She was immediately sorry she had been so blunt. "I'm sorry. I shouldn't have said that."

"Go on. You seem to know so much."

Unwilling to be intimidated by his sarcasm, she straightened her spine and met the challenge in his words. "You wear this mask of violence. You purposely intimidate people because you don't want anyone to get too close and see what's behind the mask."

"I am what you see before you, Miss Cameron, nothing more, nothing less." He rolled over onto his back, spreading his long, lean body across the blanket, pulling his hat down over his face with a shrug. "While you're working things out, I'm going to take a nap."

She watched as he settled, unable to keep from asking quietly, "What do *you* want the gold for, Mr. Montalvo?"

"I'll think of something," he said, without looking at her. "Get some rest. We'll be starting again in an hour."

Rafe sat in the shade of a cottonwood tree, his legs folded Indian style. He used his sharp bowie knife to skin a jackrabbit he'd shot earlier. But his attention drifted between his task and the woman who stood beside the river a few yards away.

They'd reached the narrow Nueces just before dusk and made camp under the trees that lined the bank. They'd filled their canteens with water, and now the horses drank peacefully from the river.

Annie bent over, dipping a piece of material she'd torn from her petticoat into the water. She straightened with an effort, walked toward a stand of trees, and unfastened the top few buttons of her shirtwaist, settling on the ground beneath a tree with a sigh.

His mouth suddenly went dry as she plunged the wet cloth inside her blouse, then ran it along her shoulder.

Desire pounded through his body. He closed his eyes in an effort to regain control, but to no avail. The sweetness of her flesh haunted him. How he ached to feel its texture beneath his hand again, yearned to trace the graceful arch of her throat with his lips.

A bead of sweat dripped from his brow. He caught it with his sleeve and tried to focus on the task at hand.

Along with other things, José had taught him to skin an animal. Rafe had done it dozens of times, but it never failed to nauseate him somewhat. This time, despite the distraction of the woman bathing just a few feet away, he managed to skin the jackrabbit without incident. He finished preparing it for the spit and carried it over to the center of the camp.

The fire was already burning and he'd rigged a spit. He took the cross pole, a slender cottonwood branch, skewered the rabbit, and placed the pole back onto its stand.

That accomplished, he glanced around at Annie to find that she had been studying him. But when he caught her eye, she looked away quickly.

"Annie, would you watch this rabbit for a minute? I've got to clean up a little."

She gazed at him dubiously. "Me? I don't know anything about cooking, especially out of doors."

"Just watch it and yell if it catches fire. I'll be right back."

She moved closer to the fire, while Rafe went back to where he'd been cleaning the rabbit. She could still see the legs and the neck of the animal as it cooked. She didn't know if she would be able to eat it once it was done, in spite of the way her stomach rumbled at its delicious smell.

She glanced across the barren landscape. Silence settled over the desert, penetrating her soul, the faint crackle of the fire the only sound that reached her ears. In that moment, she felt terribly alone and more than a little afraid. She clasped her arms over her chest, looking around for Rafe. How could he have disappeared in this flat country? Where could he have gone?

Her heart began to thud loudly in her chest as a nameless fear clutched her throat. Unreasoning panic pressed her on all sides. What if something had happened to him? What was taking him so long? Where could he be?

Then, just when she was about to give in to her fears, she saw him, walking toward her slowly, and breathed a long deep sigh of relief.

"Where did you go?" she asked when he reached the camp.

"I had to bury the part of the rabbit I didn't use to keep it from attracting wild animals—and other things."

Her stomach lurched at the image those words evoked. "But I thought . . . "

"What?"

"In San Antonio you told the undertaker that—well, that he should dump the outlaw's body at the end of town to feed the buzzards."

He laughed. "You were eavesdropping."

Annie frowned. "I'd lost something and gone back to look for it. I didn't mean to overhear."

Guilt stabbed him because he knew she was talking about the locket he'd found and still had in his saddlebag. He should have given it back to her, but somehow he couldn't part with it. He'd begun to think of it as his good-luck charm.

"Well," he said, "I'd just as soon not attract buzzards to a place where I'm sleeping. They don't kill their food, but sometimes they can get confused and think something's dead before it is."

She turned white, and Rafe regretted his frank words. Sometimes he felt a sadistic need to shock her, to prove to her how foolish she'd been to think she could have survived out here alone for more than a few hours.

Even now, a cold sickness gripped him whenever he thought of what could have happened had he not found out where she'd gone and followed her. She'd be dead by now, that much was almost certain. And if someone else had found her, she might be wishing she had not survived.

"Oh, look," she murmured in a voice full of awe.

Rafe turned to see her gazing at the horizon. The sun was beginning to set in an orange and gold splendor that could only be witnessed in the desert.

A flush crept over the heavens, sending crimson streamers in all directions, as if a huge pot of red ink had overturned on a blue and gray blotter. An army of saguaros marched across the desert, their long arms lifted toward the sky, their bodies silhouetted against a fiery background.

Mesmerized, she walked to the edge of the river to get a better view. "I've never seen anything like that before."

He moved close beside her. "It's one of the few things of beauty in this place."

"Do you really hate it so much? You've spent most of your life here."

"There are too many bad memories here for me."

"Your dream," she murmured.

"What do you mean?"

"Well," she said, shifting uneasily under his unrelenting stare, "it obviously upset you."

"I'll tell you something. If you'd seen the things I've seen in my life, you'd have dreams too."

"What things?" she asked, almost dreading the answer.

His body sagged, the bitterness left his face, and in its place was a pain so intense she could feel it across the distance that separated them.

"Things you're better off not knowing," he replied, his voice gruff with emotion.

Impulsively, she reached out, caressing his cheek with her palm. He closed his eyes tightly at the tremor that coursed through him. When he opened them again, there was fire in their depths.

"Shall I kiss you good night, Miss Cameron?" he asked. But he didn't wait for an answer.

The first tentative touch of his lips against hers sent a ripple through her body like wildfire. His lips were hot and moist as they coaxed hers apart. The fire that spread over her body gathered in the suddenly taut tips of her breasts and in the velvet recesses of her womanly flesh.

She wrapped her arms around his neck, clinging to him, pressing herself against him instinctively, wanting more contact with him, wanting his hands on her body, not protesting even when he slipped one hand inside her shirtwaist to cup her breast. She gasped sharply beneath his mouth at the feel of his fingers tugging on the hard nub of her nipple, and the fire in her loins threatened to consume her.

It was he who broke the embrace, he who came to his senses first, he who backed away and stood staring at her, his chest laboring under the force of his rasping breath. The glint in his eyes looked like murder or something equally violent. Quivering in reaction, she straightened her skirt and ran a trembling hand over her hair.

"I didn't mean to . . . " she muttered, suddenly unable to meet his gaze. "That is, I mean to say. . . . "

She didn't know exactly what she meant to say. She didn't even know what she felt at that moment. She only knew she should say something, do something.

"Don't," he said breathlessly. "It was my fault. It won't happen again."

And with that he was gone, leaving her standing there gaping after him, hoping he hadn't meant his parting words. She didn't know if she could bear it if it didn't happen again.

13

They'd been *watching* the smoke all day, a thin gray ribbon that curled its way upward toward the cloudless sky. After days of traveling across the bleak, monotonous desert, any variation would have drawn their attention, but there was something particularly ominous about this vision.

A feeling of dread sent gooseflesh over Anne's body, and though she tried with all her might to ignore it, her gaze returned time and again to that silent harbinger of ill.

She might have been able to ignore her own reaction, if not for the fact that Rafe's mood seemed to mirror hers so closely. He had been tense and silent all day.

"What do you think it is?" she asked.

"No way of knowing." He kept looking toward the horizon.

She drew her horse up alongside his and only then

noticed the thin sheen of perspiration on his face, the tautness of the muscle in his jaw. His apparent anxiety only served to amplify hers.

"Maybe it's just smoke from a chimney."

"Maybe."

He didn't have to say anything else. The way he spoke the word left little doubt what he thought. Her imagination filled in the blanks. She tried to stop her mind from conjuring one grizzly scenario after another, but she'd been in the desert long enough to begin to understand its unforgiving nature.

She knew the smoke wasn't from something as simple as a cook fire. It might be the remnants of a devastating brush fire or an entire town burned to the ground by savages of one kind or another. But there was nothing innocent about the billowing gray cloud.

They followed the trail of smoke for another hour before the smoldering ruins of a covered wagon came into view. Half a dozen buzzards circled overhead, their cries shrill and eerie in the still desert air.

Anne swallowed against the bile that rose in her throat. A tremor started in her arms and spread down her torso to her legs as a feeling of unreality, of detachment, overwhelmed her.

"Stay here with the horses while I look around," Rafe told her in a shaky voice.

She was glad for once to do as he said. She had no desire to go any closer. She'd seen death before: her father had practically died in her arms, and there had been the Union soldiers in Baton Rouge who died of yellow fever faster than graves could be dug for them. But she'd never witnessed random violence against innocent people.

As Rafe studied the scene before them, his chest

heaving with the force of his ragged breath, Anne noticed that he was trembling, and she gazed at him with a new understanding. The implacable, unreachable killer was gone, and in his place was a man capable of feeling repulsion and compassion. He seemed to have completely lost the iron control he usually exercised over his body and his emotions. And when he finally turned to her, she had the unnerving feeling that he wasn't seeing her at all.

The stark horror in his eyes set her head spinning. Those eyes were seeing something beyond what lay before them, she was sure. Something more horrible, more devastating, than she could even imagine lurked in the black pit of his memory.

As he walked toward the wagon, she had to fight the urge to call him back. He seemed so incredibly fragile suddenly. A part of her wanted simply to ride away. If there were people here, they were dead. There was nothing they could do for them.

But if they did that, they would be no better than the butchers who had killed them. Whoever they were, they had to be buried. It would be barbaric to leave them out in the open.

As he drew near the wreckage, Rafe took out his pistol and fired a shot into the air. In response, two more buzzards squawked loudly and took flight nearby.

Time passed interminably as Anne sat on her horse in the scant shade of a saguaro cactus, wiping perspiration from her face with her sleeve. A huge black carrion bird dove toward the earth, swooping down so close over her head that she ducked involuntarily.

She thought it was going to land close by, but it rose again toward the sky, then made a wide turn, and dove toward the same spot again.

With her heart in her throat, she dismounted quickly and stumbled forward, sobbing, barely able to see through her tears.

She knew she was looking at a body. Rafe hadn't seen it yet because the ground was slightly lower here and the brush was taller.

It was a woman. She was naked. There was blood. She'd been scalped.

She trembled all over, hot and cold at the same time, certain she would either faint or become deathly ill. She was hardly aware of moving, but she managed to climb to her feet. Then she was running headlong back toward her horse.

At that instant, Rafe reached her. He caught her and eased her down to the ground as she gave in to the nausea that finally overwhelmed her.

He held her gently, caressing her hair, speaking soothingly with words she didn't understand. The nausea subsided and she began to cry, clinging to him and the comfort he offered. His arms tightened around her, and he rocked her to and fro as if she were a child.

"They . . . they raped her," she murmured. "They scalped her."

"I know," he whispered against her hair. "Do you think you can stand up?"

She could only nod.

Rafe stood, pulling her gently to her feet. He supported her as they walked back toward her horse.

"Stay here," he told her. "You can stand or get on the horse, but just wait here for me. I'll be a little while. I've got to bury them."

"How many?"

"Two, probably a settler and his wife."

"No children?" She didn't think she could bear it if there were children.

Rafe shook his head without a word and went to perform his grizzly task.

She turned away, unable to watch without feeling the bile rise in her throat again. She hated the desert. She hated Texas. More than anything, she wanted to go home, back to the river. At least there she knew how to survive. She understood the rules. Here there were no rules, no laws except survival of the fittest, enforced by violence.

A cold terror stole over her. Suddenly she was afraid, more afraid than she had ever been in her life.

It was still daylight when Rafe finished burying the bodies. They traveled another hour before making camp for the night on the bank of another dry creek. He'd wanted to get her as far away from that place as he could, as if that would help blot out the horror.

Their dinner that night was beans and salt pork, but he had the feeling it could have been dirt and leaves for all Annie knew or cared.

She sat trancelike as he prepared their bedrolls for sleep. He glanced at her from time to time to make sure she was all right, but of course she wasn't.

Over and over again, she was reliving in her mind the moment when she'd discovered the woman's body. He could see it in her blank eyes. He could feel it in her silence. It was always like that the first time you experienced the merciless brutality of the desert. Nothing would ever be the same for her again.

He moved to stand over her, holding out a hand. When she didn't respond, he prodded gently. "It's time for bed. You need some rest."

Annie looked up at him, and his heart wrenched as he waited for her to return mentally from wherever she'd been. He had to admire the way she regained her composure. Annie Cameron was made of strong stuff. She was a survivor.

The thought sprang unbidden to his mind that Christina could never have held up under everything Annie had been through in the past few days. But then, Christina shouldn't have had to. If not for him, she *wouldn't* have had to.

It was one of the things that had haunted him for the past five years. Christina had been with the *comancheros* for three days and nights before he found her. He shuddered even now, thinking of all the things she had been forced to endure at their hands.

He returned to the present to find Annie reaching toward him. He wrapped his big hand around her small one and pulled her to her feet, supporting her as they walked to her bedroll, where he laid her down and tucked her in.

"Good night," he murmured, wishing there was something he could do to ease her horror. "Things will look different in the morning."

"Please." She grabbed him by the arm as he made to rise, halting him. Desperation made her voice tremble. She gazed up at him pleadingly, her face contorted as she struggled not to cry.

"Please lie down with me. Hold me. I . . . I don't think I can sleep by myself."

It was a mistake. He knew he would regret it, even as he took his boots off and slipped into the bedroll beside her, wrapping his arms around her soft, yielding body, holding her tightly against him. He tried to ignore the sweet curves that burned through his resolve. He wanted to comfort her, to hold her and feel nothing but a detached kind of compassion, but his body quickened despite his best efforts.

Oblivious to his internal turmoil, she shuddered once, then went still.

He hadn't been unaffected by what had happened today either. From the first moment he had spotted the smoke on the horizon, the memories had surfaced with sickening clarity. It had been too much like the other time.

This raid too had been the work of comancheros. He knew all the signs. Their horses had been shod, unlike Indian ponies. The wagon had been picked clean, except for trinkets that would have appealed to an Indian but that a comanchero would have recognized as worthless. They had scalped the woman but not the man. Long pale hair would bring a higher price than the man's short pate.

He hadn't said aloud what he'd thought when Annie had asked about children: that if there were, their fate would be worse than that of their parents.

Children would be taken south of the border. The girls would go to brothels, and possibly the boys as well, or they might be sold to the silver mines as slaves.

Rafe's hand moved over Annie's soft, tangled hair, and he shivered slightly. That woman they had found today could have been Annie.

It was sweet torture, lying so close beside her, their bodies pressed together. Desire flowed over him like lava. He cursed himself for the animal he was. She needed comfort, but all he could think about was making love to her, caressing the swelling breasts that pressed so softly against his chest.

She lay still beside him now, her head resting on his

shoulder, and her steady, rhythmic breathing told him
that she had fallen asleep. He kissed her gently on the
forehead and closed his eyes, struggling against memory
and desire.

Somewhere in the distance, a coyote wailed, its
lonely cry filling the still, silent night.

*He couldn't move. The heat of the sun seared his
flesh and shrank the thin rawhide straps around his
wrists and ankles. He was naked from head to foot and
as helpless as a newborn babe. He tried to open his
eyes, but the sun's glare blinded him.*

He welcomed death, yearned for it.

*A soft, brief breeze and a shadow fell over his face
and was gone. Something sharp pierced his chest. He
forced his eyes open and gazed into the face of death.*

Rafe cried out, the sound echoing across the desert.
He sat up with a jerk, startling the woman who slept
soundly beside him.

"What is it?" she asked, her voice still thick with sleep.

He couldn't speak. He sat beside her in the darkness, running a hand through his hair, trying to get his
emotions under control and still the pounding of his
heart. She touched his shoulder, and he jerked away,
leaping to his feet.

"Why won't you let anyone help you?"

He twisted his lips in a bitter smile. "Help? You
can't help me. What are you going to tell me, that it
was just a dream and that everything will be all right in
the morning?"

Her gaze dropped to his hands. He was massaging
his wrists, though he wasn't even aware of it until he
noticed her stare; and then he stopped.

"What happened to you?" she asked softly.

"Jesus, Annie!" He paced back and forth in front of her.

She sat on the bedroll, watching in awe and dread and pity. Something was eating him up inside. What secret horror lived in his mind, escaping only at night to torment him? She had thought him invincible, so untouchable that the proof of his vulnerability overwhelmed her as it had the first time she'd witnessed it.

"It might help you to talk about it," she said hesitantly, wanting him to tell her, yet at the same time dreading what he might reveal. She steeled herself for whatever was to come.

"It was while I was in the army," he began quietly, "I tracked a band of comancheros into Mexico. They set a trap for me and I fell right into it. They staked me out in the desert with wet rawhide straps." He paused, clenching his hands into fists at his sides. "Do you know what happens to rawhide when it dries? It shrinks. It would have cut through my wrists and ankles to the bone if someone hadn't come along. I . . . I couldn't move."

He had to stop speaking momentarily to regain control of his emotions and steady his voice. She almost asked him not to go on, but before she could speak, he continued in a taut voice. "I couldn't—the sky was full of buzzards. I kept slipping in and out of consciousness, but I woke up one time to see one of them sitting on my chest looking me in the eye. I . . . I couldn't move."

Her throat constricted as a terrible shudder ran through her. She closed her eyes to block the images his words had evoked.

The need to touch him, to comfort him in some way, nearly overwhelmed her. It must have cost him dearly to share what must surely be his darkest memory. He seemed so fragile suddenly, as if he could break into a thousand pieces at any moment. She made to rise, to go to him, but he seemed to anticipate her purpose and stepped back from her, holding up a hand.

"Don't. I don't want your pity. I don't want you to care about me. Don't you understand?"

"No, I don't understand," she whispered. "Why would anyone do that to you?"

"I made a lot of enemies when I was in the army."

"Someone would have to really hate you to do something like that. Why didn't they just kill you?"

Rafe released a bitter snort. "That's not El Alacrán's way."

"El Alacrán?"

"Felipe Delgado." His eyes hardened as he spoke the name. "He calls himself the Scorpion. He sets traps, and when he's caught his quarry, he likes to toy with it awhile before he destroys it."

"Why does he hate you so?" She almost dreaded the answer.

"El Alacrán and I go way back," he replied. "His mother was the daughter of a powerful man in northern Mexico. She was fifteen when the Apaches kidnapped her. Fifteen years later, the army found a white woman and her half-breed child living with a band of Mescaleros in the Potrillo Mountains.

"Tomás Delgado identified the woman as his long-lost daughter, Elena. The boy was so violent he had to be incarcerated at Fort Bliss. Tomás and Elena moved into a small house close to the fort to be near the boy while the long process of civilization began. Elena couldn't adjust to life among her own people, and the whites would not accept her."

"Why?" she asked. Her heart pounded in her chest

as her head reeled with images of what must have happened to that fifteen-year old girl.

Rafe smiled bitterly. "Most of them believed she should have killed herself."

She dropped her gaze from his uncompromising gray eyes. "Do you?"

"Doesn't matter what I think."

She looked up to find him still studying her intently. "It matters to me."

He opened his mouth to speak, then stopped, running a hand through his hair. "I don't know, Annie. How could I? I . . . I was raised to believe that life is sacred." He laughed bitterly. "Jesus, that must sound hypocritical coming from me. A man who lives off the dead talking about the sanctity of life."

He sighed, his gaze holding hers prisoner. "Indian captives, they're not usually treated . . . they usually don't survive very long. Every now and then one manages to assimilate into Indian society. I think that's what Elena did. I don't know. She ran away in the dead of night, leaving her son behind.

"Tomás thought he could civilize Felipe. He took him into his home, educated him. . . . Felipe repaid him by slitting his throat and running away with all the gold and silver and jewels he could find in the house. He became a comanchero. He raided into Texas, then crossed the border into Mexico where the army would not follow, until the army decided it was time to put a stop to it.

"We followed them across the Rio Grande, right back to their camp. We didn't know . . . there were women in the camp—and children. Captives mostly, but El Alacrán had his woman and his infant son with him. There was so much confusion—bullets flying everywhere—the baby was killed. There's no way of knowing if the bullet was army issue or not, but El Alacrán always blamed me."

"You personally? But—"

"I commanded the raid. I led the attack into Mexico, something El Alacrán never expected. He was ruined, and the only thing he ever cared about in his whole damned life was dead."

"It wasn't your fault."

"No, but it doesn't matter. It took him two years, but he finally exacted his vengeance."

She swallowed, trying hard not to think of all the unanswered questions screaming in her head.

Five years ago . . . a woman . . . El Alacrán.

There was more to the story, much more, but she couldn't bring herself to probe further. If what he'd left out was worse than what he had revealed, she decided she'd just as soon not know, for now at least.

"Who found you?" she asked.

"A bandit named José Carvajal. He nursed me back to health and taught me how to survive in the desert. He taught me a lot of things."

"I don't know what to say. I wish—"

"Don't say anything."

He looked around desperately, searching for some means of escape. His horse stood a few yards away, and the urge to jump on and ride away was almost overwhelming. But he couldn't leave her there alone. He couldn't escape her this time. There was nowhere to run. He had to face her, had to make her see that he was beyond help, beyond her reach.

"Nothing's changed, Annie."

"Everything's changed," she said, rising unsteadily to her feet. "I understand so many things now that I didn't understand before. If only you would let me—"

"You don't understand anything." The muscle in his jaw flexed. His face seemed to have been carved from granite. "You can't help me; I'm not worth the trouble anyway. There's so much . . . so much you don't know, so much I don't want you to know. If you knew me, the things I've done, you wouldn't be standing there talking to me. You'd be running as fast as you could."

She took a step toward him, stopping at the stony look that pierced her heart. "I know you. I know what kind of man you are. You're the kind of man who would take me to a doctor instead of leaving me to die in the desert."

"I couldn't leave you to die. I don't know where the gold is."

"And why don't you?" she asked stubbornly, determined to make him see his own goodness. "Why haven't you forced me to tell you where it is? You could. You know it and I know it. Because of the kind of man you are, that's why. You're the kind of man who would hold me and comfort me yesterday in the middle of a scene that must have brought back your worst memories."

"Let it be, Annie, and I mean it this time. Just let it be."

Maybe he couldn't run away and leave her alone in the camp, but he sure as hell could move to the other side of the smoldering campfire.

He retrieved his bedroll from the ground, and shook it out, to make sure nothing had crawled in, before placing it on the ground again and lying down. He turned his back to her and pulled the edge of the bedroll up to his chin, as if that would keep him safe.

He closed his eyes with a shudder and tried to close his mind. He hadn't intended to confide in her. He'd tried with all his will to maintain the distance between them. Yet something, some unknown demon, had forced him to say much more than he should have. Maybe it was the way she looked at him, as if he deserved to be cared about. But if she knew the truth . . .

When he heard Anne settle back into her bedroll on the other side of the camp, he breathed a sigh of relief. He didn't know what he would have done if she had followed him, or what might have happened if she had touched him earlier. He couldn't bear it. Tenderness was one thing he couldn't handle. It had been a very long time since anyone had felt that way toward him.

A man without compassion turns into an animal, and that was what he had become, an animal, no better than the men he hunted.

Until now, it hadn't mattered. Until now, he'd been able to keep the horrors of the past buried. Until now, he had lived for one thing and one thing alone—for vengeance.

Now he wasn't sure of anything anymore.

14

Anne pulled her hat down lower over her forehead, shielding her eyes from the glaring sunlight. Up ahead, the little town of San Juan Bautista slept in deceptive tranquility, its white adobe buildings glistening in the midday sun.

She breathed in the pungent aroma of trees, which seemed so like home yet so different. The vegetation that lined both sides of the Rio Grande was sparse and pale compared to the trees and undergrowth along the Mississippi. In every direction, the arid desert stretched to the horizon, but a gentle breeze rustled the leaves and caressed her sun-parched skin. For a moment, she could almost forget the horrors of the desert.

They had traveled all day in silence, reaching Eagle Pass and crossing the Rio Grande into Mexico, then turning northwest to follow the winding river.

For most of the time, Anne lagged slightly behind,

allowing Rafe the distance he obviously needed. She knew, as she studied his rigid back, that he was embarrassed at having confided in her. He'd described an episode in his life when he'd been vulnerable, not in control. It must have cost him.

He was so proud, so private. Yet he had given her a glimpse into his tortured soul last night. She cherished it like a gift, even as her mind recoiled in horror.

She'd known all along that he'd been through some experiences she couldn't even imagine. One only had to look into his eyes to know he'd seen and done things that were better left unexposed. And for the first time, she realized that the hard, uncompromising exterior he presented to the world was as much to keep things inside as it was to keep people out.

There were things he hadn't told her about this El Alacrán and what had happened between them. Questions still plagued her. Was El Alacrán still chasing Rafe? If he held Rafe responsible for the death of his son, would leaving him in the desert to die have been enough to settle the score? Did he know that Rafe had survived? And, if so, would he want to kill him now?

The sound of shouting, laughing voices struck a discordant note. They seemed somehow eerie against the seriousness of her thoughts.

Rafe had come to a stop on the edge of the town, and Anne drew up beside him. "Is it some kind of holiday?" she asked.

"Don't know." They were the first words he had spoken to her all day.

As they turned upon the main road into town, they saw that people lined the main street, spilling out into the surrouding countryside.

Anne and Rafe entered town at a sedate walk. The

main street was clogged with people. What must have been the entire population was there.

An old man in white shirt and trousers passed in front of them, and Rafe called out to him in Spanish. The man stopped and turned to face Rafe with a gap-toothed grin, responding in the same language.

"What did he say?" she asked as the man scurried across the street and Rafe urged his horse forward.

"It's a wedding. The daughter of the *patrón*."

"*Patrón?*"

"Probably a big ranchero whose wealth supports the village," he explained over his shoulder.

They stopped in front of the hotel, and Rafe dismounted. A man on the sidewalk stepped toward them with a smile. He clapped Rafe on the back and the two of them conversed in Spanish as if they'd been friends all their lives.

"*Gracias,*" Rafe finally said. It was the only word in the entire exchange that Anne understood.

"Do you know that man?" she asked.

"No, but it doesn't matter. Anybody who rides into town peaceably today is considered a friend." As the Mexican returned to his companions, Rafe continued, "We're invited to the fiesta."

She glanced around. It was like Carnival in New Orleans, only on a much smaller scale, of course. She couldn't remember the last time she'd been among such merry people, and she tried not to show her eagerness in front of Rafe, for fear he'd make fun of what he would surely see as childishness. He was always so serious.

She turned to find him staring up at her with an expression she couldn't read. Then he walked around to the left side of her horse, holding his arms up to her.

She placed her hands on his shoulders. His muscles

flexed beneath her grasp as he swung her to the ground in front of him. His face hovered close over hers as he held her a moment longer than was necessary. A disturbing current ran between them, and then he pulled his hands away as if he'd been burned.

"The hotel's full," he told her, his voice raw with emotion. "I saw a good place to make camp by the river on the way into town." He nodded toward the plaza, where a meal was being laid out on long tables. "You go ahead, and I'll set up camp."

"Are you sure?" she asked, sensing that he wanted to be alone.

"I won't be long."

She watched him lead the horses off, her heart aching for him. She knew he was running away—from her, from the past, from himself. Why couldn't he see what was happening? He was withdrawing more and more inside himself, and pretty soon he'd be utterly unreachable. She couldn't let that happen, but she had no idea how to prevent it.

With her heart feeling heavy in her chest, she made her way toward the plaza.

Leaning against a tree beside the river, Rafe gazed toward San Juan Bautista. He could hardly see the town for the trees and the uneven terrain. But that was why he had chosen this spot: isolated, private, defensible. He could hear the sounds of music and laughter, of happy, shouting voices.

He closed his eyes, and his mind forced him back in time to another wedding. God, it seemed so long ago, a lifetime ago. She had been so beautiful, so ethereal in her flowing white dress, her face flushed and radiant.

They'd danced the first dance together. Then he'd lost track of her as the men vied for a dance with his bride, while he stood talking with his brother about duty and responsibility and family. Every now and then he'd catch a glimpse of her as she whirled across the plaza, and she would beam a smile like sunshine in his direction.

He wished he could remember her like that: happy, beautiful, innocent. He wished he'd never met her. If he'd never met her, she'd still be alive.

"Damn you to everlasting hell!" Michael's words still reverberated in his head. "If you had been a true husband to her, she wouldn't have had to come here."

He had reacted without thinking, striking out with his fist, hitting Michael hard enough to knock him off his feet. His brother had lain on the floor, gazing up at him with eyes full of loathing as he blotted the blood from the corner of his mouth.

"She wouldn't have been on that defenseless road," Michael had murmured.

"Just what went on here between you and my wife, brother?" Rafe had demanded.

He'd never really thought about it before: Michael and Christina. He'd been too busy to pay much attention to Christina's comings and goings, and he'd seen her friendship with Michael as a godsend. It kept her occupied, gave her something to fill her time when he was away.

But then he'd gone to Michael to tell him what had happened. It was six months after her death. He'd been more dead than alive himself, and he'd gone to see Michael as soon as he'd been able. Perhaps he wanted absolution, he didn't even know anymore. All he knew was that Michael had attacked him with such venom and such passion that he had been forced to examine that relationship for the first time.

Of course Michael had denied his accusations, but Rafe had spent the past five years wondering, vacillating between nagging doubt and the sure knowledge that there couldn't have been anything between his brother and his wife. But it did no good to speculate. His brother hated him, and his wife was dead.

"You are no brother of mine!" Michael's words still reverberated in his mind, adding to the pain and desolation. Even his own brother had turned his back on him . . . .

"Amigo."

Rafe spun around, his pistol drawn, to see José Carvajal standing behind him with another man, one who was bound, his face bruised and bloodied.

"Damn, José, I could have killed you! What the hell were you thinking, sneaking up on me like that?"

José stepped forward, dragging his prisoner with him. When he was only a few feet from Rafe, he shoved the bound man forward and he fell to his knees in the dirt.

Rafe glanced past José to see another captive astride a horse, his hands bound behind his back and a gag in his mouth.

"I brought you a gift, amigo. They have been following you."

Rafe walked to the captive on the ground, lifting him to his feet by the collar. The face he gazed into was much younger than he would have guessed. In fact, he was more boy than man, probably no older than fifteen or sixteen.

"Don't you recognize him, amigo?" José asked. "Look closely."

Rafe studied the boy intently: his dark eyes and boyish mouth, his high cheekbones and hawk nose. Realization dawned, and a cold violence settled on his heart.

"Carlos." Rafe breathed the word.

"*Sí*, Carlos Delgado, El Alacrán's cousin." José motioned over his shoulder. "The other one is Diego Muñoz, El Alacrán's right-hand man."

If there was one human being in the world whom El Alacrán loved, it was his cousin. When his own son had died seven years ago, El Alacrán had kidnapped the son of his mother's brother. Carlos had been eight years old at the time, and since then El Alacrán had raised the boy as his own.

Rafe drew his knife, pressing the cold metal to the youth's throat, gratified by the look of terror in those dark Delgado eyes.

"Why were you following me, boy?" Rafe asked, his voice vibrating with menace. When the boy didn't reply, Rafe increased the pressure, nicking the skin. "I'd like nothing better than to kill you, so if I were you I'd start talking."

Carlos Delgado began to pant in fear. "The woman," he gasped. "My cousin wants to . . . to talk to her."

"Kill him, amigo," José urged.

Rafe's hand flexed on the knife. The boy's entire body shivered with fear. Innocent blood for innocent blood. The one person in the world whom El Alacrán cared for was under his knife.

His vision blurred and Annie's face floated before his eyes. She believed in him. She saw something in him that no one else had seen for a very long time. What would she think if he did this? If he killed an innocent boy?

He imagined the expression in her eyes when she looked at him, when she finally understood what he was, a man without conscience, an animal capable of killing in cold blood. Damn her for trying to make him something he wasn't.

He pulled the boy up to his full height and lifted the knife.

"Do it quickly, amigo," José urged.

"No! Please!" the boy begged, his eyes bulging, his Adam's apple rising and falling as he struggled to swallow.

Rafe's hand began to sweat. His heart pounded violently in his chest. He would be justified. Christina would be avenged. An eye for an eye, an innocent life for an innocent life. The urge to kill pounded in his temples, coursed through his veins.

At last the time had come for sweet vengeance. He waited for the feeling of triumph and euphoria to wash over him. It didn't come.

Wasn't that how all this had started? If he killed Carlos Delgado to avenge Christina's death, would he be any better than El Alacrán? Where would it end?

Annie's words returned to him. *I know what kind of man you are. You're the kind of man who would hold me and comfort me yesterday in the middle of a scene that must have brought back your worst memories.*

With an anguished bellow, he flung the knife to the ground so that the blade stuck in the sand.

"Take him," Rafe ordered, shoving the boy toward José. "I won't have his blood on my hands too."

"I was right, amigo, you are going soft. What do you want me to do with them?"

Rafe couldn't think clearly. He could hardly speak. His breath came in gasps as he struggled to regain control of his emotions. He'd nearly killed an innocent boy. Not so long ago he would have done so, before Annie had come into his life and complicated it.

"Just get him out of my sight," Rafe said. "I'll decide what to do with both of them tomorrow. I want them alive, amigo. *¿Comprende?*"

"*Sí*, just as I thought. You are going soft."

Anne stood at the edge of the street behind a hitching post, where she could get a good view of the horse races down the long, dusty street between the buildings. The tables had been cleared away after the fiesta, and now everyone lined the streets, many placing bets on whichever horse they thought to be the best.

Handsome young men in silver-studded finery lined up across the street on their spirited horses for each race, which would take them through the plaza, around the buildings in a wide circle, and back into the plaza for the finish.

When it began she clapped her hands and shouted for the winners along with the crowd, but as the riders returned after the last race, she began to search the sea of faces for Rafe.

She hadn't seen him since he'd gone to set up camp, and she was getting concerned. It shouldn't have taken him so long, unless he'd run into trouble.

Maybe he'd decided not to come back. Always when he was out of her sight there was that fear, though she knew he couldn't get the gold without her. Now she didn't believe he wanted the gold at all. There was something else driving him, something dark and dangerous.

Last night, when he'd told her about his nightmare, they had stepped across an invisible threshold; there could be no turning back. She sensed he had revealed more to her in a few moments than he had to anyone in a very long time—maybe ever.

He was so closed up inside, so guarded. In spite of her resolve not to become involved in other people's problems, in spite of the fact that Rafe Montalvo was the last man who could give her what she wanted, the last man she should care about, she was determined to break through that hard exterior of his. She wanted to know what caused the flashes of pain she'd seen in his eyes from time to time, what drove him to kill for a living. She wished he would just come back. . . .

She searched the crowd again, but he was nowhere to be seen.

Rafe stood at the bar in the small cantina, a glass of tequila in his hand, his elbows resting on the rough-hewn surface.

How much would he have to drink to forget about Annie, to dull the pain that was becoming his constant companion?

Lifting the glass, he tossed its contents down his throat, then poured another from the bottle that the bartender had left in front of him. He was nearly halfway to the bottom of the bottle and still without results.

It was his curse to have an unusually high tolerance for alcohol. When he'd been a young man in the army, it had come in handy. It was amazing what you could find out when everyone around you was drunk and you were still sober.

He pictured the faces of the men he'd known at Fort Bliss, his friends. He hadn't thought of them in years.

Why now? They hadn't been a part of his life since the day he'd fallen from grace. There was hardly a man among them who would sit down and have a drink with him today.

He tossed down another shot of tequila. As he lowered his head, he caught sight of his reflection in the mirror behind the bar and scowled.

"Rafael Sebastian Holden y Montalvo," he murmured, raising his empty glass in a mock toast. "Fallen angel." He laughed, bitterly.

For a fleeting moment, he thought he recognized the man in the mirror, thought he saw something that reminded him of the young West Point graduate who had returned to the West to right every wrong and personally see to it that justice triumphed.

Then he turned away with a sneer. Justice? Men like El Alacrán were beyond justice. Survival of the fittest, that was the law of the desert, and the only justice he'd ever found had come at the end of a gun—or a knife.

He still couldn't believe that Carlos Delgado had been under his knife that very day, and still lived. The perfect vengeance for Christina's life, and he had not taken it.

Closing his eyes, he relished the vision of El Alacrán's face as it would look when his beloved cousin's severed head was delivered to him. It would be a sight worth seeing—but somehow Rafe just didn't have the stomach for killing an innocent, even if the blood of the Scorpion flowed in his veins. José was right; he was definitely going soft, and it would cost him.

He pushed away from the bar, and stumbled toward the door. From outside, he could hear the sounds of laughter and cheering and music, and his mood grew even darker.

Annie was out there somewhere. She deserved to be happy. She shouldn't be here with a man like him, a man who could barely control his lust and wasn't accustomed to being required to do so. He didn't know how much more of her nearness he could take.

He tried to remind himself that she was a pawn in a deadly game, but the words didn't ring true any longer. She had a name, she had a face he would never forget, and she had a body he wanted to know intimately.

Annie, Annie, why did you have to get mixed up in this mess? Why didn't you just stay in Louisiana or Mississippi where you'd be safe?

He pushed open the cantina door and stepped outside. As soon as his eyes adjusted to the waning sunlight, he began searching for the one face that could make him forget the horrors of the past, at least for a moment or two.

She was standing on the edge of the crowd, clapping and cheering with the rest of them, her face glowing with joy as he'd never seen it. His treacherous heart leapt into his throat as he made his way slowly toward the only ray of hope in his dismal existence—toward Annie.

15

The sun began to fade, sending long gold and red streamers across the sky in its wake. The horses were tethered and lanterns lighted in the trees. Several men carried benches to the middle of the plaza and set them down to form a square. A small band gathered at one end and began to tune their instruments.

The women removed their mantillas and formed a line, while the men made a row behind them. For a fleeting instant, Anne imagined that Rafe was one of those young men, so innocent, so carefree. But that was absurd. There was too much darkness in Rafe, and she doubted that he had ever been innocent. She couldn't imagine those eyes ever reflecting anything but pain.

A discordant blast from the band turned slowly into a sweet, haunting melody. The men and women stood watching as the groom led his bride in the first waltz.

Anne wrapped her shawl more closely around her, and watched the newly married couple glide gracefully around the makeshift dance floor, seemingly unaware of anyone but each other. She couldn't help the sigh of longing that escaped her parted lips.

Longing for what, she wasn't quite sure. She'd spent most of her life convinced that men were nothing but trouble and misery and that women were profoundly better off without them. Still, something about the way the happy couple moved together, looking at each other with such devotion and adoration, struck a yearning in the depths of her soul. What would it be like to be loved like that? Completely? Unselfishly?

She searched the crowd for Rafe Montalvo. He stood across the square, leaning against a rail of the corral, talking with a group of men. A shiver trembled up her spine as he glanced up and locked his gaze with hers.

Anger pricked her when she tried to imagine where he must have been—probably inside the cantina. But something in his face, even from this distance, sent a chill of apprehension and excitement down her spine.

Did he keep his distance because he was afraid he would have to talk to her if he got too close? It was a question she couldn't answer, but she did know that his eyes never strayed from her for more than a few minutes. It was disconcerting, to say the least.

As the first dance ended, a wild cry went up from the spectators, and the plaza erupted in applause. A feverish fandango burst quickly from the band; the two lines of men and women joined in the dancing with a wild abandon that took her breath away. The rhythm and pulse of the music flowed into Anne until she was clapping and tapping her foot with the other spectators.

Panic seized her when she gazed across the plaza to find that Rafe wasn't where he should have been. She looked around, but he was nowhere to be found. Some of her joy evaporated. Suddenly all she wanted was peace and quiet and Rafe by her side.

The frenzied tempo of the music gave way to a placid waltz, but Anne hardly noticed. The tiny hairs on her arms stood on end. She was strangely breathless, as if she, too, had been dancing. She didn't have to turn to know that he had come to stand beside her; she could feel his presence as surely as if he'd reached out and touched her. She turned slowly to look at him.

Without a word, he reached out, wrapped an arm around her waist, and pulled her into the square. His eyes never left hers. Their hands joined, her small one inside his large one, as they moved around the clearing to the rhythm of the music.

How could a man of such violence dance with such skill and grace? He held her close against him, guiding her gracefully over the hard-packed ground. The flickering lantern light accentuated the planes of his face and made his dark hair appear even darker, but his gray eyes glowed as he looked down at her, and her pulse quickened.

Cut off from the rest of the world by his arms and his muscular body, she closed her eyes, surrendering to the sweetly haunting music. He held her gently, as if she were something precious. And when she gazed up into his eyes again, they had lost their cold remoteness and burned instead with a fire that spoke of hunger and need.

The heat of his body reached out to her, engulfing her in warmth and strength. She clung to him, pressing her body fully against his, willing herself to forget for just a while that he was a gunfighter, a man who could never give her what she wanted. Right now, he was everything she needed.

She thought she heard him whisper her name, the sound like a soft, caressing breeze on a hot summer's night. His chin rested against the top of her head, and she laid her cheek against his chest. His heart beat strong and fierce against her temple. She knew in that instant that she never wanted to be without him, even for a single day. The realization terrified her because she knew that eventually he would leave.

Oblivious to everything around them, they continued to sway together long after the music died away. The band began another fandango, and the dancers started to whirl around them.

"The waltz is over," he murmured, the sound rumbling in his chest. He held her away from him, and she tipped her head back to gaze into his eyes.

"Yes."

The noise and the crowd receded. He reached out to tilt her face toward his. She knew he was going to kiss her before his lips gently touched hers.

A groan passed his lips and shuddered through her body. She grasped his shirt and pulled herself closer to him.

Rafe backed away from her as she leaned toward him. Taking her by the hand, he led her through the dancers and out of the square, into the shadows where the lights could not follow.

They reached the edge of the river where Rafe had set up camp. He pulled her into the circle of his arms and kissed her, his mouth traveling down the column of her throat, even as he tugged her shirtwaist out of her skirt.

Slowly, slowly, he told himself, fighting the urgency of his own desire. This was Annie, not some whore, not a faceless body he could use for his own pleasure with no regard for her. *Don't frighten her. Don't hurt her.* But the blood pounded in his veins with relentless power, threatening to blot out everything but his own need.

His hand moved up under her blouse, closing around a soft, firm breast. She gasped at the contact, gazing up at him with lips slightly parted, her eyes dark with passion. A familiar hardness began to build between his legs, and a groan rumbled up from his belly as he kissed the hollow of her neck.

Straining against him, she returned his kiss with a hunger that coursed through his painfully aroused body. He lifted her shirt. She shivered but did not protest until he bent his head, capturing a sweet, swollen nub between his lips. Then she cried out in shock and jerked away.

She watched the rise and fall of his chest as he struggled for breath, marveling that she had elicited such an acutely physical reaction in him. Slowly, he moved toward her, as if he feared he might startle her into flight. Her heart drummed in her chest with such force that she could scarcely breathe, but she didn't back away. There was an inevitability about what was happening between them, as if it had always been meant to be.

He didn't touch her except to undo the buttons that ran down the front of her blouse. When he had unfastened the last one, he pushed the garment open and slid it down her arms. He had removed it before she reacted, folding her arms over her breasts, turning her face away from him, suddenly shy, suddenly afraid of the fire in those pale glowing eyes.

She was torn between incompatible urges: to press herself against him and to keep her nakedness hidden from him. (He wanted to see her, all of her. He wanted to touch her, all of her.) She hadn't known it would be like this, this complete giving of herself to someone else. And while it frightened her to her core, her body cried out for his touch.

"Let me see you, Annie," he whispered against her ear.

She didn't resist when he took her wrists and drew them gently apart. She felt the heat of his gaze as he looked at her as no man ever had before. Pulling her chemise over her head, he dropped it to the ground. Warm hands encircled her flesh and calloused thumbs caressed her sensitive, nipples sending a flash of something like pain plunging downward, across her belly, between her thighs.

"So soft," he murmured. "So sweet."

He twisted a hand in her hair and gently pulled her head back. She gazed into his eyes, into the barren wasteland that was his soul. The desolation tore at her heart and took her breath away. She wanted to take away the pain, the darkness.

She lifted her lips to his, her kiss like a whisper, her soft curves molding to the contours of his lean body. He held her more tightly, drinking her essence like a starving man. His hands went to the small of her back and fumbled for the fastenings of her skirt, then unhooked them quickly. It fell to the ground, leaving nothing but her thin pantalettes to protect her. He lifted her in his arms, carried her a short distance to the river, and laid her down gently in the scant grass that grew along the bank.

Fear rippled through her as she thought of the creatures that must call this place home—insects, snakes, spiders. But the urgency of her desire overrode everything else when he knelt beside her.

She knew he was naked, even though she averted her gaze in embarrassment. Was it too late? she wondered in sudden panic. Too late to stop, to turn back?

His mouth captured hers again, and she forgot her fear. His tongue traced her lips while his hands worked to divest her of her last garment.

Her world was filled with him. He stretched out beside her, supporting his body with one hand while his other hand stroked her breasts, moving down her belly and across her hips, his touch feather light. She moaned as sensations pulsated through her, and her body yearned for fulfillment.

She gasped as his fingers found the triangle of downy hair that grew at the juncture of her thighs and moved downward into the recesses of her core. She nearly cried out at the savage thrill that leaped through her tingling body. His eyes bored into hers while his fingers explored, arousing a response that terrified her with its intensity.

"Stop!" she finally cried.

He continued touching her, caressing her. "Did I hurt you?"

She couldn't answer. An unfamiliar spasm ripped through her being, leaving her speechless, mindless. She could hear herself moaning, but she couldn't stop until her body reached an apex of sensation.

He shifted his weight, and she felt the pressure of his knees coaxing her legs apart. He lowered himself between her thighs.

Her flesh encircled him as he eased inside her, slowly, gently, even though a raw insistence urged him to take her quickly and end the unbearable agony. But he was determined to be patient, to give as much pleasure as he received.

It was then he encountered the barrier, the thin but insistent membrane, and he went still. He'd known it would be there, though he had nearly forgotten in his frenzied need. The thought shot through him like a hot wind that this was the one pure thing in his wretched existence, and he was about to defile it.

He couldn't stop. He needed her as he had never needed anyone or anything in his life. His body convulsed with a blinding hunger as he fought the urge to thrust into her, to break through that barrier, to feel the sweetness of something untouched, something pure. He needed to feel connected to her, if only for a short while. He almost believed—hoped—that she could redeem him.

"Oh, God, Annie, I can't give you anything," he managed to choke out, hating himself for what he was doing. He was everything dark and vile. She was everything bright and beautiful. He had no right to touch her, to want her so desperately.

She answered him by wrapping her arms around his shoulders, pulling herself up to him so that her soft breasts brushed his hard chest and her lips fitted themselves to his. He moaned deep in his throat as a shudder ripped through him. The urgency to be inside her consumed him. His breath hissed between his teeth. His heart pounded painfully in his chest, blood rushing through his body to his groin.

She clung to him as he pushed her back down to the grass, a war raging inside his rigid body between the insistence of his need and his desire to be gentle, to cause as little pain as possible.

Why, Annie, why? he kept asking silently, even as

he made that irrevocable thrust. She cried out sharply, and he willed himself to absorb her pain.

She had gone rigid, lying beneath him, trembling in reaction. He pressed a kiss to her temple, smoothing the hair from her brow with a trembling hand, fighting the burning need to move, to thrust deeper inside her, to feel her flesh tight and soft around him.

She had known there would be pain, but what she hadn't expected was the absolute invasion of her body and her soul. He surrounded her, absorbed her, as she absorbed him. She wanted to know what he felt, what he thought when he looked down at her, their bodies locked together, his flesh inside hers. In his eyes, she saw pain, her pain, and she wanted to reassure him that she would not break.

And then he moved, and she released a long, low gasp of surprise mingled with pain and pleasure as he entered her further, pushing deeper, her body stretching, opening to receive him until he lay fully inside her. She felt the sleek caress of his naked body as he withdrew from her in a long, silken movement, his mouth trailing along her collarbone, his lips teasing their way down the valley between her breasts.

He stopped the slow retreat from her body, remaining inside her. His mouth continued its feast, extending its quest to the soft mound of a breast. She arched her hips toward him and he remained still, so that it was she who took him.

Her breath came in soft, painful gasps as she felt herself stretching once again to accommodate him. She sank back down to the ground and he followed her, maintaining the connection between their bodies, deepening it when her hips rested on the ground.

He didn't have to pretend this time that she was

someone he cared about. He didn't have to keep his eyes shut tightly to block out the reality. She was soft and sweet and guileless, and she'd given him the most precious thing she had to give—her innocence.

All the emotions and all the memories he'd kept so carefully buried for so long rose inside him and devoured him. He felt himself slipping into a black hell as all of his defenses began to crumble, leaving his soul open like a raw wound.

Her hand on his face brought him back from the abyss. He closed his eyes, leaning his cheek into her palm.

Wetness touched her fingers and her heart constricted. "It's all right," she whispered, because she didn't know what else to do, to say.

He pressed a kiss into her palm. A hand slipped beneath her shoulders and lifted her up against his chest. Her arms went around his strong muscled back, clinging to him as he moved inside her. The cadence of his breathing turned shallow and raw. It frightened her, his wildness, his loss of control. She tried to remind herself that he would never intentionally hurt her, but it was all she could do not to cry out as the rhythm of his body increased and the thrusts became fiercer, deeper. She knew that he needed her, and tonight his need outweighed hers. He clung to her, devoured her with the fervor that grew to a shattering climax, and cried out with the release that tore through him.

The music from the village faded away, and Anne heard the howl of a coyote in the distance, sweet and sorrowful. Rafe's heart hammered against hers as she listened to his rapid, shallow breathing.

His breath quieted eventually, and he turned on his

side, drawing her soft, moist body against him, her back pressed against his chest. She came into the fold of his embrace so sweetly, so eagerly, that his heart plunged into his stomach with regret that he could never be what she needed, while she was everything he wanted.

He wrapped an arm around her, his hand closing over her soft, vulnerable shoulder.

"I'm sorry, Annie," he whispered against her hair. "I hurt you and I'm sorry."

"My father's mistress told me it always hurts the first time."

What Terese had said was that there were always tears the first time, but they were supposed to be her tears, not his.

"I could have been gentler. It's just been so long. . . . Why, Annie?" He finally asked the question that had plagued him throughout their lovemaking.

"I wanted it to be you," she murmured.

"I don't understand. Why me?"

She hesitated. Her heart knew the reason, but she wasn't sure how he would react if she told him.

He waited in silence until she finally replied. "Because I love you."

A slow, bitter sigh hissed between his lips. She regretted her truthfulness when his arms fell away from her. She pushed herself up, bracing her weight on an extended arm so she could look down into his eyes. Her long, loose hair brushed against his chest. He lifted it in his right hand, caressing it. His other hand cradled his head. He refused to look at her.

"You can't love me."

"But I do. You don't have to—to say anything. You don't have to feel. . . ."

"You know what I am." His voice sounded as dry and coarse as desert sand.

"Yes."

"Don't tell me you believe in me or that I'm something I'm not."

"And don't you try telling me you're not! You kill people for money. You have no home to speak of. You've lived a harsh, rugged life by any standard, yet you waltz as if you were born to it."

He turned to face her. "A whore taught me."

"I don't believe you. No whore could have taught you to dance like that. It's as if there's another man deep inside you—"

"He's buried in the desert, Annie. There's no one else in here now but me."

"All right. I don't care. I love you anyway."

He began to rise, but she tried to block him.

"Don't!" she cried. "Don't leave me, not now. We won't speak of it again, I promise."

She wrapped her arms around herself as if suddenly aware of her nakedness.

Rafe cursed himself silently. He must be the most insensitive son-of-a-bitch who ever lived. He'd taken his pleasure, and now that she needed him, all he wanted to do was escape. He took her by the shoulders and laid her down on the ground, reversing their positions.

"Don't move," he whispered.

He rose and walked to the horses where he quickly untied his bedroll from behind the saddle and threw it over his shoulder. He lifted his saddlebags and carried them with his other hand, as he walked back toward her, touched by the way she averted her gaze from his nakedness. He couldn't get used to this new

Annie. She was always so self-assured, so bold and intrepid, it was odd to see her so timid.

He dropped the bedroll and fumbled in his saddlebag.

"Here," he said, dropping to the ground beside her.

She sat up with a gasp at the feeling of something cold against her breast. It was her lost locket. She opened her eyes, gazing at him in wonder.

"You can add theft to the list of my sins," he said, wrapping the bedroll around her trembling shoulders. "I wanted to give it back to you before, but I started thinking of it as my good-luck charm."

She touched the locket with a sad smile. "My father gave this to me the night he died. He'd won it gambling, and when he gave it to me it still had someone else's picture in it."

"You once said something about the man who killed your father. I got the impression you knew him."

"Borden McKenna." The name was like a curse on her lips. "My father befriended him when he was down on his luck. Papa was always bringing home strays of one kind or another. I was in Baton Rouge and Papa was in Natchez when they met. Papa sent him to fetch me to Natchez when it was safe."

Anger surged through him at the thought that her father would have sent a stranger to escort his daughter anywhere. How had he known he could trust the bastard? "But he hardly knew the man, from what you've said."

"My father's judgment wasn't the best. But Borden was a handsome, charming Irishman. He didn't have to resort to molesting women. They fell at his feet."

"Including you?" He wasn't sure he wanted to hear the answer to that one. He didn't want to think of Annie loving another man.

"I should have known better."

"You were innocent. Your father should have known better. He should have kept you away from a man like that."

"Borden McKenna could charm a drunk out of his last drink. He deceived my father as he deceived everyone else. He told me he loved me, and then he shot my father in cold blood."

"Both of them were fools." Rafe said in a low, pain-filled voice.

"I loved my father. He had his faults, but he loved me. My mother died in childbirth in St. Louis when I was five. My father blamed himself. He was never the same after that."

Rafe was silent, and Anne knew he was somewhere far away. The muscle in his jaw tightened, as if he was having a hard time controlling himself. She wanted to comfort him, to make him tell her what he was thinking, but she knew he would only become angry if she asked.

She held the locket out to him. "Here. You keep it."

He blinked his eyes, focusing on her with an effort. "It belongs to you. It holds special meaning for you."

"But if it brings you luck . . ."

"It's yours." He settled on the blanket beside her. Relief burst inside her as his arm encircled her and he pulled her closer. She'd been afraid he was still angry.

A sense of peace filled her heart. She cursed herself for her inability to stop herself from asking the one question sure to raise his ire again.

"Who is Christina?" she asked softly.

He stiffened. It was a long time before he answered, in a flat voice, "She was my wife."

"What happened to her?"

"She's dead."

Tension gripped his body, belying the detachment in his arid tone. Anne felt it in her own body.

"How?"

"Comancheros."

She shuddered at the violence in that one word, remembering the man in the saloon in Castroville and Rafe's accusation.

Five years ago . . . a woman . . . El Alacrán.

So that had been El Alacrán's revenge. He had killed Rafe's wife. That was the part of the story Rafe had left out.

"I'm sorry," was all she could think of to say.

He heaved a great sigh. "Where are we going, Annie? We're in Mexico now. Do we just keep going south until we get to Bolivia or do we change directions?"

"I don't know," she said truthfully. "The gold is behind the altar of a small church in a place called Concepción."

Rafe could hardly believe she had told him her most guarded secret, the location of the gold, and he had nearly told her his. She trusted him, damn her. He wasn't worthy of her trust, but she had given it to him anyway. Now he could ride away and leave her behind, didn't she realize that? Didn't she know what he was capable of?

"Do you know where Concepción is?" he heard her ask softly.

It was a moment before he could speak, and when he did, his voice sounded raw and unfamiliar in his own ears. "It's about a hundred miles southwest of here in El Alacrán's territory."

Anne's skin crawled. *Five years ago . . . a woman . . . El Alacrán.*

"You mentioned him before. Is he involved with the gold?"

He laughed bitterly. "Involved? He stole it first, and then one of his own men stole it from him. Luis Demas, the man who died in San Antonio was the man who stole it and the man who hid it. El Alacrán wanted him alive. If Demas had had any accomplices, you can be sure they would have told him anything he wanted to know."

He thought of Carlos Delgado, and his mission to take Annie to El Alacrán, and knew that the comanchero still hadn't learned the location of the gold.

"You don't want the gold at all, do you? You want El Alacrán," she said.

"Maybe you're right."

"I know I'm right."

"Annie, I want you to promise me something. If anything happens to me, I want you to promise me you won't go after the gold alone. You can't face a man like El Alacrán."

She trembled against him and murmured through her tears, "Nothing's going to happen to you."

"I know," he said, not wanting to frighten her, "but I need you to give me your word. If anything happens to me, take the money in my saddlebags and go west to Las Cruces. My brother's name is Michael Holden. He'll take you in."

"I thought you said he hated you."

"He does. But he won't turn you away. He is a man of honor."

"But there's nothing there for me."

"There's nothing here for you but death. Don't you understand?" So much for not frightening her. Why did she have to be so stubborn? "Promise me."

"All right, I promise."

Rafe smoothed a strand of hair from her face. "You're right, Annie, nothing's going to happen to me. I promise."

He crawled inside the bedroll with her and they lay side by side, bare chest to bare chest. A familiar heaviness gathered between his legs. Tears glistened on her long lashes, and he kissed them away.

"Hush, Annie, don't cry. I didn't mean to upset you. Nothing's going to happen to either of us. Don't cry." He kissed her eyelids, her lips, her cheeks. Her tears tasted salty on his mouth.

"Did you love her very much?" she asked in a small, jerky voice.

"Who, Annie?"

"Your wife. Did you love her very much?"

"I don't remember." Pain, like a knife, twisted in his heart. "Yes, I loved her."

Her heart broke in two. She didn't know if she was crying for Rafe's loss or for her own.

16

The sun felt warm on her face when Anne opened her eyes the next morning. She stretched like a lazy cat, wincing at the slight pain between her thighs. Memory returned in a rush and she sat up, clutching the rough blanket over her naked body.

Suddenly wide awake, she glanced anxiously around the camp until she saw Rafe kneeling at the edge of the river. A heavy sadness settled on her heart as she watched him stand and screw the top onto the canteen he'd been filling.

He was in pain; she'd known it before last night. But last night all the barriers had come down. She had seen past the pride and anger into his dark, tormented soul.

She remembered the other parts of last night, his gentleness, his fervor. And even though there had been pain and a little embarrassment, she wanted it again, wanted to feel connected to him again, wanted to hear his voice full of passion whispering her name. Her stomach fluttered at the thought.

He walked toward her, and her breath caught in her throat. What did you say to someone who'd seen you naked, who'd touched you intimately, who'd been inside you? How could she face him, knowing he knew all her secrets?

Her face flushed as their eyes met. Quickly she turned away, adjusting the blanket, feeling vulnerable in her state of undress, especially since he was fully clothed. He appeared so at ease, so normal, as if nothing had happened last night, as if he was accustomed to such things.

How many other women had he been with? His wife, for one, and he had loved her. He'd admitted it, even though the admission had cost him dearly. Was Anne just another woman to him? Just another body? She shuddered at the thought that he might have compared her to other women and found her lacking.

He hunkered down beside the remnants of a fire. She watched from the corner of her eye as he poured coffee into a tin cup.

"Coffee?" he asked calmly.

She looked directly at him for the first time, and the glint in his pale eyes set her heart pounding. She reached out with a trembling hand to take the cup, careful to hold the blanket in place, concentrating on his steady hand because she could no longer hold his gaze.

"There aren't a lot of towns where we're going," he told her matter-of-factly. "I'll need to buy a pack mule to carry supplies."

The coffee was tepid and bitter, but she drank it, hoping it would steady her nerves.

A long silence wrapped around them. The pressure

of his eyes drew her like a magnet, but she refused to look at him.

"Annie," he said softly, "I . . . last night . . . I'm sorry. If I could undo—"

"Please don't say that." She looked at him, her throat burning with unshed tears. "I'm not sorry. I don't want to undo it."

He ran a hand through his hair, staring into the distance. The muscle in his jaw moved and he cleared his throat. "You deserve better."

"I wanted it too. I could have stopped you—" He turned his gaze on her again, and something in his eyes made her shiver. "Tried to stop you. Please don't apologize. I don't want you to be sorry."

He gave a crooked smile. "I don't know if I'll ever understand you." He stood, stretching his long legs. "We need to be leaving soon. The horses are saddled."

"I . . . I need privacy," she stammered. "Will you turn your back?"

That crooked smile deepened, and she knew what he was thinking. He'd already seen everything there was to see of her. But it was broad daylight now, and she didn't think she could bear to have him watch her dress.

He picked up the coffeepot, kicked dirt on top of the fire, and started toward the river. "I'll finish packing."

She waited until he reached the river before standing. With the blanket still carefully wrapped around her, she managed to step into her pantalettes and had her shirtwaist firmly in her hand before she dropped the blanket. She had never dressed so quickly in her life, and in no time she was fastening her skirt.

The sound of footsteps behind her told her he had not waited for her to tell him she was ready. Out of the corner of her eye she saw him walking to the nearby horses.

She brought him the blanket as he stuffed the coffee pot inside his bedroll. Without speaking, he took it from her, folded it, and crammed it inside the bedroll with the coffee pot.

"How long were you married?" she couldn't help asking.

"A year."

He finished securing the bedroll, then mounted up.

"We don't have any more time to waste. Let's get our supplies and get moving."

Rafe kicked his horse into a slow trot, stopping far enough away that she couldn't ask any more questions. A sickening knot formed in the pit of Anne's stomach. He had loved a woman once and, judging by the fact that he wouldn't discuss her, he must love her still.

She walked to her own horse and mounted after a moment's struggle, turning the animal and starting toward him.

He'd been married, this man who wanted the world to believe he needed no one and felt nothing. He'd been in the army and he'd been married. And he'd nearly been eaten alive by buzzards. He danced like an aristocrat and killed people for a living. He was from New Mexico and his brother hated him.

That was the extent of her knowledge about Rafe Montalvo, that and the fact that he had a conscience, no matter what he wanted people to think. He had a conscience, and he could be gentle, and he cried when he made love.

She didn't think she would ever understand him. There were too many shadows, too many contradictions. It was as if he were two men at once, the man he presented to the world and the man inside.

He's buried in the desert, he had said. How true was that? Did she really want to know all his secrets?

Leaving their horses tied outside, they entered the general store and walked around inside, surveying the merchandise. She looked longingly at an ivory-handled hairbrush and ran a hand over the bristles. When she noticed Rafe watching her closely, she returned the brush to its place on the table, blushing in embarrassment.

But instead of scowling at her and reminding her that she didn't belong in the desert, he smiled. "I'm going to the livery stable to buy that pack mule. You stay here and look around. See if there's anything you need. I'll be back."

Rafe stepped into the street, his heart almost light. For the first time in years, as he walked along he actually noticed things about the world around him other than whether or not it held any danger. A dozen or more men worked in the plaza, restoring it to its normal state after last night's festivities. Half a dozen women gathered at the well in the center of town to draw water. An old man sat in the shade of a tall tree in the plaza.

The darkness was still there, but it seemed distant this morning, like something that belonged to someone else. He'd seen the way Annie had looked at the hairbrush with such yearning, and he decided right then and there to buy it for her as a surprise.

Once inside the stable, it took a moment for his eyes to adjust to the relative darkness. At first he thought there was no one there, but then he caught a movement near the end of a long row of stalls. A big, powerfully built man walked slowly toward him, wiping his hands on a soiled apron.

"What can I do for you?" the man asked as he reached Rafe.

"I want to buy a pack mule."

"Got two out back. I'll bring them around if you want to wait here."

Rafe nodded. The man walked back in the direction he'd come, and Rafe's thoughts returned to Annie. Just remembering their lovemaking sent the blood pounding through his body.

She was like light in a dark tunnel, drink to a thirsty man. He'd even thought of telling her everything, but he knew if he did she would never let him touch her again. He never wanted to let her go, and an acute pain stabbed his heart when he realized that one day he would have to.

The slight noise behind him didn't penetrate his consciousness at first. When it did, he knew it was too late. It was the sound of a gun cocking. Was he about to be shot in the back? If so, he'd try going for his gun. He just might have time—

"Turn around real slow," a voice said behind him. "Lift your hands where I can see them."

Damn, he'd been taken completely unaware. He'd let down his guard for a few minutes, and it might well have cost him his life—his *and* Annie's, he realized with a sick dread. He didn't believe she could survive here without him.

He turned slowly, and the man who held the gun proved to be no stranger. Tom McCoy smiled broadly, flashing a row of uneven yellow teeth. "Long time no see, Montalvo."

"What the devil do you want, McCoy?"

"I think you know. Hell, I been following you all the way from San Antonio, you and that pretty little gal of yours. I wonder if she'll like me as much as she likes you."

Rafe made an involuntary move toward the outlaw, and McCoy lifted his gun in warning. "Wouldn't do that if I was you. I'm supposed to bring you in alive, but I could say you drew on me. Now, pull that pistol out and drop it real slow."

"He ain't come out of the barn yet!" A voice called from outside.

McCoy glanced away for a flicker of an instant, long enough for Rafe to pull his pistol. He fired, and the bullet tore through McCoy's chest. The other man drew, but Rafe didn't get off another shot before his head exploded in pain and the world went dark.

Anne strolled between the rows of merchandise, running a hand over crisp red-and-white calico, fingering a length of satin ribbon, touching the soft bristles of the hairbrush she'd admired earlier. She picked up a small bar of lilac soap and held it beneath her nose. It smelled sweet and clean.

How she longed to bathe in it, wash her hair with it. What would Rafe think if she smelled like flowers instead of trail dust and sweat?

With all her heart, she wanted him to love her, and she knew he did not. He didn't even believe she loved him, for that matter.

She couldn't forget the tears he'd shed last night. They haunted her. She wanted to know everything about him, but she knew there were things he hadn't told her, terrible things.

Her thoughts were shattered by the sound of a gunshot. It could have been anything, anyone, but a prickling of fear brushed the nape of her neck and the hairs on her arms stood on end. Dropping the bar of soap, she ran for the door.

In the street, people were pointing toward the livery stable. Her heart skipped a beat.

Rafe!

She stepped down from the sidewalk, but before she could take another step, someone seized her from behind, covering her mouth with an iron hand.

He dragged her into the alley beside the store, in spite of her attempts at escape. Her booted foot made contact with her assailant's shin, and he cursed in Spanish, tightening his hold on her. She tried to bite his hand, tried to twist out of his hold. He kept his hand clamped over her mouth and pinched her nostrils shut.

She couldn't breathe. She struggled in panic, her lungs aching for oxygen. In the depths of her mind, she knew she was going to die, and there was nothing she could do about it. Her head began to spin, her body weakening until darkness consumed her.

Another blow smashed into Rafe's face, and he welcomed the blackness that followed. He relished it. It took away the pain, the awareness that Annie was in danger and there was nothing he could do about it.

The next instant he was sputtering and gasping for breath. Water covered his head, his shoulders, his chest. He blinked his eyes open to see one of the outlaws standing over him with an empty pail.

Someone jerked him back up on his knees and a man he knew as Braxton hunkered down beside him. "Rafe, ol' buddy, you don't look too good. You feeling all right?"

"Why don't we just kill him?" someone asked. "He don't know nothin'."

"No," Braxton growled to the man without taking his eyes off Rafe. "I've been waitin' a long time to have

Rafe Montalvo where I want him. I'm gonna enjoy this before he dies. Besides, I ain't so sure he don't know nothin'. Charlie, let's see how fast our friend here can run. Bring me a rope."

Anne stirred from a deep, bottomless sleep, a low moan in her throat. Before she could open her eyes, a hand clamped over her mouth, the same hand that had pinched the breath out of her earlier. She was lying on her side on the ground, a man's body pressing against hers from behind. She trembled and tried to pull away, not knowing who it was but knowing it was not Rafe.

"Señorita," a voice said close to her ear. She could feel his warm breath against her neck. "I am a friend. Be very still and don't make a sound or you will get us all killed."

Her memory returned in a rush. She had run out into the street at the sound of gunshots from the direction of the livery stable.

Rafe. Where was he? Where was she, for that matter?

It was nearly dark, so she must have been unconscious all day. She was on a hill, looking down into a small canyon at a group of men gathered outside a ranch house. One man down there struck another hard in the face. He did it again, and Anne flinched involuntarily. The assaulted man crumpled to the ground, but someone threw water on him and he was hauled back to his knees.

Rafe!

The name stuck in her throat. She tried to rise, but the man who held her kept her still. He pinched her nostrils with his thumb and forefinger again, and she began to struggle with all her might. If he cut off her breath again and she passed out, she wouldn't be able to help Rafe.

"Are you loco?" The voice rasped in her ear. "Be still and quiet like I told you or I will smother you again. *¿Comprende?*"

She nodded and went still, fighting against the dizziness, beating at his arm with her fist until he released her nostrils. He kept a firm hand on her mouth, though.

"I will let you speak if you promise not to make noise. If those men find out we are up here, they will catch us and then Rafael is done for. *¿Sí?* Can you be quiet?"

He released her in response to her nod of agreement. When she was able to breathe normally again, she whispered, "We have to help him."

"There is nothing we can do," came the calm reply.

She faced her attacker for the first time. He lay on the ground behind her, but even so she could see that he was a short, rather round man. Thin, wiry brown hair sprang out of his head in disarray, which was also the way he wore his clothes. He was Mexican, that much was evident from his appearance and his accent.

The gleam in his eyes when he looked at her sent a shudder of unease through her body. They were round and brown and intelligent, completely emotionless. She didn't trust him, but then she turned and looked again at the scene unfolding beneath them, and she knew he was Rafe's only chance for survival, whoever he was.

"Who are they?" she asked.

"Those men? Filth, scum. They have been trailing you since Ubiquitous."

"How do you know?" she asked sharply.

The man smiled a bit sheepishly, revealing a gold-capped tooth. "Because I have been following them."

"Who are you?"

"I am José Carvajal. Rafael and I go way back."

"He mentioned you."

"Of course he did. We are like brothers."

Her attention returned to the canyon. Someone rode up to one of the men who stood over Rafe and dropped a rope to him. He made a loop and dropped it over Rafe's head, careful that he placed his captive's bound arms over the rope. He jerked on the rope but Rafe didn't move. Two other men grabbed him by the arms and dragged him to his feet.

Anne tried to rise, but José grabbed her and held her down. "What are they doing? We have to stop them!"

"There is nothing we can do," he said again.

The other end of the rope was tied to the pommel of the saddle. The leader stepped back and gave the signal, and the rider took the slack out of the rope.

"They're going to drag him! They'll kill him!"

"Be quiet, señorita, or they will hear," José Carvajal urged. "They will not kill him unless he tells them what they want to know. Rafael knows that."

Tears slipped unheeded down her face. If only she could run to him, somehow make them stop. She hated this feeling of helplessness and terror. She fought with all her strength as José dragged her away. He carried her to the other side of the hill and lay on the ground almost on top of her, his hand still covering her mouth.

"It is better that you do not watch, señorita," he said. "There is nothing we can do right now, but Rafael is strong."

She sobbed beneath his hand, quaking with the force of her emotions. How could anyone endure something like that? she wondered. She could only pray that he would.

*   *   *

"You must eat something," the Mexican said between bites of cold beans. He ate them straight from the can because they couldn't chance a fire. The outlaws were still searching for her, or so José claimed.

Huddled in a ball of misery, Anne watched in disgust as he ate with his fingers, licking them clean every now and then. Her gaze swept over the small camp, stopping on two men who sat tied to a tree, their hands and feet bound, their mouths gagged.

She nodded toward the men. "Who are they?"

"Because of them, I wasn't around this morning when Rafael was captured. The older one almost got away from me, and I had to chase him down. He is a comanchero named Diego Muñoz. The boy is Carlos Delgado, the cousin of Rafael's old enemy."

"El Alacrán."

"What do you know about El Alacrán? Rafael told you about him too?"

"Yes."

"I do not believe you."

"Then how would I know about him?" She kept her eyes on the boy, who sat a few feet away, and wondered if he was hungry.

"Rafael would never . . . so what do you know about El Alacrán?"

"He's the one who stole the gold. He set a trap for Rafe once and left him to die in the desert."

"El Alacrán is a very dangerous man because he is loco. Men who are crazy and have power are always dangerous."

"They have been enemies for a long time."

"Rafael made it his business to put an end to El Alacrán's crimes in Texas and New Mexico as soon as he returned from West Point."

"West Point! No wonder—"

"What?"

"He just isn't what he seems to be."

José laughed softly. "He is exactly what he seems to be, señorita. He was *un aristócrata*. His father was a powerful American soldier who married a Mexican woman and settled in New Mexico. Rafael had every privilege. Of course, I didn't know him then. I knew of his family. Everyone knew the Holden y Montalvos."

"But if his father was American, why is his name Montalvo?"

"He changed it after—after the trouble. He took his mother's name."

She looked at Carlos Delgado again. When he caught her eye, he glanced away quickly. "Do you think he's hungry?" she asked.

José shrugged. "So what if he is? He should be dead."

"Dead? Why?"

José threw the bean can on the ground beside him and wiped his hands on his pants. Anne thought she saw dawning comprehension in his gaze, but comprehension of what she couldn't imagine.

"I killed the other two men who were with them. Diego, I figured we could use him to bargain with if we needed to. I took the boy prisoner as a gift for Rafael."

"A gift?" The implication in his words sent a shiver down her spine.

"*Sí.* The boy's life could have settled an old score between El Alacrán and Rafael. But Rafael, he is getting soft."

"But he's just a boy. How—"

"In the old days, Rafael would have killed him." He looked at her with accusing eyes.

"I don't believe you."

José studied her so intently she wondered if her feelings for Rafe were written clearly on her face. Finally, he shrugged. "Believe what you want. It takes a hard man to survive what Rafael has survived. A soft man does not live long in the desert. If you do not want to eat, you can get some sleep. There is only one bedroll."

She cringed at the thought of crawling into a bedroll where this dirty little man had been, but the air was already beginning to grow chilly.

"What about you?" she asked.

"I will see to the horses and then keep watch."

"You've got to sleep sometime."

"And let those bast—and let those outlaws sneak up on us?"

"You take the first watch, then wake me up for the second."

José laughed. "I think not."

She pulled the gun out of her pocket, and José's eyes widened. "*¡Dios!* You had that the whole time?"

"I can use it too." She smiled. "You've got to sleep or you won't be of any use to Rafe."

José glanced at the gun and then back to her face. "*Sí,*" he said, and walked away to take the first watch, but Anne's words halted him.

"If you'd made camp at the top of the hill instead of here with the hill between us and them, we could have watched them from the camp," she pointed out.

"But if I had made camp on top of the hill, they would have been able to hear the horses," he replied. "Get some sleep, señorita, and do not try to outsmart a fox."

Anne crawled into the bedroll but found it impossible to sleep. She kept thinking about Rafe and what he must be going through. She couldn't bear it. Had they fed him? Was he still bound, lying on the hard ground, hungry and cold like the boy who slept nearby? Was he even still alive?

No, she couldn't allow herself to think he might be dead. He was alive, he had to be. He was alive, and tomorrow they would save him.

If she thought she could find her way, she'd go down to that ranch house tonight and find him. . . . And do what? José was right, as much as she hated to admit it. There was nothing they could do right now. They'd have to wait for better odds. She only hoped Rafe could hold out that long. If he died, she would want to die too.

She closed her eyes and rolled onto her side, and the tears came freely. She didn't know how long she lay there before she finally cried herself to sleep.

If Rafe had done one good thing in his life, he just might have saved Annie's life, he thought as he slipped in and out of consciousness. If she'd done what he'd told her, if she'd taken his horse and his money and headed for Las Cruces, she'd make it. There was some satisfaction in knowing that even though he had been unable to save Christina, he had saved Annie. It seemed somehow fitting that he should give his life for her. It would absolve him. If only she made it, it would be worth it.

He welcomed death, even though he hadn't been able to carve El Alacrán's heart out in front of him as he'd planned. El Alacrán's punishment would have to wait for hell, he decided, slipping into a velvet darkness where he dreamed of holding Annie and making love to her and hearing her whisper his name.

*　　　*　　　*

"I'm tellin' you, Frank, he don't know nothin'."

"I say we kill him and. . . ."

Voices floated around Rafe, but he didn't know who was speaking or even where he was. All he knew was that the longer it took him to die, the more time Annie would have to get away. But even though he had told her exactly what to do, he couldn't help feeling betrayed. She'd said she loved him, yet she'd been willing to leave him behind. He knew it was irrational, but all rationality had been long since beaten out of him.

"I've had enough," a disgruntled voice said. "I'm goin' after the woman."

"What makes you think you can?" Braxton said. "No one's been able to find a trace of her."

Rafe smiled, though he wasn't sure if his lips had responded. Good girl, he thought, you got away.

"I'll go back to town. Someone's bound to have seen her leave."

"I'm with Hank." Another voice joined in. "He don't know nothin'. If he did he'd have talked by now."

Braxton watched as more than half his men moved toward their horses. He pulled his revolver and fired into the air, and they halted.

"You can't kill all of us," Hank said.

"No, but I'll start with you." Braxton leveled his pistol and shot Hank dead. The other defectors drew their weapons, and Braxton's men drew theirs.

"We can all kill each other, or you and your boys can put your guns down and let us go peaceably," one of the would-be deserters said.

Braxton stared at him for a long moment, measuring his intent and his determination. Satisfied that he meant to fight to the end, and knowing he and the men who had remained loyal to him were grossly outnumbered, he uncocked his pistol and lowered it.

"Get the hell out of here, then."

Nine of Braxton's thirteen remaining men mounted up and rode off, and he could do nothing but watch in cold fury. Before the dust had settled, he found an outlet for his anger. He walked over to where Rafe Montalvo lay on the ground and kicked him hard in the ribs.

From her vantage point, Anne cringed but Rafe barely moved. "You've got to do something. There are only five of them now," she said to José.

"Unless there are more inside the house. Besides there is only one of me."

"I can help."

Her captor only snorted his dismissal and her anger flared. He had cleaned his gun, and now he lay on the ground close by, reloading it with a calm detachment that made her blood boil. "Are you going to sit here and let them kill him?"

"I am going to wait until the time is right," he said, his attention riveted on the pistol in his hand. "A little patience goes a long way, señorita. You would do well to remember that. I was once young and impetuous too, and I nearly got myself killed many times. Now I am older—not old, mind you, but older—and I know better than to go running into a situation without a plan."

When his words elicited no response from her, he looked up, only to find that she was gone. He lurched forward, looking down into the canyon below, and swore savagely as he watched her ride slowly into camp, her gun drawn.

*   *   *

"He doesn't know where the gold is," Anne said in a clear, strong voice. "I do. Let him go and I'll tell you."

One of them moved toward her, and she shoved her pistol at him. "I wouldn't," she warned.

"I don't believe she'll shoot," another one said.

Anne decided to prove him wrong. Leveling the pistol at him, she pulled the trigger.

The man cried out as the bullet ripped through the flesh of his thigh. He fell to the ground in a shower of curses, rolling around, clasping his injured leg as blood began to seep through his fingers.

"Goddammit, she shot me!"

She screamed as she was grabbed from behind and hauled down from her horse, but another shot rang out and she fell with the man who had grabbed her. She stood quickly, turning to see that he was dead, his eyes staring sightlessly at the sky.

Another man fell as José rode into camp, his pistol blazing, his eyes on fire. She pointed her gun at the man closest to her. He was about to fire at José, having completely discounted her as a threat, and she squeezed the trigger and dropped him.

The man she had hit in the thigh tried to rise, and José finished him off. With the next shot, he wounded the leader, Frank Braxton. She ran toward Rafe. Braxton rose up, injured but not dead. He pointed his gun at Rafe, and Anne screamed and lunged forward.

Rafe screamed too, but the sound ricocheted inside his head. The blood pounded in his brain. He couldn't move. Helplessly he watched as she hurled her body in front of him.

Two shots rang out. He tried to call out to her, to stop her, but his head began to spin, and he passed out knowing that Annie was dead and he had caused it.

17

Rafe knelt on the ground. *The smoke from a burning wagon filled the air and scorched his lungs. He held Annie's head while she vomited.*

When he looked down, she was gone and there was a knife in his hand. He moved it over the rabbit's carcass, peeling back the hide with practiced skill.

"If your knife is very sharp and you are very careful, you can remove the hide in one piece without nicking the inside layer of skin," he heard José's voice saying.

His hands trembled violently, but he managed to hold the rifle steady long enough to squeeze the trigger. A shot exploded, echoing through the empty desert.

He walked through the tall brush around the burning wagon. There was a body, a woman. He had to bury her. He rolled her over and Annie's dead eyes stared up at him.

He was falling through a dark tunnel, nothing to

hold on to, nothing to stop his fall, nothing but cold darkness.

"There was nothing you could do," a voice echoed in the tunnel. "There was nothing you could do."

"I couldn't move," he heard himself reply.

"There was nothing you could do."

Slowly, reluctantly, he woke up. He wanted to go on floating in the tunnel forever. He wanted to be dead, never to wake up again or feel the pain in his gut.

Why, Annie? Why? The question reverberated in his mind, sending him back through memory. He was lying beside her in the grass, caressing her breasts, kissing her soft, sweet lips.

He had to wake up; he had no choice. Though he tried to resist, the light drew him like a magnet. He blinked, opening his eyes to a shower of sunlight pouring in through an open, unadorned window. The light intensified as it bounced off the white adobe walls that surrounded him.

Squeezing his eyes closed tightly, he tried to blot out the memory of Annie throwing herself in front of a bullet intended for him. Thoughts kept tumbling in his mind—that he would never see her again, that she had died for nothing. She had died to save him, a dead man. How could he ever live with that?

"Annie," he whispered through swollen lips.

It was another nail in the coffin that housed his soul. He yearned for death more vehemently than he ever had in his life. Annie was gone, gone forever.

Something tickled his hand. He brushed it aside, only to have it return. He brushed it away again, but it persisted. When he tried to move, pain sliced through his being, consuming him. Lifting his head with an effort, he saw the woman sitting in the chair beside the bed, her body hunched over, her head resting on the bed beside him. He couldn't see her face, but the pale red hair was unmistakable.

Maybe it had all been a nightmare, a terrible nightmare. Or was he dreaming now, dreaming that Annie was alive? If he could just touch her . . .

Despite the pain that made it difficult for him to breathe, let alone move, he managed to lift his arm enough to lay his hand on her head. She stirred and raised herself up. Her eyes were swollen and rimmed with dark circles when she looked at him, but then she smiled and the signs of worry and fatigue seemed to disappear.

She was real. Somehow she was alive. He had so many questions, but he could feel his mind slipping away into the shadows.

Just as the darkness enveloped him again, he thought she had to be the most beautiful woman in the world.

Rafe sat up in bed, his shoulders propped up by a mountain of pillows. Annie dipped the spoon in the bowl of broth and raised it to his mouth, her small hand trembling slightly.

She hadn't done what he'd asked. She'd promised to go to New Mexico if anything happened to him. If she had, he would be dead right now. And wasn't that what he'd wanted? To die?

The spoon touched his lips and he ate obediently, though his eyes remained on her slightly flushed face. She looked tired, his angel of mercy. When she smiled his heart lurched.

She'd told him she loved him, this beautiful, stubborn, indomitable woman, and for a moment he let himself imagine that it was true, that all the years of brutality hadn't eaten away the fabric of his soul. For a moment, he tried to forget there were things she didn't know about him, things that would make her turn her back on him forever. She was light in an infinite darkness, but he wondered if it wouldn't have been better to have never seen the light than to have seen it, only to have it taken away. He'd lost so much already, he didn't know if he could survive another loss.

"Where are we?" he asked, his voice soft and tense.

He closed his eyes tightly, trying not to remember that terrible moment when he'd seen Annie jump in front of a bullet meant for him, the moment he'd known she was dead.

"A deserted ranch house near San Juan Bautista." She wouldn't meet his gaze, and he couldn't help wondering why. She seemed embarrassed, even timid. His throat constricted with an emotion he couldn't name and didn't want to explore.

"How—"

"We—"

"Who is we?"

"José Carvajal and I." She looked at him finally, and he could read her emotions in her eyes. She cared about him, for some reason he couldn't understand. He'd made love to her. He'd been the first. That must be it—infatuation. She'd almost died for him, because . . . because what?

"He helped me get you away from those men and bring you in here," she was saying, but, immersed in his own thoughts, he barely heard her. "He said they knew about the gold."

She pressed the spoon to his lips again and he forgot to eat. He was remembering it all again, that split second before the world had gone black, when he'd seen Annie fall and thought she was dead.

Nothing made sense anymore. He'd wanted to die for her, and she'd nearly died for him. It was more than he could bear to think about, Annie dying for him. What could have prompted her to do such a thing? He wasn't worth it, not worth her life. Nothing was worth Annie's life. She would have died for nothing.

Annie's hand faltered and he gasped as the hot soup spilled on his bare chest. Instinctively, he tried to jerk away, and the movement caused a fiery flash of pain that blazed along his rib cage.

"I'm sorry," she whispered. Setting the bowl down on the bedside table, she reached for a towel and caught the hot trail of soup before it reached the white bandage around his midsection.

She tried to concentrate on her task as she cleaned the spill, but she couldn't help remembering the feel of his chest against hers, the texture of the hairs that curled sparingly across his breastbone. The need to touch him, to kiss him, to assure herself that he was real nearly overwhelmed her. She had almost lost him.

"What happened?" he asked, his voice thick with emotion. "I thought you were dead, Annie. Braxton wasn't dead. I saw you jump in front of his bullet."

"José shot him and Braxton's bullet went wide."

"You could have been killed, Annie. Why would you do something so foolish?"

"I couldn't let him shoot you." She turned her head away from the pain and desolation in his pale eyes.

"Promise me you'll never do anything like that again," he said.

Anne picked up the bowl and turned to face him again.

"Promise me," he repeated.

She reached for the spoon, but he grabbed her wrist. "Promise me."

After dinner, Anne returned to Rafe's room, stopping before the door at the end of the dark corridor. She shifted an armload of sheets to one side so she could knock with her free hand.

Whoever had deserted this place had left behind most of their worldly possessions. José said they'd probably been greenhorns from the East who gave up and went back home.

For some reason it made her sad to think of it, although she could certainly understand. This was a savage, unforgiving land, a place where only the strongest flourished, and everything, even the men and women, had to be prickly in order to survive. Sometimes even that wasn't enough.

If ever a man had thorns, it was Rafe Montalvo. Yet he'd almost died. He knew this land and its hazards, yet it had nearly devoured even him.

He'd been hurt pretty badly. His chest and arms were bruised and cut. Patches of skin had been scraped off his legs. According to José, he'd bruised his ribs. It would take him a while to recover, but recover he would—this time.

He could have been killed. In the darkness of the night while she'd tended him, she had realized she couldn't stand by and watch him die. She couldn't endure another episode like that.

She also believed that he cared for her in his own way. Maybe it would be enough. Maybe she would be able to convince him to give up his quest for vengeance, to just walk away.

When there was no answer to her knock, she pushed the door open and stepped inside.

Rafe sat on the bed, his back to the door. His torso was bare, except for the bandage wrapped around his ribs, stark white against his sun-darkened skin. She walked around to face him, clutching the towels to her chest like a shield.

"You must be feeling better," she said with a smile.

He didn't move, didn't respond. His gaze seemed fixed on some distant object he could see through the window. A steely tension radiated from his body, and she took a step back from its impact.

"I brought you some clean sheets. If you'll sit in the chair . . ."

When he turned to glare at her, the fury in his eyes took her breath away. Pain like a knife twisted in her breast at the contempt in his expression. She wanted to touch him, to say something, to ask why he was so angry suddenly, but she dared not. Violence simmered just beneath the surface calm, and she didn't want to be the one to unleash it.

And then he gazed out the window again as if nothing had happened, his indifference more devastating than his anger.

Shaken and confused, she put the linens on the bedside table and began untucking the sheets. When the time came, she had no doubt he would move to the chair and allow her to complete her task. Besides, she couldn't leave him, not like this, not until she figured out why he'd reverted to a stranger today, a cold, menacing stranger who hated her for no apparent reason.

"Leave it," he said, without turning around.

"But the sheets were on the bed when we brought you here. You've bled on them—"

Without warning, he swung out with his arm, knocking the sheets and the lamp from the nightstand. The lamp shattered and kerosene went everywhere, all over the floor and the bedding.

"Leave me alone!" he growled.

She recoiled from the violence in his voice and the savage bitterness in his eyes. "What's wrong?" she asked. Her heart hammered in alarm. She didn't know whether to flee or stand her ground because she didn't understand what had caused his outburst.

"You should have let me die," he said quietly. "You promised you'd go to my brother if anything happened to me."

"And you promised nothing would happen to you."

"I lied."

"So did I." Her eyes widened as a thought struck her. "Is that it? Are you angry because I injured your stubborn male pride?"

"I told you," he said through clenched teeth, "I'm not angry. Leave me in peace, Annie. You've done enough for me. Now I want you to leave me the hell alone."

She started at the sound of the door opening, though Rafe hardly seemed to notice. José stepped through the portal, shoving Carlos Delgado into the room in front of him. The smile vanished from José's lips as his gaze fell on Anne.

"*Buenas tardes, señorita,*" he said with a nod of his head.

Anne looked from the Mexican to Rafe. "What are you going to do?" she asked, a cold dread clutching her heart.

"Leave us," Rafe said, without looking at her.

"I will not. I want to know—"

"Get out, Annie. Now."

She shivered under the deadly chill of his voice but refused to back down. Was he capable of killing an innocent boy to avenge his wife's murder? She didn't want to believe it, but the merciless glint in his eyes chilled her to the marrow.

"If you do this," she said, her voice trembling, "you'll be no better than El Alacrán."

"José," Rafe demanded, "get her out of here."

"Please! Don't do this! This isn't the way to settle anything!"

José grabbed her arm and hauled her to the door. She turned as they reached the portal and gazed pleadingly into José's hard, cold eyes. "Please. Don't let him do this!"

José said nothing, just shoved her out the door and slammed it shut, turning a key in the lock.

Rafe jerked around at the sound of her fist pounding on the door.

"Damn you!" she cried, her voice barely audible through the thick wood. "Damn you!"

Rafe rose carefully and walked to where the boy stood just inside the door. The naked fear in the youth's wide brown eyes disgusted him.

"You too, amigo, out," Rafe said to José, without taking his eyes from the boy.

"But, amigo—"

"Get Annie away from the door." When José didn't move to comply, Rafe turned a murderous glare at him.

The Mexican backed away, muttering under his breath in Spanish, and opened the door. Anne nearly fell into the room. José grabbed her and backed her through the portal.

"*Please* don't do this!" Anne cried as José dragged her away. "*Listen* to me, Rafe!"

The door closed with a loud crash. Rafe waited for a

few moments until the sound of scuffling moved down the hall and dissipated.

He turned back to the boy. Without a word, he moved to the bureau and retrieved his revolver from its holster. He hated himself for enjoying the sense of power he felt in the boy's fear. Slowly, he started removing cartridges from the gun while the boy watched in mute terror.

As he returned to the boy, he spun the cylinder, saying, "There's one bullet in this gun. Now, I'm going to start pulling the trigger. Who knows when the bullet will come up? Where is your cousin?"

He pressed the gun to the boy's temple. Carlos Delgado squeezed his eyes shut tightly, his entire body convulsing with fear as perspiration beaded on his forehead.

Rafe pulled the trigger and Carlos cried out. His eyes filled with tears that spilled down his cheeks. "Please! Don't kill me!"

"One down and five to go. Answer my question. Where is your cousin?"

"I don't know!"

Rafe pulled the trigger again. "Wrong answer. Four chances left."

Carlos was sobbing now. "You're crazy! Why are you doing this?"

"Ask your cousin, if you live long enough. Now, start talking."

"I can't!"

The hammer clicked again. "The odds are narrowing. Three left."

"He'll kill me if I tell you!"

Again Rafe pulled the trigger. "And I'll kill you if you don't."

"All right, all right, I'll tell you! J-just don't shoot. Don't pull the trigger again. H-he's in Chihuahua."

"City or province?"

"Province."

"Where?"

"I don't know."

Rafe fired again. "Just one left."

"*¡Madre de Dios!* He is north of the city. He has a fortress near the Rio Conchos. He will kill me if he finds out I told you."

Rafe held the gun to the boy's head, his eyes narrowing as Carlos Delgado trembled. He pulled the trigger for the sixth time, and the boy fell to his knees on the floor at the hollow sound of metal against metal.

"You are loco!" he sobbed.

"I must be," Rafe agreed. "Otherwise I would have killed you."

The door to Diego Muñoz's room banged open, flooding the small room with light. He shielded his eyes as Carlos Delgado flew through the opening and landed at his feet. Behind him stood Rafe Montalvo, his face grim.

Without a word, the bounty hunter grabbed Diego by the arm and hauled him toward the door. Stumbling, nearly falling, he struggled to keep his balance with his hands tied behind his back.

They didn't stop until they were outside. Rafe Montalvo dragged him toward the stable, where he spotted his own horse standing outside the wide front doors, saddled and ready to ride.

When they reached the horse, Rafe shoved Diego's chest against the animal and drew a long knife, which he used to slice through Diego's bindings.

"What are you doing?" Diego asked, rubbing his wrists as he turned to face the other man.

"What does it look like? I'm letting you go."

"I don't understand."

"You're going to Chihuahua," Rafe said casually. "I've got a message for El Alacrán, and you're going to deliver it."

"But I don't know where he is," Diego said nervously.

"Well, that's too bad because there's a little town about a day and half's ride from here called Concepción. If El Alacrán isn't there in four days, his cousin's going to die. Maybe I should just kill him now."

"*¡Perro!* If you kill the boy, El Alacrán will kill me."

Rafe smiled. Fear could be a powerful weapon when used correctly. "If you're lucky."

Diego's eyes widened and he paled noticeably.

"Better get going," Rafe said as he sheathed his knife. "You've got a lot of territory to search. Four days, then the boy dies."

"What about my gun?"

"What about it?"

"You can't expect me to leave without it."

"You'll manage."

Diego hesitated, studying Rafe's eyes as if searching for some sign of weakness or mercy. Finding none, he cursed under his breath and swung up in the saddle.

"I'll tell him, amigo. And when El Alacrán finds you, he'll make you sorry you were ever born."

With that, he wheeled the horse around and galloped through the stable yard.

* * *

Rafe rose before dawn the next morning and dressed in the darkness. Then he took up his saddlebags and bedroll, wincing with pain as he straightened up. He was becoming accustomed to the ever-present discomfort. Like the pain in his soul, he was learning to adjust to it.

His horse whinnied softly as he entered the stable. After dropping his saddlebags over the stall door, he petted the animal on the nose, pushed the door open, and led the horse out. Farther down the row of stalls, he found Carlos Delgado's roan and led it out, too.

As he saddled the roan, he thought of Annie with a bittersweet pain. He remembered teaching her to saddle a horse, her tenacity and courage in the face of her fears. He remembered how she'd grabbed the saddle and tried to carry it to the horse, in spite of her weakened condition. Once she set her mind on something, there wasn't a power on earth that could sway her.

Crazy woman, he thought, crazy, stubborn woman.

He didn't want her to care about him. He didn't want anyone to care about him. To care about him was to be in peril. Annie had almost found that out the hard way. To care about him was to embrace a dark, bottomless nothing.

He wasn't worth caring about, couldn't she see that? He'd become an animal, worse than an animal. It made it easier that way to do the things he had to do— to live under the most wretched conditions, to survive when his every human sensibility sought death, to kill.

With a weary sigh, he slipped the bit into the roan gelding's mouth. The mere fact that she cared about him changed everything. He was no longer worthless if she cared about him, if she were willing to die for him. Either that, or she would have died for nothing. He couldn't bear either alternative.

The only thing he knew with any certainty was that he had to get away. He had to put as much distance as possible between them. She made him feel things he didn't want to feel. Better not to feel anything, he decided, than to allow himself to care about her.

It seemed he couldn't cut off a single emotion—such as pain—without shutting them all off. Similarly, he couldn't feel a single emotion—such as joy—without feeling them all, and there were things he never wanted to feel again, ever.

He finished saddling the roan and was throwing the blanket over the chestnut's back when he heard soft, measured footsteps on the hay-strewn floor.

"Running away again?"

18

Rafe closed his eyes as her voice trembled up his spine. He turned slowly to see Annie standing behind him, her face a study in agony and confusion. Swearing under his breath, he turned back to his task before he started remembering everything that had happened between them.

"That's right," he murmured.

She walked slowly toward him. He could hear her movements, though he didn't turn to look at her.

"You were going to leave without even saying good-bye?"

He could tell by her voice that she had come to stand near him. Ignoring the pain in his ribs, he lifted the saddle and swung it up on top of the blanket with a grunt.

"Right again."

"You don't need me anymore," she said to his back,

each word a stone on his heart. "I told you what you wanted to know."

He turned and walked toward her. She retreated until her back met the wall and she could go no farther. Guilt twisted in his heart at the fear in her eyes, but he couldn't stop himself. He couldn't face her questions. He'd hoped to get away without seeing her again. It would have been so much easier that way.

"Right the third time," he said. If he confirmed her accusation, maybe she'd be so hurt and angry that she would leave him alone. "I seduced you. I used you to find out where the gold is, and now that you've told me—"

The crack of her palm against his face almost felt pleasurable. It sobered him, braced him for what he had to do.

"Bastard!" she cried. She drew back to slap him again, but he caught her wrist and held it still.

"You should have believed me, Annie," he murmured against her ear, trying to ignore the softness of her hair and the sweet scent of her flesh. "I am what you see, nothing more." His voice was husky, his body growing hard with desire, despite his best efforts. "You try to see something good in everyone, but sometimes it just isn't there. I'm empty inside. I use people, I kill people, and I just keep on living. I have no conscience."

"I don't believe you," she managed to say, running her tongue over dry lips.

He still held on to her wrist with his left hand. With his right, he clutched her chin, forcing her head back. His lips came down on hers in a brutal kiss that was meant to hurt her and to brand her as his, at the same time. He closed his eyes, struggling against the demons that rose up inside him, trying to capture the feel and taste of her, knowing it was the last time he would ever kiss her.

He ignored her struggles, pushing her against the wall, pinning her with his weight and his strength, crushing her soft breasts with his chest. She gasped for breath, but he would not relent.

She jerked her wrist free, and pressed her hand against his chest, trying with all her might to push him away.

His free hand plunged down into her blouse and closed around a breast. His hips began to move against hers as he caressed a nipple with his thumb and it hardened beneath his touch.

His tongue sought the inside of her mouth but she kept her teeth closed defiantly against him. Her body quivered beneath his; he recognized the first signs of surrender in the softening of her lips and the caress of her hands on his back. It nearly drove him beyond reason. If not for the pain in his midsection, he would have undressed her and taken her right there against the wall.

He stumbled away with a growl as sanity returned to his fevered mind with the force of a bucket of ice-cold water. In just a few moments, he would not have been able to stop himself, in spite of the pain in his battered body, in spite of the pain it would cause in her heart if he made love to her again and then walked out of her life forever. Once was bad enough, but he'd done worse things and managed to live with himself.

"Maybe you're right, Annie," he said, moving back to his horse, feeling defeated and as desperate as he ever had in his life. "Maybe I do have a conscience. Maybe that's the problem."

"You're going after that man, El Alacrán, when you can barely move."

"It's none of your concern."

He reached beneath the horse's belly and found the girth, then worked at securing it. He had to get away from here, from her, from the tears in her voice and the comfort in her arms.

"It *is* my concern. If someone saves your life, you're their slave forever, remember?"

In spite of his grim mood, he smiled, remembering when he'd told her that. "Not in Mexico. Besides, I'd say I'm still one up on you."

Anne reached out and grasped his arm, her touch searing his flesh through the fabric of his shirt. He turned to look at her and winced at the pain in her eyes.

"You could have been killed, and for nothing," he muttered, his voice trembling with emotion.

"For you."

He jerked away. "For nothing. For a dead man. You are everything light and beautiful, and I am everything dark and ugly. I have nothing to live for. You have everything."

"How can you say that? Why can't you let go of whatever is eating you up inside?"

"There is nothing in here," he said, pounding his chest and causing a physical pain that did nothing to lessen the pain in his heart. "That's what I'm trying to tell you, Annie. Your life for mine is not a fair trade. I can't stand the pain of living. Damn you for what you've done!"

"What have I done besides love you?"

He didn't know how to describe it to her, this feeling of powerlessness that possessed him. He didn't know how to tell her that because she was willing to die for him, he now felt a strange obligation to live for her.

"I don't care if I live or die, but you do. You do, and
. . . God, I don't know how to explain it. Your caring
forces me to choose life, or your life becomes meaning-
less. Do you understand?"

"No, I don't understand. I don't understand why you
would want to die or why you would think yourself so
worthless. I know you still love your wife. I know you
still grieve for her, but—"

The laugh that rumbled up from his chest sounded
hollow and maniacal, even in his own ears. "Still? I
never grieved for her. I never had time. I was too busy
trying to survive and forget."

"Forget what?"

Something inside him broke. The hole in the dam
around his emotions had been too long neglected, and
now they burst through in a torrent. He turned on her
with a swiftness and violence that left her no time to
react before he grabbed her by the arms and pushed
her against the wall so hard he heard her breath hiss
between her teeth.

"I killed her," he said, shaking her with every word,
oblivious to the tears that spilled over her long lashes
and trailed down her cheeks. He struggled for breath,
for sanity. "I killed my own wife!"

His whole body shuddered, his breath coming in
great gulps. He released her and she fell back against
the wall, watching him in shock as he stumbled away
and began regaining the control he usually kept over
his emotions.

Her own breath hung suspended in her throat. Her
entire being trembled with dread. She searched his eyes,
but they had turned to stone. "It's not true. You're
lying."

He backed away with an inhuman growl. His face

had gone deathly pale; his gray eyes were as hard as granite. He ran a hand through his hair, and she saw the pain flash across his face as he expelled a ragged breath.

She waited, her heart still, her mind whirling, waited for an explanation, but when none came, she created her own. "You . . . you couldn't save her. You went after them, but you got there too late."

She searched his eyes for confirmation of her words, but there was none.

He turned away with a bleak expression on his face. Returning to his horse, he pushed the right stirrup over the animal's back.

"She was on her way back to Fort Bliss from Las Cruces," he began, his voice so soft she had to strain past the thundering of her own pulse to hear. "She'd been visiting my brother."

His powerful back expanded and contracted as he took a deep, painful breath. It was a long time before he spoke again, and as the brittle silence stretched on, she realized he'd been transported. He was reliving the past now.

"She was traveling under military guard, as always," he finally continued. "But that didn't matter to El Alacrán and his men."

They had abducted his wife, Anne knew. They had abducted her and killed her. Rafe hadn't been able to save her. That was the source of his guilt. She closed her eyes, trying not to imagine the horror of being kidnapped by men whose brutality knew no bounds. How terrified his wife must have been, how profoundly helpless.

Her skin crawled as she tried not to think of the things they must have done. She looked up and met his gaze, knowing he could read her thoughts on her face. The expression in his eyes confirmed her worst fears and spoke of things beyond her realm of understanding.

"Christina and her escort were late arriving at the fort," he went on, his voice soft and calm, though the muscles in his neck strained to the breaking point.

Turning back to the saddle, he worked the girth strap through the metal ring.

"The day after they were supposed to arrive, I took a party and we scoured the road from Las Cruces."

He gave one last jerk to the cinch.

"When I arrived at the scene of the ambush, one of the soldiers was still alive. He'd been scalped, but he was still alert enough to tell me that El Alacrán and his comancheros had taken Christina with them."

He turned to face Anne again with the eyes of a man who has seen things no one should have to see.

"They crossed into Mexico," he said quietly, his voice taut. "The rules had changed since the last time. He knew the army wouldn't pursue, and he knew I would."

The muscle in his jaw tensed and flexed as he paused to rein in his emotions.

"And I did, even though I knew it would mean a court-martial. I trailed them through the desert for days."

She didn't know if she wanted him to continue. Moisture beaded on his forehead and he wiped it away with his sleeve, the motion causing him to wince in pain. His chest rose and fell with labored, rhythmic breathing. The violence in his eyes terrified her, but she knew she couldn't stop him now that he had begun.

"I kept coming across scraps of her clothing along the way." His voice trembled and nearly broke, as a shudder ripped through him.

"They wanted to make sure I didn't lose them. By the time I found her I was wild with fear and worry and anger."

Anne slid down the wall and sat on the floor, unable to support her own weight any longer, clenching her fists until her nails bit into the flesh. But the pain did nothing to protect her from the impact of his words. Tears rolled down her cheeks and dropped unheeded to her blouse.

"They'd left her in the back of the wagon they'd stolen when they took her," he said, his voice coarse and dry like desert wind.

He'd begun to massage his wrists in an unconscious gesture. She doubted he even knew she was there as he continued to relive the horror of that day.

"The sky was full of buzzards." He covered his ears with his hands as if to block out the sound. "I've never seen so many in one place," he added, shaking his head in wonder.

He raised his gaze toward the ceiling as if he could see them hovering overhead, watching, waiting. Then he dropped his hands from his ears.

"There must have been thirty or more."

Rafe looked back down at Anne. Nothing was left of the mask he had worn so carefully to hide his emotions. Lines of strain creased the corners of his mouth. A naked torment shone in his eyes, the eyes of a wounded animal.

"She was alive," he said softly, as if he still couldn't quite believe it.

There was a long fragile silence. His whole body seemed to slump. Anne had to strain to hear his words. His dead voice chilled her.

"Somehow, I don't know how, she was alive. They

. . . they'd skinned her . . . . They'd skinned her alive from the neck down."

His words shattered her. A sob broke through her control and her body convulsed in reaction, trembling with horror at the images that flashed in her mind. She swallowed the bile that rose in her throat. She wanted to cry or run away or cover her ears and pretend he hadn't said it, pretend she hadn't heard. . . . It hadn't happened. It couldn't have. Things like that didn't happen.

"They were so careful," he went on, in a voice that trembled slightly.

"Please stop." Tears trailed down her cheeks, and she covered her ears to block out his words.

He reached her in two strides. He took her by the wrists, hauling her to her feet, pulling her roughly against him. She shrank inwardly from the awesome devastation in his eyes.

"They'd skinned her alive," he said between clenched teeth. "Is your curiosity satisfied now? I didn't know what to do. I don't remember how it happened, but I had my rifle in my hands. I raised it and put a bullet in her head."

"Let me go," she whimpered. "I don't want to hear—"

"It was a trap. They captured me and staked me out in the desert to die, and I would have died if not for José. The buzzards, they were in such a frenzy—"

She screamed to drown out his words.

He shook her viciously, grinding out his words. "Not a night goes by that I don't think of her eyes staring at me as I pulled the trigger."

He released her and she fell against the wall. Then he walked to his horse, lifted the bridle, and slipped the bit into the animal's mouth.

"You didn't have any choice," she whispered. She felt too battered inside to offer more.

"Don't," he said, his back stiffening. "I had a choice. I had a lot of choices and I made all the wrong ones, and an innocent woman paid a terrible price for my stupidity. I thought I could change the world. I thought I could crush a man like El Alacrán. I was a fool. You have to think like an animal in order to kill one, and that is what I have learned to do."

She walked up behind him and placed a trembling hand on his shoulder. She felt the shudder that ran through him before he jerked away.

"Don't, Annie," he growled. "For God's sake, don't."

He pushed her hand away, struggling for control. He fastened the strap on the bridle and ran a sleeve across his face.

"Let her go," she whispered, fighting her tears. "Killing El Alacrán won't change anything. Can't you see this is destroying you?"

His face was a mask of anguish and self-loathing. "Why couldn't you have let me die? Why couldn't you have done what I told you to do and left me behind?"

"Because I love you."

He smiled, the most bitter, hollow smile she had ever seen. "Annie, you can't love someone who's dead."

Slowly he led the horses from the barn.

She stumbled toward the open door and collapsed. Her head spinning, she clutched the door frame for support. A terrible ache filled the very depths of her being, as if her body and soul had been turned inside out, exposing all her emotions, all her nerve endings. She struggled for air as she watched him stride across the stable yard.

He left the horses tied to the hitching post before the house and went inside. He was going to get Carlos Delgado, she knew.

She closed her eyes to block out the pain, but all she could see was Rafe lifting a rifle, sighting down the barrel, killing the woman he loved. He'd had to do it, but she knew that hadn't made it easier.

Easier? Dear God, the horror of finding someone you loved in that condition would be enough to destroy anyone, and then to have to end her life to end the pain, the unbearable, unimaginable pain.

She should follow him, stop him, but she couldn't. She could hardly move, and even if she could, she knew he would never listen to her. He was going to meet his destiny, and there was nothing she could do.

She felt a spasm of agony in her heart as she thought of where he was going. He was going to meet El Alacrán, the monster who had shattered his life with an act of unspeakable violence.

Skinned alive!

He had said he couldn't forget Christina's eyes, so she had been conscious when he found her, conscious and aware that there was nothing left for her but agony and death, nothing to keep her company but her own tormented soul.

Anne shook her head to dispel the unbearable images. What would be worse, to be the victim or to be the one who found her? Christina's pain was over; she was dead. But Rafe had had to live on.

She took a deep, ragged breath that ended in a sob. The memory had haunted him all these years. He hated himself for what he'd done, hated himself for failing Christina, for not saving her. She wanted to comfort him, to tell him it wasn't his fault.

How could he have known? Until that hideous day, how could he have known that men were capable of such horrors?

He was going to die, she knew with a sickening certainty. He hadn't been speaking figuratively when he'd called himself a dead man. Her blood ran cold as she realized what he planned to do, what he had always planned to do. He would kill El Alacrán and die in the process.

Her control broke and she began to weep, silently, bitterly. It didn't matter that he wasn't fit to meet his nemesis. He didn't expect to survive—or want to. All he wanted was to make certain he sent El Alacrán to hell.

The world seemed to be collapsing around her. Rafe emerged from the house with Carlos Delgado in tow, his hands bound behind his back and a gag in his mouth.

Rafe forced him to mount one of the horses before he swung up into the saddle himself. She watched them ride away until they were nothing more than a faint puff of dust on the horizon.

19

Concepción shimmered in the heat reflected from the desert sand. A slight breeze stirred a cloud of dust and sent a tumbleweed careening down the street. A single buzzard circled high in the sky, its screeching the only sound in the stillness.

El Alacrán held up a hand as he and the dozen men with him neared the edge of town. The place was quiet, empty, deserted, yet he could feel the pressure of eyes upon him. The hairs on his arms and neck prickled as he guided his horse into town. He looked up at a second-floor window of the deserted cantina, but he saw nothing beyond the dirty glass windowpanes.

Both sides of the street were lined with squat adobe buildings, one not much different from another, with high windows and open doors and crumbling staircases. At the far end of town stood a small church, its once-white walls now faded and dirty, one of the bells missing from the twin arches above the front door.

A movement caught his eye, and he swung his head to the left, noticing a wooden structure at the far end of the street near the church.

"What is that?" one of his men asked.

"A gallows," said Diego Muñoz, who rode beside him. "He built a gallows. In less than three days he built a gallows—alone."

"We will hang him on it!" El Alacrán laughed loudly, and most of his men joined in.

Diego Muñoz remained sober. "It's not empty."

A shiver of apprehension traveled down El Alacrán's spine, but he managed to subdue it.

"Carlos!" He let out an animal growl and spurred his horse forward, but before he could make any progress, a bullet whizzed past his head so close he could feel the air on his cheek.

Bullets riddled the ground in front of the horses and the riders pulled back fiercely on the reins. Through a cloud of dust, he saw Carlos on the gallows. Another shot resounded and the trap door beneath his cousin fell away.

"No!" El Alacrán bellowed.

Carlos's legs dangled in the air. He kicked frantically, screaming at the top of his lungs. His wrists were tied above his head to the same beam as the noose.

The chaos subsided and quiet reigned. El Alacrán searched the upper windows in all the buildings but could see nothing. Sweat beaded on his forehead, and his gut twisted in helpless fury. There was a cat-and-mouse game going on here, only this time he was the mouse instead of the cat, and he didn't like it one little bit.

"Come out, *cobarde*," he shouted.

"I don't see anything," Diego whispered.

"He said—he said—" Carlos shouted haltingly as he struggled to take the pressure off his throat, "he said he'll kill me if—if you don't tell your men to leave town. He said—he said he wants you alone. Help me, *primo!*"

Rage smoldered inside El Alacrán, impotent fury. He clenched his teeth and weighed his options. He had none.

"You heard him," he snarled. "Leave me."

"But jefe—"

Another gunshot rang out. Carlos screamed, and one of his hands came loose. He coughed and choked, struggling to pull himself up.

Instinctively, El Alacrán urged his horse forward and another bullet whirred past his ear, this one taking his hat off. Trembling with anger and frustration, he watched as Carlos managed to take the pressure off his neck by grabbing hold of the rope that bound his other wrist and pulling himself up. He couldn't hang on like that for long.

"Get out," he murmured to his men in tight rage. This *picarón* had the upper hand.

El Alacrán had the advantage of superior numbers, but as long as Carlos's life was at stake, there was precious little he could do but play along—for now.

"But—"

"Now! Go!" he shouted, then added more quietly, "Watch. You will find a chance to move back in. I am depending on you."

Diego swallowed convulsively. "*Sí*, jefe."

He wheeled his horse around and signaled to the others, and they moved back up the street to the perimeter of the town.

El Alacrán looked around him but still saw no one. "What now, Rafael?" he called out.

He waited for several minutes, always conscious of Carlos dangling from the hangman's noose. When there was no answer, he nudged his horse forward, moving slowly up the street toward the gallows.

The lone church bell began to ring, stark and eerie in the desert silence. El Alacrán smiled as he drew even with the gallows, in spite of the grimness of the moment. Rafael was in the church. He was trapped, whether he knew it or not. He would never get out alive.

No one outsmarted the Scorpion. Rafael should have learned that.

The ringing of the bell subsided. El Alacrán dismounted, his gaze fixed on the door of the church as he took a step toward Carlos.

"He booby-trapped the gallows," Carlos told his cousin. "If you try and cut me down, we'll both die."

Two gunshots exploded as the rope around Carlos's neck and the one around his wrist broke and he fell through the open trap door to the ground below.

He scrambled to his feet, tearing the noose from around his neck. He didn't move toward El Alacrán but stood beneath the gallows, massaging his wrists.

"He said if I didn't hang, I was to walk down that street to the edge of town and not come back."

"Go, *primo*," El Alacrán said.

Carlos walked past his cousin, then turned around to face him again. "Did you do it? Did you do what he says you did to his wife?"

El Alacrán faced him unblinkingly. His expression hardened, and his eyes took on a maniacal glint. "This is not your fight. There are things you can't understand. It will soon be over. As soon as you are safely with the men, I want them to surround the church. Tell them."

Carlos studied his cousin's visage for a long moment before turning and running up the street.

"Wide is the gate and broad is the road that leads to ruin."

El Alacrán looked up to the bell tower above. Rafael Montalvo stood leaning against a wall, his hat pulled down over his face so his features were indiscernible. A flame ignited as he struck a match and lighted a cheroot.

"Narrow is the gate and hard is the way that leads to life," Rafael went on. "In case you had other ideas, I'd go in through the front door if I were you."

El Alacrán glanced briefly over his shoulder to see that his men still waited at the end of town. When he looked back at the bell tower, Rafael was gone.

"¡Perdición!" El Alacrán ran a sleeve over his sweat-soaked brow. He told himself it was foolish to be uneasy. He had nearly fifteen men behind him. As soon as he walked through that door, they would move in. There was nothing to worry about.

As he pushed the door open, he heard an explosion that seemed to come from behind the church. Fire sped toward him around both sides of the building, two flaming paths that met behind him. Acrid smoke burned his eyes and caused him to cough. Quickly he stepped inside and closed the door behind him.

Just inside the door, he paused, blinking until his eyes adjusted to the dimness, focusing on the man at the front of the church. Rafe sat on the altar, tapping his left foot, resting his left arm on his bent knee.

As the comanchero walked slowly up the middle aisle of the church, Rafe studied him closely. El Alacrán had changed little over the past five years. He was tall and lean and clothed in silver-studded black. His aquiline features and high sharp cheekbones proclaimed the Apache blood that flowed in his veins. The cruel edge to the mouth was unmistakable.

In a flash, Rafe's mind sent him back five years to the desert. He was staked out on the ground, his body naked, the sun already beginning to sear his flesh. He was crazy with horror and fury and self-loathing. He could hardly see past the sweat that trickled into his eyes, the sun that glinted off the belt buckle of the man who knelt beside him.

"You are lucky, my *inexperto niño.*" El Alacrán's face had loomed over him, his lips curved in a demonic smile. There were other men there who had beaten him and stripped him and staked him to the ground, but they seemed inconsequential. Now there was only one: El Alacrán. His face was emblazoned on Rafe's mind for all time.

"I don't want to kill you, *pequeño.* I only want to warn you. I'll even leave water for you." He laughed. Rafe turned his head to see the canteen on the ground ten feet to his right. . . .

El Alacrán's laughter followed Rafe back to the present.

"Rafael—*¡mi compañero!*" El Alacrán exclaimed, taking another step toward him. "Your mother would be proud of you. You ride into town and the first thing you think of is going to church. I see you have been expecting me. I am impressed with your cleverness. A ring of fire? How—?"

"Not that it matters," Rafe said calmly, "but Concepción used to be a mining town. Sulfur. They manufactured gunpowder in a factory not five miles from here."

El Alacrán laughed. "Very clever."

Silence stretched between them as they measured each other. Rafe had learned a great deal about judging

an opponent since the last time he'd seen El Alacrán.
He'd learned how to read a man's eyes to determine
how far he would go, how crazy he was or how frightened. The eyes he examined now held no fear, but he
could see flashes of madness in their onyx depths, and
he stifled a shiver. The madness did not block out the
intelligence, however, and the two were doubly dangerous when taken together.

"Rafael." El Alacrán tried to appear self-assured and
completely in control, but Rafe sensed an uncertainty
in his manner, as if he knew the man before him now
was every bit his match. "You have been trailing me for
five long years. You have managed to kill many of my
most trusted men. Now we are finally face to face, just
the two of us. Don't you have anything to say to me?"

When Rafe didn't reply, El Alacrán continued.

"You are alone. As honorable as ever, I see. You have
come to settle things with me, no? Rafael, haven't you
learned? Look at you. You have nothing. No wife, no
home, no money—nothing. Even the army has turned its
back on you. Then look at me. I have prospered greatly
since last we met. Honorable men die young."

"I have come here to die," Rafe said evenly. "Haven't
you figured that out? A man who doesn't care if he lives
or dies is a dangerous man."

El Alacrán laughed. "A brave man, too. Cowardice was
never your shortcoming. Recklessness, perhaps. But
your true shortcoming, the one which has destroyed
you, is that there are things you care about more than
your own life. You cared what happened to your beautiful wife. You even care what happens to a girl you
hardly know, a nobody. Yes, I can see that you are harder
now, stronger. But you cannot be ruthless, Rafael. You
cannot be ruthless."

A sudden explosion rocked the building and El Alacrán jerked around, surveying the balcony and church rafters until he realized the sound had come from outside.

"I may not have learned much about desert survival at West Point, but I learned a great deal about weapons and ammunition," Rafe said evenly. "Black gunpowder makes one hell of an explosive. They should have stayed out of town. There are charges scattered everywhere."

Another charge exploded, as if to confirm Rafe's words. El Alacrán's eyes widened, the first sign of fear he'd shown. Rafe relished it.

Rafe inclined his head toward a sound from above. He surveyed the landing, and though he saw nothing, he knew someone was there. One of El Alacrán's men had made it inside through the roof, something Rafe had anticipated. That was why he had decided to wait on the altar. He could see the entire landing from his vantage point.

A movement overhead caught Rafe's eye at the same time that the church door flew open and a shot felled the man on the landing. Drawing his pistol, he shot a second man who fell over the rail into the pews below. He whirled around as El Alacrán pulled his gun, and both men dove for cover in opposite directions.

Rafe wrapped an arm around his rib cage to ease the pain as he crawled between a row of pews toward the wall, his heart pounding, the blood rushing through his veins. He knew he had to guard his back and keep out of sight while he figured out what was happening. He'd shot only one of the men on the landing, and he'd be dead right now if someone else hadn't shot the other. He didn't need to be distracted by trying to figure out the identity of the shooter. He needed to concentrate on El Alacrán.

A scraping sound reached his ears. It came from behind him. He leveled his gun in the direction of the noise, but he couldn't fire. He waited, knowing that a second's hesitation could mean the difference between life and death, but also knowing that the other person in the church might be José . . . or Annie.

Had they followed him? What other explanation could there be?

The sound of staccato gunfire outside the church reached Rafe's ears, and in the next instant a head popped out from between two rows of pews close by.

"Annie," he murmured as she slid along the wall toward him. "What the hell are you doing here?"

There was no time for a reply. This time when Rafe heard something dragging along the floor, he knew it was El Alacrán. He peered over the backs of the pews, ducking back down to avoid a bullet.

The shot ricocheted harmlessly against a wall. As Rafe fired back, El Alacrán dove for cover.

"Shit!" Rafe swore. "Goddamn you, Annie, why the hell did you come here?"

"If I hadn't, you'd be dead."

When Rafe raised up to shoot again, El Alacrán was ready for him once more. The bullet whizzed by Rafe's head; then he returned fire. He had barely ducked again when Annie fired, and he heard the comanchero swear viciously.

"You saved my life again," Rafe said, but there wasn't a shred of gratitude in his tone.

"I guess we're even now."

"Rafael!" El Alacrán laughed, the sound bouncing off the wall. "Since you can't keep your women alive, you have decided to arm them so they can defend themselves, I see. Does this one know what happened to the last one?"

Rafe took advantage of the opportunity to get off a shot, taking El Alacrán off guard, but the other man still managed to dodge.

"Señorita, did he tell you what happened to his wife? He was too busy playing soldier to take care of her. She had to go to his brother for love!"

Anne gazed at Rafe. He had gone still, except for the flexing of the muscle in his jaw. He turned toward her, but she could read nothing in his expression, nothing but fury and hatred.

"She used to travel the road between El Paso and Las Cruces regularly, remember, Rafael? A dangerous stretch of road. You should have prevented her from going so often. But I guess you were too busy being a soldier to notice."

"Where is José?" Rafe whispered anxiously.

"Outside," Anne replied in the same hushed tone. "There were other men—"

Rafe held up a hand to silence her.

"Señorita," El Alacrán called, his voice coming from a slightly different direction. "You need a real man. I know how to treat a woman, don't I, Rafael? Rafael has led you into a trap. He will not escape with his life, but you—I plan to take special care with you. I wonder if you will scream like the other one?"

His words struck Anne's soul like hailstones. She struggled for breath, fought against the panic welling up inside her. She had to stay lucid and reasonable for Rafe.

Rafe started to rise, but Anne laid a calming hand on his arm and he turned to look at her, his eyes wild with rage. She shook her head, her hand caressing his arm. Slowly the murderous glint in his eyes faded and he nodded, assuring her that he was again under control.

A shudder ran through him as he imagined what El Alacrán could do to Anne if given the chance. Despite the way she handled a gun, she was no match for El Alacrán and his kind.

Rafe knew that if he died, Anne would be destroyed. He had to think. When he'd set his elaborate trap, escape had not been a part of his plan. All he'd known was that he would kill El Alacrán, and whether he himself survived or not didn't matter. Now he had to think of a way to get them out of this, even if it meant that his vengeance would have to wait.

"Did he tell you that he killed his wife, señorita? He shot her in the head with a rifle. One shot through the brain."

The direction of El Alacrán's voice told Rafe that the comanchero was moving along the opposite wall toward the door in an effort to trap them in the church. He didn't know about the back door. But even though El Alacrán couldn't trap them, Rafe didn't want to let him out of the church where he might escape.

Rafe grabbed Anne by the hand and dragged her along the wall, trying to be as quiet as possible. El Alacrán fired his gun, and Anne screamed when the bullet nicked the wall only a few inches from her head.

Rafe jerked her down and they huddled in the aisle near the wall. He held her close and felt her heart beating furiously against his chest. He could hear the terror in the way she gasped for breath and he silently cursed her for being here. He wanted to berate her nearly as much as he wanted to comfort her, but there wasn't time for either.

"Annie," he whispered, "do as I say for once. Stay here and keep your head down." His arm tightened around her trembling shoulders before he released her. "I don't know where José is—if he's even alive. But, Annie, if I die . . ."

He hesitated at the tremor that ran through her body. How could he tell her that her only choice might be to end her own life or face unspeakable torture and inevitable death at the hands of El Alacrán? He looked into her dark pansy eyes, perhaps for the last time. It tore his soul apart to think of her dead, and he couldn't even contemplate what might happen to her if she lived and he did not. But she lifted her face and looked into his eyes and he knew she understood.

Reaching behind her neck, she lifted a gold chain and lowered it over Rafe's head. He dropped the locket that dangled from the chain down the front of his shirt, touching a finger to her lips. She closed her eyes as he slipped away down the aisle toward the front of the church.

Rafe fell to the floor as two bullets struck the pews closest to him, splintering wood. El Alacrán fired again, and he ducked out of the way. This time the shot struck wood behind him and he heard Annie gasp.

"Stay down, Annie!" he cried.

"Annie!" El Alacrán called.

Anne fought the nausea that rose in her throat at the sound of her name on the comanchero's lips. She shivered as she fought for control. There was something horrific about this man—this monster who was capable of skinning an innocent woman alive, leaving her to suffer so that her husband could find her and kill her— knowing her name, speaking her name.

"You can live if you come to me now, Annie," El Alacrán said. "Follow my voice. I'll get you out of here. I am a wealthy man. A million dollars can buy a lot of happiness."

Someone cursed and Rafe heard what must have been a gun hitting the floor and a fist hitting flesh.

"Annie!" he cried. "No!"

The scuffling stopped. Rafe's heart pounded like a drum in his ears as he waited, dread twisting in his gut. What had she done?

"Rafael! I'm coming out! Don't shoot or you might miss and hit your friend!" It was El Alacrán's voice.

"Amigo, don't shoot!"

Rafe cursed with relief at the sound of José's voice. He collapsed against the wall, his lungs filling with air, his eyes filling with tears.

He stood when he felt steady enough, his gun hand hanging at his side, as El Alacrán straightened and walked toward him shielded by José's body. The comanchero held a pistol to José's temple and was smiling in triumph.

"Don't worry, José," El Alacrán said. "Rafael is a man of honor. He would never let you die."

"I thought you were outside," Rafe said, playing for time.

"I came in through the back door, amigo. You should have been more careful. One of the explosions shook the lock loose."

"Drop your gun, Rafael," El Alacrán warned. He walked toward Rafe, his eyes never leaving his enemy's.

Rafe knew he'd be a dead man as soon as he dropped his gun. As long as he held onto it, there was hope, hope for Annie. If he had to sacrifice José for Annie . . .

"What are you going to do with so much gold?" Rafe asked. "There's enough for all of us."

"One can never have enough gold, Rafael." El Alacrán laughed. "Drop your gun—now."

"I told you he was a greedy bastard," José said. "Shoot him, amigo. You can hit him. Shoot him."

"José will be dead before you can lift your arm," El Alacrán assured Rafe.

"Well, the way I see it, we're all dead either way," Rafe reasoned.

The comanchero shrugged. "But perhaps I will let this one live and it will go easier for your woman. I will take excellent care of her, Rafael, you can depend on it."

El Alacrán cursed as a shot exploded to his left. He grabbed his arm and blood immediately began seeping between his fingers. José took advantage of the moment, falling to the floor.

The comanchero turned, the gun still in his right hand as he gripped his left arm. He gazed at the woman who stood pointing a pistol at him.

Anne squeezed the trigger and the loud click told her that she had run out of bullets. A smile spread over El Alacrán features.

"Felipe!" Rafael called sharply, using El Alacrán's given name.

His gaze still fixed on Anne, El Alacrán lowered his gun hand to his side. "*Perdición,* Rafael, I forgot she had a gun."

In the blink of an eye, El Alacrán whirled around toward Rafe and raised his gun again. Rafe fired and the Mexican fell to the floor with a loud thud.

The pistol slipped from Anne's numb fingers.

"*¡Ay, Jesús!*" José cried, struggling to stand and wiping the dust from his pants. "You could have killed me! What made you so sure you could hit him?"

"I wasn't," Anne replied, her gaze on Rafe as he moved slowly toward the prone form of El Alacrán. "But I knew it was our only chance."

"*¡Dios!* I could be dead right now!"

Anne hardly heard him. Her attention was riveted on Rafe as he knelt beside El Alacrán. He reached down and rolled the comanchero over, placing a finger against the jugular vein.

Rafe's body slumped, and all the life seemed to drain from him as he lowered his head, and closed his eyes.

The very fiber of his life seemed to be unraveling. He reeled slightly, disoriented, confused. El Alacrán was dead—too quickly dead—and he, Rafael, was still alive. He looked at the gun in his hand, the gun that had killed El Alacrán. It hadn't happened as he'd planned it at all.

"Goddamn you, Annie," he said. Fury rose in his throat, choking him. "Why couldn't you stay out of it?"

"I . . . I did it for you," she murmured behind him, but he barely heard the words through the fog of rage that slowly enveloped him.

He leaped away from the hand that touched his elbow and turned, grabbing her by the shoulders, shaking her hard, not caring if he hurt her. "If you wanted to do something for me, you should have stayed at the ranch like I told you!"

"Rafael!" José cut in, but a look from Rafe quieted his protest. "There is a wagon outside. I'll hitch two horses to it. The gold, señorita, where is it?"

Anne kept her gaze on Rafe as she replied. "Behind the altar. There are some loose boards: a secret compartment, I think."

José moved away toward the front of the church.

"If we hadn't come, you'd be dead," Anne said, drawing his gaze back to her tear-streaked face.

"Did it ever occur to you that I wanted to die?"

He flung her away from him and turned, running a hand through his hair.

"Yes, it occurred to me," she murmured, massaging her shoulder where his fingers had clutched her. "But I couldn't let—"

"You had no right to interfere! This had nothing to do with you! You made me kill him too quickly. I had plans for El Alacrán, and you ruined them!"

Something inside him broke. Rafe struck out viciously, kicking the corpse in the side.

"Filthy bastard!" He kicked the corpse again and again.

"Rafe, stop! He's dead!"

He glared at her.

Anne took a deep, steadying breath and wiped at the tears that slipped silently from the corners of her eyes. "You killed him. It was what you wanted."

He holstered his pistol and walked toward the door without looking at her.

"Where are you going?" she asked, her voice trembling.

"*¡Madre de Dios!*" José's voice boomed in the sanctuary. "Just as you said! More gold than a man can count!"

Rafe stopped but didn't look at Anne. She could see the tightened jaw muscle and the clenched hand at his side. "You got your gold."

He halted just outside the door at sight of Carlos Delgado. He was the only one of El Alacrán's men still alive, and he was standing near the bottom of the stoop with a revolver in his hand.

"I don't want to kill you, boy," Rafe said softly.

Carlos dropped the gun and took a step back. "The killing stops here today."

Rafe nodded and strode past the boy. Anne ran to the door and watched as he swung up into the saddle and galloped away.

Epilogue

Rafe watched the sun set behind the brick and stucco mission on the dusty road to Las Cruces, wondering how he'd come to be here and why he couldn't just turn and ride away.

He hadn't meant to come here. For the past six months, he'd drifted aimlessly in Mexico, but there was nothing there but memories, all of them painful. The setting sun had drawn him like a magnet until he'd found himself at the place where the Rio Grande turned north into New Mexico and he'd known where he had to go.

Uncertainty gnawed at his gut. He had no idea what he would find here, how he would be received. The last time he'd been ordered never to return.

He nudged his horse into a slow walk, postponing the moment of confrontation. What would he say? How could he begin to explain? Would he get the chance?

As he rode his horse through the open gates, a dog barked close by, announcing the arrival of a stranger. Dismounting before the priest's quarters, he looped the reins over the hitching post and stared at the hard, silent door. Part of him wanted to turn and ride away, but he knew that whatever had brought him here would give him no peace until he faced up to his past.

He stood at the door, afraid to knock, afraid not to. His gaze moved to the church across the way. He'd attended mass in that church as a boy, and he'd been married there.

He scowled. The past was better left buried, he well knew. He'd been a fool to come. He turned away and was taking a step toward his horse when the door opened.

"Did you want something, my son?"

The voice of the man behind him made him shiver. He closed his eyes against memory and pain and turned slowly to face the speaker.

"Hello, Michael," he said.

Michael Holden hadn't changed at all in the past five years. Tall and slim like their mother, Michael's features bore the unmistakable mark of their Latin blood: pitch-dark hair, deep brown eyes, dark skin that appeared even darker in contrast to the white collar around his neck.

"Or should I call you Father Michael?"

Michael frowned, then his face relaxed in recognition. "Rafael," he whispered.

Rafe didn't move. He stood watching his brother's face, so like his own yet so different. He tried to gauge his brother's reaction while his own blood pounded with both hope and dread.

Father Michael Holden expelled a breath. "It is you."

Rafe ran a hand across two weeks' growth of beard,

realizing how unkempt he must appear. Michael had always been so clean and fastidious.

"You look well," Rafe said, because he couldn't think of anything else.

When last he had seen Michael, his brother had been a novice. Rafe had heard he had taken vows and become the priest at the mission. And even though he had never doubted it, he had not been able to picture Michael in austere black, a white collar around his neck. At least he wasn't wearing robes at this hour.

Michael didn't reply. In his eyes, Rafe saw pain and a deep sadness. The lines on his face seemed to deepen as he stepped toward Rafe and threw his arms around him. Hesitantly, Rafe returned the gesture, his arms going around his brother in an awkward embrace.

"I can't believe it's you!" Michael exclaimed. "I can't believe you've come back!"

"Neither can I."

The two men pulled apart, staring at each other for several moments before Michael seemed to remember himself. "Come inside, Rafael. Come inside. We have a lot of catching up to do. Has it been five years since . . . ?"

"Since you ordered me off the mission." Rafe stopped at the door and Michael turned to face him with a ragged sigh.

"I was a little crazy. Please forgive me. I've had a lot of time to think things over. Will you come in?"

Michael sat in a chair beside a large window in the parlor, his white collar on the small table beside him. He stared at the piano against the opposite wall with a faraway glint in his eyes. "She used to come to the ranch for the music. You knew that. We both loved music. Did you ever hear her play?"

His heart a knot of emotion lodged at the base of his throat, Rafe stared into the glass of amber liquid in his hand before taking a sip. "No, I . . . I guess I never had time."

"She had a natural gift." Michael shifted his weight nervously, then turned to look at Rafe. "I loved her, you know. Not . . . not like a man loves a woman— although if I hadn't already chosen the priesthood, and if she hadn't been your wife—I loved her as a sister. It hurt . . . it hurt when she died."

Rafe walked to the piano and touched a low key. "You blamed me. I blamed myself."

"I was crazy with grief. She was traveling home from a visit to me at the ranch. I guess I needed someone to blame besides myself."

"I guess we were both a little crazy. I said some things—"

"I blamed you because I didn't understand," Michael interrupted.

"I'm not so sure. You were right about one thing: I was too damned busy. I should have—you made her happy in a way I never could. I was too obsessed with chasing—"

"She loved you, Rafael."

"I know. She loved you too."

Silence stretched between them, silence accentuated by the soft ticking of a clock. Rafe turned his glass up and drained it, wondering what to say. He crossed the room and stood behind Michael, gazing out the window, though the glass only reflected his own image.

"Did she suffer?" Michael asked haltingly. "I mean, those men: I know what they were capable of."

Without volition, Rafe dropped a hand to his brother's shoulder. "No, *mi hermano,* she did not suffer." He walked to the sideboard and placed his glass beside the sparkling bottle of liquor. "It's getting late."

"You can stay in the guest room upstairs. It's not luxurious, but it should be comfortable."

"Thank you." Rafe made his way toward the staircase and was halfway up when his brother's voice halted him.

"Rafael," he called quietly, "I heard you'd become a bounty hunter."

Rafe faced him and waited.

"It shows in your eyes," Michael continued. "Death . . . and guilt, I think. God has forgiven you. It is time you forgave yourself."

Rafe nodded. "Good night, Michael," he said, ascending the stairs, leaving his brother to gaze after him.

Anne helped her housekeeper, Rosa, extinguish the candles downstairs before taking a lantern and slowly mounting the stairs to her room. She paused in the doorway, still unable to believe the luxury around her. She'd purchased the finest furnishings from the East and had them shipped overland to Ubiquitous. And why not? She could afford it.

She had made quite a splash in placid little Ubiquitous eighteen months ago when she had shown up out of nowhere to pay off the mortgage on her aunt's house and buy the town bank into the bargain. A smile of satisfaction curved her lips as she thought of Mr. Thaddeus P. Sampson and the expression on his face when he'd learned he would be working for a woman, the woman he hadn't had time for just weeks earlier.

She knew she was the topic of most of the gossip in the small town, and she cared not at all. She knew everyone wondered and speculated as to how she had come to have so much money. She'd professed to be from Natchez, widow of a fallen Confederate soldier and planter, who had packed her trunks with gold and jewels and headed to Texas to take refuge with her only living relative, Marguerite Tremaine, only to find she had died.

If they only knew the truth!

She and José had loaded a million dollars in gold into a wagon left behind by the comancheros. Disguised as a peasant couple, they had filled the wagon with produce to hide the gold, managing to hook up with a caravan returning from the coast with supplies for San Antonio. It had taken two months, but they'd managed to make it back to Ubiquitous after a harrowing, exhausting journey.

As for José, he'd loaded his saddlebags with as much gold as he could carry and taken off for parts unknown almost as soon as they'd reached Ubiquitous. She hadn't seen him since.

Politicians and ranchers had paid court to her, but she had remained aloof, and she knew she had that to thank for the rest of the gossip that circulated about her. The widow Cameron, known throughout the area for her charity and her coldness toward suitors.

She had tried to care, to be flattered by their attention, to forget. . . . She'd even considered marrying the mayor when he proposed to her last year, but her heart was hollow. There was nothing left inside her that didn't belong to another man, a man she would probably never see again.

Blood money, she thought. Blood money allowed

her to live this life of luxury and ease. So much had
been sacrificed for this money that she hadn't been able
to enjoy the bounty without some form of penance. It
had been Confederate gold, after all, so what better
way to assuage her conscience than to provide for wid-
ows and orphans created by the war? Besides, she
derived a real pleasure and fulfillment each time she
saw the strained, bitter face of a child turn into a smile
as a result of her generosity. For the first time in her
life, she was doing something worthwhile.

She removed her gown, placed it carefully across a
stuffed chair, then sat before the vanity and lifted the
ivory-handled brush to her hair. She couldn't use it
without thinking about Rafe and wondering, with a
twist of her heart, where he was, if he had found whatever he'd been seeking, if he ever thought of her.

He'd sent the brush to her after he'd left. She knew
he'd purchased it in San Juan Bautista. She remembered admiring it in the general store, just before Rafe
had been captured by the outlaws who had nearly
killed him.

How she'd longed to run that brush through her tangled hair, how she'd longed for a piece of lavender
soap. Now she could have all the soap and all the hair-
brushes money could buy.

But she would gladly trade everything she had if Rafe
Montalvo would walk through that door right now.

There were too many things in her life that reminded
her of him, far too many. Not a day went by that she
didn't think of him. Not a night went by that she didn't
long for him. Even after eighteen months of waiting and
watching the road, she still couldn't let him go.

Her gaze swept the vials and bottles on her dresser,
the silver dish that held the jewelry she'd collected

since that terrible day. Some of it she'd purchased herself; the rest had been gifts from admirers anxious to discover the mystery of the cold, aloof widow.

Her heart stopped.

There among her other jewelry was her locket, the locket her father had given her so long ago, the locket she had put around Rafe's neck that day in the Concepción church.

With her heart in her throat, she whirled around, her gaze sweeping the room, searching for a hiding place. She ran out into the hall, glancing anxiously up and down the long corridor, but no one was there.

She flew to the end of the hall and down the stairs, her feet hardly touching the steps, and went from room to room: the dining room, the kitchen, the parlor, the music room. No one.

She stood in the foyer, clutching the locket to her heart, her breath coming in gasps. Damn him! He'd been here! He'd come into her house, left the locket, and gone without a word.

"Damn you, Rafe Montalvo!" she said aloud as she turned and yanked the front door open, running out into the night.

"Damn you!" she cried, tears trailing down her cheeks.

By the time she reached the top of the stairs again, she had her emotions under control to a degree, although her heart felt heavier than it had since that day so long ago when he'd ridden out of her life. But maybe now she knew he had come back and hadn't even spoken a word to her . . . maybe now she could put the past behind her and get on with her life. But she knew it would be impossible.

She stopped at the door next to her own room, hesitating as she struggled for calm, and turned the knob carefully, trying not to make a sound. The room was dark, but she could clearly make out the figure of a man. Her heart stopped beating for a fraction of a second. Then she recognized him and the blood began to pound through her veins.

"Rafe," she whispered shakily.

He didn't turn to look at her. He was too intent on gazing at the baby in the cradle. She heard a faint whimper and knew the baby was awake.

Slowly, soundlessly, she crossed the room to stand behind him. She ached to touch him as tears clogged her throat, but she didn't dare, not yet.

"She won't break," Anne assured him.

"She's . . . she's beautiful," Rafe murmured, his voice husky with emotion.

"Pick her up."

He backed away slightly. "No."

She smiled and stepped around him. Slipping her hands beneath the familiar little body, she lifted the baby from the cradle.

"It's just Papa," she said. The baby gurgled and made incoherent sounds, the sweetest sounds he had ever heard.

He looked at Anne in wide-eyed wonder, and she realized that he hadn't known until she called him Papa that the baby was his.

"You mean, she's . . . ?"

"I've waited for you, Rafe," she said as she rocked the child gently. "There's been no one else."

"You must hate me."

A sob escaped her lips at the pain in his eyes. "Where have you been?"

"I . . . I didn't know what to do," he whispered.

She turned to face him, but he didn't look at her. His gaze seemed fixed on some distant object.

He seemed older and more vulnerable. He was as lean as ever, perhaps a little more so than before. His face was covered with a growth of beard, as it had been the first time she'd seen him. His eyes reflected a profound emptiness. It startled her because she had never been able to see into his soul so clearly, not even the night they'd made love under the stars.

She touched his face and he pressed his cheek into her palm, his tears warm and wet on her fingers.

"For a while, I just drifted; then I went back to New Mexico," he said slowly, softly, in the voice Anne had feared never to hear again.

He's here. He's truly here. He's come back.

"I had to settle things with my brother," he went on, "and with the army. I went to Fort Stanton and pleaded my case. Because of the extenuating circumstances, they agreed to pardon me if I'd serve in the Union army and fight in the war for six months, which I did. I'm a free man now, in more ways than one."

"That's good, Rafe, that's good. Here, you put her to bed," she said, holding the sleeping baby toward him.

He took the infant with great care, gazing at her as if mesmerized as he carried her to the crib, and then placing her gently on the mattress.

"I could stand here and watch her all night long," he said.

"Her name is Marie, for my mother. I hope you don't mind."

"I wasn't here," he said, his voice breaking slightly as he turned to gaze into her eyes. "You went through it all alone."

A shadow of remembered pain crossed her face and was replaced by a smile, a new smile. Her face was the same, her hair, her soft skin. But her eyes were the eyes of a woman full grown, a woman who had survived hardship and travail and emerged stronger, resilient.

"You didn't get a chance to watch me get fat," she said.

Rafe went to her. He fell on his knees, wrapping his arms around her hips, burying his head against her flat stomach. "Oh, God, Annie, I need you. I've missed you. I tried to forget, to stay away."

"Why?" she asked, as she ran her hands through dark hair that curled around her fingers.

"I thought you'd be better off without me. I had to find out who I was, what I was."

"And?" she asked.

"Please tell me you have room in your life for me now."

Anne wrapped her arms around his head and held him close to her. "There will always be room in my life for you," she assured him. "Always."

Desert Song by Constance O'Banyon

The enthralling conclusion of the passionate DeWinter legacy. As Lady Mallory Stanhope set sail for Egypt she was drawn to the strikingly handsome Lord Michael DeWinter, who was on a dangerous mission. From fashionable London to the mysterious streets of Cairo, together they risked everything to rescue his father, the Duke of Ravenworth, from treacherous captors.

A Child's Promise by Deborah Bedford

The story of a love that transcends broken dreams. When Johnny asks Lisa to marry him she knows it's the only way to make a new life for herself and her daughter. But what will happen when Johnny finds out she's lied to him? "A tender, uplifting story of family and love...You won't want to miss this one."—Debbie Macomber, bestselling author of *A Season of Angels*.

Desert Dreams by Deborah Cox

Alone and destitute after the death of her gambling father, Anne Cameron set out on a quest for buried treasure and met up with handsome and mysterious Rafe Montalvo, an embittered gunfighter. They needed each other in order to survive their journey, but could newfound passion triumph over their pasts?

One Bright Morning by Alice Duncan

Young widow Maggie Bright had her hands full raising a baby and running a farm on her own. The last thing she needed was a half-dead stranger riding into her front yard and into her life. As she nursed him back to health, she found herself doing the impossible—falling in love with the magnetic but difficult Jubal Green.

Meadowlark by Carol Lampman

Garrick "Swede" Swensen rescued a beautiful young woman from drowning only to find her alone, penniless, and pregnant. He offered Becky his name with no strings attached, but neither of them dreamed that their marriage of convenience would ever develop into something far more. When Swede's troubled past caught up with him, he was forced to make the decision of a lifetime.

Oh, Susannah by Leigh Riker

Socialite Susannah Whittaker is devastated by the death of her best friend, Clary, the sister of country music sensation Jeb Stuart Cody. An unlikely pair, Jeb and Susannah grow closer as they work together to unveil the truth behind Clary's untimely death, along the way discovering a passion neither knew could exist.

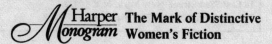